Praise for *Hieroglyphics*

"A good novel can perform the same perception-bending trick as a lockdown: slowing time, throwing light on shadowed corners, reminding us of the interdependencies among us that we once took for granted . . . Vibrant, engaging . . . [In *Hieroglyphics*] McCorkle, a generous, humane writer, knows that facing death allows us, as this terrible pandemic has, to focus on what is essential: how to take care of our vulnerable, and to appreciate the connections that sustain us." —*The New York Times Book Review*

"A moving and deeply appealing novel." —*People*

"Throughout, McCorkle weaves a powerful narrative web, with empathy for her characters and keen insight on their motivations. This is a gem." —*Publishers Weekly* (starred review)

"A bard of Southern fiction weaves a layered tale around a married couple who retire from Boston to North Carolina amid a beehive of secrets. A hidden journal, a childhood house, a long-ago fire: All emerge as keys and touchstones in McCorkle's shimmering prose." —*O, The Oprah Magazine*

"*Hieroglyphics* is suffused with a deep and heartening understanding of human resilience and strength. A beautiful and emotionally satisfying novel." —Brad Watson, author of *Miss Jane*

"Gathers layers like a snowball racing downhill before striking us in the heart with blunt, icy force." —*Kirkus Reviews* (starred review)

"No one has a more captivating storytelling style than McCorkle, and her narrative gifts are on full display in *Hieroglyphics*. As in her previous novel, *Life After Life*, she does a masterful job of weaving a whole from many parts. Revelations about all the characters arrive slowly, finally reaching a conclusion that is fully satisfying, as soaked in love and sorrow as every human life."

—Chapter16.org

"*Hieroglyphics* is a novel that tugs at the deepest places of the human soul—a beautiful, heart-piercing meditation on life and death and the marks we leave on this world. It is the work of a wonderful writer at her finest and most profound."

—Jessica Shattuck, author of *The Women in the Castle*

"Jill McCorkle at her best—a masterful storyteller noting the complications of life with a heart full of empathy."

—*Garden & Gun*

"Wise and tender, *Hieroglyphics* captures life itself: the experiences that shape us and bind us to one another, and the moments of terror and grace we carry in our hearts. Jill McCorkle's new novel is a triumph." —Claire Messud, author of *The Burning Girl*

"A thoroughly existential story that inspects mortality, the passage of time and the inadequacies of human communication . . . [McCorkle's] mastery of words as a vehicle to deliver raw emotions never wavers. *Hieroglyphics* dwells in nostalgia and the inevitable pain that's built into the contract of life, but like a good therapy session, it proves rewarding." —*The Atlanta Journal-Constitution*

"The real joy of *Hieroglyphics* is its intricacy, the pieces of four stories assembled into a mosaic of love and pain and redemption . . . The plain and elegant style pulls the reader through its shifts and counterpoints. You emerge bedazzled, blinking in the bright sunlight of now and carrying the shards of their experiences in your heart. McCorkle is a gracious stylist who hides a whip-smart gift behind her Southern charm. She knows how to tell a good story."

—*Washington Independent Review of Books*

"McCorkle offers a poignant meditation on the timeless question: Is there existence beyond the grave? Her metaphors expand her reach beyond the simple clichés that our lives are a blink in time, and her tale dramatizes how attaining meaningful understanding has always been the true challenge between wife and husband, parent and child. McCorkle testifies to the ageless nobility of human beings who want the next generation to do better. A deeply moving and insightful triumph."

—*Booklist* (starred review)

"McCorkle is known for being a funny and astute chronicler of everyday life. [*Hieroglyphics*] is a layered and powerful meditation on parenthood, loss and family history, and yet it has the easy feel of an entertaining neighbor spinning a tale on the porch while shelling peas."

—*Savannah Morning News*

"Jill McCorkle's novels are always worth the wait. That's certainly true of *Hieroglyphics*. Few books are so honest and true to life, yet so ultimately uplifting. She's a master of the art of weaving a story, through just the right details, nuances and anecdotes, for us to decipher as we read."

—*News & Record* (Greensboro, NC)

"Jill McCorkle has long been one of our wryest, warmest, wisest storytellers. In *Hieroglyphics*, she takes us on through decades, through loss, through redemption, and lands in revelation and grace. As always with McCorkle, the story feels so effortless and true that we might well miss what a high-wire act she's performing. But make no mistake: She's up there without a net, she never misses a step, and it's spectacular."

—Rebecca Makkai, Pulitzer Prize finalist for
The Great Believers

HIEROGLYPHICS

HIEROGLYPHICS

A NOVEL

Jill McCorkle

ALGONQUIN BOOKS
OF CHAPEL HILL
2021

Published by
Algonquin Books of Chapel Hill
Post Office Box 2225
Chapel Hill, North Carolina 27515-2225

a division of
Workman Publishing
225 Varick Street
New York, New York 10014

This is a work of fiction. While, as in all fiction, the literary perceptions and
insights are based on experience, all names, characters, places, and incidents
either are products of the author's imagination or are used fictitiously.

Library of Congress Cataloging-in-Publication Data

Names: McCorkle, Jill, [date]– author.
Title: Hieroglyphics : a novel / Jill McCorkle.
Description: First edition. | Chapel Hill, North Carolina :
Algonquin Books of Chapel Hill, 2020.
Identifiers: LCCN 2019059067 | ISBN 9781616209728 (hardcover) |
ISBN 9781643750538 (e-book)
Classification: LCC PS3563.C3444 H54 2020 | DDC 813/.54—dc23
LC record available at https://lccn.loc.gov/2019059067

ISBN 978-1-64375-138-2 (PB)

10 9 8 7 6 5 4 3 2 1
First Paperback Edition

For Claudia and Rob—
there are no words or symbols that can adequately
express my love

Languages die like rivers.
Words wrapped round your tongue today
And broken to shape of thought
Between your teeth and lips speaking
Now and today
Shall be faded hieroglyphics
Ten thousand years from now.

—CARL SANDBURG, "Languages"

Shelley

❧

LATELY, SHELLEY HEARS things in the middle of the night, hinges creaking and papers rustling, but it could be anything—the dog, her son, a mouse, the wind—and she forces her mind to stop right there so she doesn't imagine possibilities that would terrify her, like a killer or a ghost. It doesn't help that that old man rides by so often now, his green Toyota slowing in front of the house and then circling the block.

"I grew up here," he said that first time—now over a year ago—when he parked and came up to the door. His dress shirt was damp with perspiration, and he wiped his face with a handkerchief he then tucked in his shirt pocket. "I would love to see inside if convenient.

My wife, too." He pointed to the car, where an old woman lifted her hand in a wave and smiled with what seemed the same weary patience Shelley feels when dealing with her son.

"I moved here when I was ten," he continued. And though with tired, kind eyes he seemed harmless enough, Shelley kept the chain in place while he told her a few more things: There used to be a big sycamore tree, and the cemetery nearby was contained in the old gated part, thick with pines and magnolias, and not like now, sprawled all the way to Highway 211 where they are building a Taco Bell. He said his mother and his stepfather died in the house, which was certainly not something she wanted to hear and she certainly didn't want Harvey to hear. But of course he did.

"People died?" Harvey asked, and stepped closer to the door. He was playing Superhero and had a beach towel around his shoulders and a Batman mask his older brother, Jason, had worn one Halloween when he was much younger.

"Long ago," the man said, and waved his hand, clearly trying to put Harvey at ease. "They were old."

"Were they mean?"

"Not at all." The man looked like he was about to say something else, but Harvey ran back into the living room, where he was watching Nickelodeon while jumping on the sofa, something Shelley had given up trying to control.

She told the man she had lived there only a little over a year herself, and then thought if she didn't say anything else, he would figure out it was not a good day and leave—which he did, but not without asking if he could come back again at a better time. He told her it would really mean a lot to him, and when Shelley looked out toward the car, the woman nodded and waved, this time as if to encourage her to let him in. He pulled out a photo of himself as a young man with his mother, standing right there in front of the house. He seemed like someone she would like, but what if she didn't? What if she didn't and then he wouldn't go away?

"Perhaps when my husband is home," Shelley said. "That would be best." She'd whispered so Harvey wouldn't start asking about his dad again.

Now, there's a creak down the hall, a thump, and she hopes Harvey is fast asleep and doesn't hear this: the wind, the mouse, the dog. *Please let him sleep through the night*, she thought. She is exhausted these days, and so is it any wonder that she screwed up at work the way that she did? Is it any wonder at all?

Sometimes when she can't sleep, she thinks of old numbers: all the addresses where she has lived, numbers on mailboxes and spray-painted on curbs, some she wishes she could forget, numbers of telephones perched on tables or tethered to walls she will never see again, emergency numbers, numbers important for a child to memorize. Or she distracts herself by thinking of old jingles and ads, like *I don't want to grow up, I'm a Toys "R" Us kid*, or *I am stuck on Band-Aid*, or *Where's the beef? Body on Tap. Gentlemen prefer Hanes.* It's one of those things that once she starts, she can't stop, more and more stuff crowding in and getting stuck, and usually she can get lost in there. *Jordache. Jhirmack.* Usually she can close her eyes and find sleep.

"I'll be back," the man said that day. And every time since, Shelley has pretended that she's not home. She had told him that he could come inside on a day when her *husband* was home, and she is still waiting for that day. It's been over a year since she has even talked to Brent, but she still finds herself thinking that it could happen; he could have a change of heart and show up at the door.

"How will Dad know where we are?" Harvey asked when they left Atlanta, and she told him not to worry, that she sent the address. What she didn't say was that she sent it telepathically, because she really wasn't sure *where* to send it. Brent had said he was moving to Alaska, but the last time he sent a check that got forwarded, it was postmarked Alabama.

Harvey asked did she think his dad would ever come back, and she said yes, yes, she did; she just didn't say as *what*.

When Brent said he thought it was best if they went their separate ways, he said it was clear she wanted that, too, because she had done nothing to try and change his mind. In a trial, someone would argue that he had manipulated the truth to his own advantage. "Don't you have anything to say?" he asked her.

"Don't ever beg, Shelley," her older brother once told her. He was in high school and worked at the bowling alley on the weekends, and smelled like cigarettes and floor wax and fried food when he draped his arm around her. "They'll always disappoint you."

They were on the small back porch, right off the kitchen, where their parents sat smoking over their empty plates; he whispered, finger up to his lips, then pulled several bills from his back pocket and counted out just enough for her to order something on paperback day at the middle school. People who ordered nothing looked weird or poor, and her brother understood this.

"Here," he said. "Get something good." And she did; she got a book called *Dear Patti: Advice for Teenage Girls* and a book of tongue twisters she practiced for months after—*red leather, yellow leather* and *she sells seashells*—things she sometimes teaches Harvey when he can't sleep, or says to herself when hoping to conjure that image of her brother and better days, or to not think at all.

Frank

BEFORE THEY WERE even old enough to worry about losing their memories, Lil had quizzed Frank about their special word. "Do you remember?" she would ask, leaning in close for him to whisper in her ear and prove it, like he was some kind of imbecile or hadn't taken that long-ago conversation seriously.

"Of course I remember," he told her. "I thought of it. Do you remember that?"

"Do you remember where we were?"

"Of course I do."

By the time they had packed up their lives and started driving to North Carolina, she said only, "Do you," and he said, "Yes."

"How do you know what I'm going to say?" she asked.

"Because I know you."

But then she asked some other questions, silly things that made them both laugh. Did he remember the name of the man who used to pump their septic tank all the while whistling show tunes in rhythm with the grinding machinery of his pump? Did he remember what went in the recipe for those grasshoppers he made on Saint Patrick's Day a hundred years ago? Crème de menthe and then what? Did he remember her phone number from when they first met?

The whole car ride was filled with such questions, and it was a good way not to feel the sadness they both were feeling, miles falling behind them like all the years they'd lived there.

Retirement has not been all that others told him it would. They had said he would love not reading student papers or typing a syllabus, but that wasn't true. He had missed it, and now, even a decade after the fact, he still does. He misses the schedule and the order of it all, the year neatly divided into terms—pauses for the holidays and summers—those chunks of time all the sweeter because there *was* an end in sight and he had to cram all that he could into those isolated weeks or summer months.

He'd loved having a topic in mind, an idea, and then setting about researching and reading. It was peaceful down in the library stacks, the smell of old paper and glue.

Do you—

Yes.

Do you remember when you looked pale as a vampire because you practically lived in that tomb of a library?

It's been hard to get anything new started lately, an idea for a paper or article, though he still keeps up with all the readings, or tries to, all the discoveries he would have sent students to the library to explore. As a younger man, he would have wanted to build a vacation around it: the Egyptian boat carvings in the ancient city Abydos, dating back over thirty-eight hundred years; or the pyramids found within a pyramid in Mexico; the mosaic of Noah's ark in Israel; or the one he feels most drawn to these days, the lost city of Neapolis, submerged off the coast of Tunisia since the fourth century AD.

"Can't you find something old to excite you in Hawaii or Antigua?" Lil had asked after saying she did not want another hot, sandy vacation unless there was a great big ocean and good seafood within walking distance. "And what about Cape Ann? Plenty of old things there."

They always said they would go to Paris, and Lil was quick to add that they also needed a return trip to Florence. But now, Frank's main focus is on exploring the place he'd lived as a boy: the house, the yard, that old root cellar his stepfather dug out near where he'd had his garden.

"Just go knock on the door," Lil had said the first time they rode by. They had barely moved, and she insisted they go see it, that he bring the photograph of himself with his mother, taken in the front yard. "They'll let you in," she said. But so far, that hasn't happened.

Lil

⤜

August 10, 2016
Southern Pines, North Carolina

You two have always wondered why I spend so much time filling these notebooks (Frank, you, too, if you're reading this!), but it is simply a part of my life, a way to clear my mind and to remember. Sometimes I just record the weather, something simple about the day. It is so easy to let everything run together. I had years that were that way, and I find such loss troubling; better to try to define something, the premature blue dusk of a winter afternoon or the long, clear light of summer, that kind of light that makes you feel immortal. And I guess that's why we hold on to our bits and pieces in the first place, because we aren't immortal, and though denial fills our days and years, especially those that have slipped away, that kernel of truth is always lodged within.

We all are haunted by something—something we did or didn't do—and the passing years either add to the weight or diminish it. Mine has been diminished, perhaps because I've spent time thinking about it all. It might sound silly, but I see these bits and pieces as my contribution to evolution, the unearthing and dusting of the prints and markers that led me here. Some seem to bulldoze right through life and up to their headstones, but I want to take my time. I want to find the right words.

I imagine my recipient to be you two, or perhaps your children, and I hope this is so, rather than some stranger who comes in and hoists old boxes into a dumpster, or rakes away the remainders of my life, like the sad debris in the aftermath of a flood or fire. I will never get over the sight of what we left behind at our home of over 50 years to move down here, a mountain of cast-off things—old towels and linens, papers and books and shoes and pots, side tables and lamps, hoses and hoes, packets of seeds I meant to plant, and a rubber squeak toy that had been safely hidden away in the back of my closet by one of the dogs long dead. And so much more: things not needed, things long forgotten, cans of cream-of-whatever soup and V8 juice (why?) and peas that had sat there forgotten for years, and things that never should have been there in the first place, like Tuna Helper, or those things in my closet like that geometric-print minidress I bought in the '60s, hoping to look like Petula Clark or Judy Carne—a perky-pixie kind of dress that I never had the nerve to wear and instead looked at it there at the back of the closet for years, along with a wiglet and a long frosted fall and some jackets with shoulders resembling a football player's or Victorian monarch's. We divided it all into Goodwill, consignment, recycle, or landfill.

But there were also the things I couldn't let go of—letters, reminders, souvenirs—and I am taking my time, relieved when I find something that might have gotten lost in that mountain of debris, like one of your drawings from first grade or the stub from a movie I'd forgotten I even saw, or a note from my father.

When the moving van pulled away that afternoon and we got in the car and turned southward, the space within the car seemed so empty, vacant, our suitcases and silver chest in the trunk, an overnight bag and thermos of coffee on the back seat, and I had that terrible feeling that I had forgotten something. Because I was thinking of all the times the car was filled with you two, your belongings, your music and voices, the dogs, while going to school or on vacation, or just to the grocery store where I bought all of those things that I then put on the shelf there in our dimly lit pantry—on the red gingham contact paper I spent one snowy afternoon 40 years ago cutting and sticking in place—all those things that I placed there and then forgot about.

I like to imagine that I will be your cornerstone, a reminder of what was. The old building crumbles away, and yet there I will be (me, my life, our life) like when you were assigned time capsules in school. Remember? You both were in elementary school and were asked what you would take to leave on the moon. And then *your* children did it again with the turning of the century, and asked us to write a letter about what has changed in our lifetime. Your father wrote a lot! And he even made a timeline about all that had changed about cars and appliances, the telephone and the mail.

I have been writing notes and saving bits and pieces since long before you both were born, my attempt at explaining my life to myself, perhaps. I have so little of my own mother and have spent much of my life yearning for more. This habit of mine, trying to hold on to those days, was simply a way to reassure myself and to recall every detail of her—all I knew of my parents' life together and all I knew of her death. I was afraid of forgetting, a fear that has never diminished, and now I *am* forgetting things. There's no denying that I am forgetting. We all joke about it at a certain age (you will, too) but there's a line you cross when you don't talk about it in the same way. I am 85 years old, so what do I expect? You're all grown; your children are even grown, so what do we expect? That's what I keep saying to your father: "What do you expect?" We have both already moved past the estimated life expectancy for men and women in this country. We have both long passed the ages our own parents were when they died.

Sometimes, I feel like my life is all laid out before me: dots connecting, patterns shaped and designed, words naming and classifying me. We all have those moments when we are so aware of where we are; there are the moments when we feel graced and blessed, and there are likewise those when we say, "What am I doing here?"

I have tried to imagine my mother on that last night of her life. Surely, she asked, "What am I doing here? Oh God, what am I doing?"

I asked myself that same thing in that empty-feeling car, your father silent behind the wheel, as we got on I-95 and instead of heading north to Gloucester, as we had a million times before, we went south and kept going the rest of the day, neither of us saying much and yet both aware of the sad, questioning cloud hanging over us. And after a restless night at a Holiday Inn somewhere in Maryland, we rode much of the next day, until we got here and met the movers—belongings we had had for years looking so different in the warm, bright light.

Remember how you were here to greet us, Becca? You were our reason for coming, and we are happy to have this time near you and your family, but I still wake some days and think: "What am I doing here?" Even though we have been here for over a year now, I panic, and then I try to rationalize it all, to name the reasons and the benefits of living here. We have followed the migratory path of the snowbirds we once saw as traitors—the weaklings, your father and I called them as we stood armed with our snow shovels and salt. And, yes, ice and cold are hard on brittle bones, and, yes, help is needed when dealing with worn-out hearts and lungs and words that won't come. The love and attention of a child nearby cannot be underestimated—please know we are grateful, Becca. And yet there remain those parts of me that simply refused to come along, and they pull my mind this way and that all day, especially when I'm in here sorting through it all and trying to give it some order. I try to collect and hold on to them, but it is like grasping the wind, and yet those are the parts—what I knew as a child—that seem the truest parts of me.

Home. I hear that word and I am in my bed in Massachusetts. I went to bed as one girl and woke up another. I hear the word "home" and it is 1942, that late dark before I woke to learn that my mother had not come home. Even after all these years, I hear that word and that is where I am transported.

I guess I have always drifted back there, so often that I have memories tucked within memories, like carpool lines, moments of waiting, when something pulled me backward. I recall clearly waiting for Becca during her swim practice those cold early mornings before school, the air smelling of chlorine; there were echoes and splashing and a kind of false warmth when outside it was winter, snow on the ground. And I remember being there, not just once but many times, too hot in my coat but not wanting to shed everything, because the whistles were blowing and it was time for practice to end and the day's work to begin. But I closed my eyes, and there in the dozy haze with the sounds of water, I drifted from our suburban comfort into that second story of my childhood home there on School Street; last I checked, it was still there—a simple wooden house, tan with dark-brown trim, a steep center staircase, and a radiator by the door, where we laid our gloves and scarves.

I can close my eyes and know every square inch. I know the sound of my father's footsteps leaving for his job at Waltham Watch, and then his return in early evening, already dark in the winter months. His movements through life were as precise as the timepieces occupying his days, the close fine-tuning of parts, a focused ability that reassured me but I suspect had the opposite effect on my mother. I remember her standing, hands on her hips and toe tapping. "Tick-tock, tick-tock," she said, moving her hand like a pendulum, impatient to get out and go wherever it was we were going.

I remember hearing them laugh in the room next to mine, leaving me to feel both comforted and left out. My mother's laugh is one I can still hear on a good day, and yet I can't even begin to describe it to you. I tried to imitate it once, alone in the car while I watched the rush of children swarm from your school, and my voice was thin and tinny, nothing like what I was hearing in my head. Still, I place my memory of it there, one to handle as gently as a piece of recording tape. These days, there would be a real recording to keep, but not so for my mother; her voice is only in the heads of those of us who knew her. Now, there is no one who shares this with me.

I remember my bedspread: nubby chenille in a pale yellow with a big, heavy blanket on top of that, the radiator ticking like the Tin Man's heart, like your father's artificial valve. For many years now

when I couldn't sleep, I've lain awake there beside him and listened.
It's a sound like the radiator of my childhood, the window above it
encased in ice, crystals visible in the glow from the light on the corner, where there was a local grocery. I even know the owner's name,
Mr. Rosen, his white apron always stained with blood as he leaned
across the counter, his smile boyish and funny as he reported neighborhood gossip, who he saw doing what when, while he slipped
penny candies into your open palm.

"Earth to Lil," your father would say, or one of you would call,
"Mom? Hello?" and I woke to this life, both glad to be in it but
also sad to leave that long-ago moment; I would wake, and there
you were, Becca, chlorine on your skin and hair, body goosefleshed
and shivering, as I wrapped a big towel around you. I remember the
moment so clearly, and yet I can't tell you what might have been on
my mind that day or what coat I wore during that period of time. It
might've been the camel-colored one, or it could have been that red
corduroy I wore for so long, the one that led your dad—those times
he acted silly (rare times!)—to sing that old song "Hey there, Little
Red Riding Hood, you sure are looking good."

It's so clear to me—the laughter, your childhood voices, your
father's young face and headful of dark hair—but I can't recall how I
felt when I woke that day, what I did after your swim practice, what
dance classes I taught that day, or what ancient this or that your
father was fixated on and lecturing about at the time. And what did
he and I talk about then? The news of the day? The weather? What
needed to be fixed? If so, then I can assure you that so much of life
never changes.

What I do recall is that while back in my childhood room, I
saw my mother's hairbrush; it was simple and plain, so unlike her,
just brown boar bristles, and she tossed her head side to side as she
brushed and fluffed, the auburn heft of her hair falling chin-length,

very fashionable. It was on my dresser, and I was surprised and delighted to see it there. It was there like a promise, because she brushed her hair before bed, 100 times, as she had read somewhere was the thing to do. She would have needed to come back into my room to get it, and I would have heard the door creak on its hinges. I would have seen her there in the dim light of the hallway lamp we left on all night because our stairs were so steep and the landing so small; I could almost see her there. And that is what I remember, straining my eyes against the darkness to see her there, the brush on my dresser, above which the mirror reflected light from the street below.

It's mysterious how fluid time has become for me; I wake and pour a glass and have no idea what I'll find.

We all have those objects that keep us feeling connected to a person or time long gone. For me, it's that hairbrush and my mother's little ivory pin shaped like a Scottie dog, with rhinestone eyes, and the watch my father methodically took apart and then put back together in the nights after my mother died. For your father, it's a toy badge, a box of his father's fishing lures, and his grandfather's stethoscope.

Remember how you loved to play with that stethoscope, listening to your own hearts and the gurgles of your stomachs? Jeff, you loved it so much you wrote a school report in the sixth grade so that your father would have to let you touch it. You loved school reports and projects; so many vinegar-and-baking-soda volcanoes over the years! You loved reading about how the Frenchman who invented the stethoscope did so because he felt uncomfortable pressing his ear up to women's breasts. Remember? You said, "S'il vous plaît open your shirt," in a silly accent modeled after that cartoon skunk. I thought it was funny, but that was the kind of thing your father got impatient and irritated about; he was always much harder on you, Jeff, something I have never understood. Did he want you to be something you weren't? Did he envy that you could be a young man without feeling the weight of the world? I have your yearbooks right here on the shelf, too, and you look so young, hair down in your eyes and that denim jacket you wore all the time.

When I was in high school, our yearbook had a page that said "Faces" with lots of little thumb-sized pictures, and we all very carefully wrote the name of the person under each picture. I was included in one with three other girls: Doris Banks and Lois Starnes and Jean Burr. I still like to look at those girls, the wavy curls with great big bows pinned to the side, a style that seems to have returned, infinite recycling.

Darling Lil, 2 sweet 2 be 4gotten.

That was written so many times in my yearbook, but I suspect it wasn't true at all, both the sweet part and the forgotten. I stayed in touch with many people over the years—through Christmas cards, changes in address, the occasional swapping of birth announcements, and then wedding and retirement, and then the obituaries started rolling in and have continued.

Stay sweet, Cutie-Pie.

My best friend in elementary school was Bettie Conroy; she lived down the street, and I went to her house almost every afternoon after my mother died. Then at some point, it was like I just stopped going, and I don't remember why.

Bettie had a doll I loved, and she would let me hold her if I promised to be very careful—a bridal doll, all white lace and veil. And we roller-skated, our keys on strings around our necks, the scritch-scratch sound of those old metal wheels on the sidewalks.

Remember all those times I took you all to Wal-Lex for birthday parties or just on a Saturday afternoon? I always thought about skating with Bettie just a few blocks away. A different time, a different life, and yet it felt like the two overlapped, a double exposure of me in two places.

"What happened to your mother?" Bettie asked one of those days, and though her mother shushed her, she also stopped stirring to listen. We were there in the kitchen because she had promised to let us crack and break the eggs. "I mean did you see her?" Bettie said.

I focused on the recipe her mother had on the counter, something from *Woman's Day*, a magazine my mother had also sometimes bought. *Cheese soufflé, costs 63¢; 6 large servings*, the recipe said. *Warn the family that the soufflé must be served immediately!*

I nodded but gave nothing else; it felt like a betrayal, and I was still harboring the hope that it had all been a terrible mistake, that it wasn't my mother after all.

Maybe that was the last day I spent at Bettie's; I have tried so many times to remember what came next, but I can't, just as I now sometimes look at the Faces page and, even seeing the names written there in my own youthful handwriting, can't place them. Your father often says, "Of course you can't remember! We're old as dirt, Lil," and we laugh.

In fact, when we moved here, I got a chalkboard and wrote "Faces" at the top and then listed the neighbors we met and described them. Lucy next door: slight stoop to the shoulders, hair has a pink tinge. Her husband, Raymond has big ears and wears his pants too high and was a dermatologist. They have a koi pond in their backyard and talk about it all the time. The Parkers down the block, originally from upstate New York, but if we have anything in common who would know, because they spend all their time golfing

and visiting their kids, somewhere even farther south than where
we are now. The Warrens, much younger than everyone else on the
street and always offering to help, even when you had no idea you
needed any.

Faces has helped us to remember all of their names and something about them. I wrote of the Parkers: "Fans of black hair dye
and facial procedures." And of Ron Todd, the divorced realtor who
sold us this house in between various dental procedures he described
in great detail, I wrote: "A man, a plan, a root canal."

Remember all those palindromes you kids knew? I had made
your father laugh, something that has become harder and harder to
do; he used to always make jokes about his heart, about kicking the
bucket, circling the drain, but those jokes have dwindled with all he
has going on, and so any levity is good. I'm hoping to do some more
palindromes, but in the meantime, he said I need to keep Faces hidden in the bedroom, in case any of our neighbors pop in, something
we are finding people do around here a lot.

And I am not complaining, Becca, because you (and Ron Todd,
of course) helped us find a great place to be, but I would be lying if I
didn't say that there are times when the heat and humidity is killing
us, as is the constant chatter and hospitality and all that hugging.
Oh my. Your father has done much better with that part than I have;
he once lived here, after all, and has a greater tolerance for those
who invade your personal space. I extend my hand and hope for the
best. I avert my eyes if I sense a talker up ahead. Just the other day,
a woman at the dry cleaners said to me, "The humility is just awful,
ain't it, sugar?" and I said, "Oh my God, yes. The humility is terrible
these days." And don't even mention the tea, thick with sugar and
God knows what; you can feel your arteries closing in resistance.

In short, I am homesick and I am timesick. I would be lying

not to say that. It is possible to feel content and resolved and still be homesick. I miss all that no longer is, which is why I paste and piece all these scraps together. Sometimes, I hold a ticket or photo, a piece of paper, while willing myself back to where I first held it. I know that might sound silly, but it's what I do. I want to hear your young voices, the dog scratching to come in; I want to call my father on the telephone, finger in that rotary dial one number at a time—TW3-3642. Let me take this Playbill and arrive at the theater, or this receipt and find myself there in the produce aisle of Star Market. Then, after the show, after I check out, after I sit and let the car warm up, I drive those familiar streets home and find everything just as I left it, the kitchen door creaking behind me.

The cornerstone always goes in the northeast corner, something my father told me about years ago. I don't recall why we were talking about it; perhaps it came up because of that popular cartoon of the singing and dancing frog trapped there—you know the one, "Hello, my baby, hello, my honey"—only the frog refuses to perform for the greedy man who hopes to make a fortune, except when it is just the two of them. What I recall is my father telling me it all had to do with the Masons, and something about coming out of the cold darkness of the north into the dawning light of the sunrise, and something to do with the summer solstice and the longest day, but now for me, the memory is all about my parents at a time when there seemed to be no threats whatsoever to our life.

We were at our kitchen table, a small white porcelain surface, and it must have been spring, because the window facing School Street was open and there was a single jonquil in a jar on the table. I don't know what we ate (the plates are empty), and my parents are both smoking (Chesterfields, an ashtray shaped like a little frying pan between them). "I bet that's why graves face that way," my mother said, and my father nodded, both of them seeming pleased to be teaching me something, although it doesn't always hold true; I have been to many cemeteries in my life, and there are a lot of graves not facing east. Even recently, when I went with your father to ride by that house where he once lived, we went in the cemetery where he played as a boy, a shady lovely place, Whispering Pines, but there seemed no rhyme or reason whatsoever to the way people were placed. His mother is facing north, in fact, which Frank said was unintentional but certainly made sense.

We were once on a trip, one of those far-flung places your father wanted to see—Egypt or Morocco or Peru; so much has run together for me, though I do remember that he was writing something about fishhooks from thousands of years ago. We were somewhere, brilliant-blue sky and sun and sand, when I suddenly froze in panic of what I had left written for you to find, should something happen to us. I kept a journal then, or my version of one, a legal pad tucked in my bedside table drawer, where I often documented the date and the weather or made lists of this or that: what to buy at the store, what people want for Christmas. Should I attempt a real ballet for the recital or just keep doing flowers and bees and sunbeams? Should we get a second dog so we are never without one in the house? Should I leave your father? The whole time it was all I could think about, picturing you two, your own adult lives barely beginning, having to read all that I had to say.

I recall that I had written "Frank—the pros and cons." But now I'm not remembering the details listed there. What I do remember is burning the list in the kitchen sink as soon as we got home.

"Will you snap out of it?" your father said, the bright, exotic place devoured by my panic. "You could just as easily go to the grocery store and never come home."

"Yes," I told him. "Yes, that's right." Or I could just as easily say I was going out to teach a dance class on a cold November night and wind up in a club burned to cinder.

October 17, 2016
Do I need to draw you a picture?

I woke today with that question stuck in my head. It is something my mother said, each syllable clearly enunciated, when she felt unheard or misunderstood. She would stand there with her hands on her hips for emphasis.

My father and I often told her that, yes, she did. Her stories were often so confused-sounding, as if she couldn't tell it all fast enough, high-speed versions about this or that neighbor and what was going on, too many pronouns to keep up with who was who.

Once, after a particularly long-winded tale that left my father sighing in exasperation, she went and got a piece of paper and a pencil from the kitchen drawer where she kept the grocery list and drew a picture of a stick woman (Mrs. McCarthy two houses over, who had seven boys), then drew an arrow to the stick woman's stomach. "'Another bun in the oven,' is what I said. I heard it from Mr. Rosen, whose wife teaches one of those boys, whichever one is in fourth grade," she said. She tapped the pencil in place and then repeated very slowly, in a way that made us laugh, "A bun in the oven. Hoping for a girl." Then she laughed and said if she were Mrs. McCarthy, she'd be hoping Mr. McCarthy might find a hobby like stamp collecting or something and take a year off, and my father said he doubted collecting a few stamps would make a difference but certainly there *was* something he could do.

The older I got, the better I understood it all, my mother point-ing to her galoshes by the back door and the two of them laughing and touching each other's arms in a way that reassured me. I sat there at that small kitchen table picturing a fat baby girl (redheaded and freckled like all the McCarthy boys) baking away in the oven, while my mother did a little variation on the Lindy Hop, which she had been practicing, her stocking feet moving while she sang "I Got Rhythm." *Who could ask for anything more?*

That baby was named Norman, and then the very next year they welcomed Maureen McCarthy, who ended up working as the librar-ian in your high school. "Small world," she and I would say each time we ran into each other, and seeing her always triggered that memory of my mother dancing there in the kitchen, finger pointing to those galoshes that remained by the back door for way too long after she died.

It's so mysterious where our minds take us. Your father has said that if he could attend one more archaeological dig in his life, it would be a tour of my brain and all that is hidden there. I told him that it's a gold mine and that he would need every available tool!

Sometimes, the most insignificant thing can become important. For instance, there was no reason to save a receipt from Stop & Shop, except that it got mixed up with lots of other scraps of paper stuffed in a drawer, probably one of those times I emptied my purse and thought I would sort it all out later, but later never came. It was a day I bought baby food and I also bought Barbasol, my father's brand of shaving cream. It would have been one of those many days I went between my two lives, there with you and your father, and then back to School Street to check in on my father. I never intended to save it (why would I?) and yet, years after the fact, the figures nearly faded, it reminds me how I felt so responsible and torn some days, back and forth, back and forth. Tick-tock, tick-tock.

Hours to days to weeks to years.

It seems I never get to the bottom of that one box filled with notes. I keep finding things.

June 4, 1967
Mom, thank you for not making Rudolf leave even though he ate some of the kitchen floor and scratched up the hall door. He loves me and I love him. He threw up on the floor and is good now. He is sorry. Your son, Jeff Wishart

I never would have made him leave. He did love us—that beautiful, selfless soul, with the perfect poodle coat. The scratches were still there when we left, too, not as obvious—we sanded and painted—but still there. Poor Rudolf died long before those shirts that keep dogs calm in a storm were invented; that would have made such a difference for him. Whenever I say that, your father says it sounds like I'm talking about the polio vaccine or antibiotics, and I say yes, that's exactly what I'm talking about.

Spring 1988? (pretty sure this is right)
Mom,
I appreciate your questions and offerings of advice and opinion. I do, but I also beg that you please understand my need to handle this my own way and in my own time. You have never been divorced, and so there is a lot you really do not know, even if you have read a lot of books. Trust me on this. Your whole life has been defined by losing your mother

young and wishing that she had been there to advise you at
every turn (or thinking you do), but that is not my story. I
hope you will understand when I say that I do not need any
more advice. I just don't. I am doing fine and need for you
to treat me like the adult I am.
Love, Rebecca

June 21, 1982
Dear Mrs. Wishart,
I only met your father once but my father was a long time
co-worker of his—Sam Merriweather, you may have heard
his name. He died several years ago. He always said James
Porter was one of the nicest and most honest people he ever
met and I thought you would like to know that. He said it
was especially amazing given all that he had gone through.
People say he was a fine gentleman and I thought you would
like to know that. I know he will be missed.
Sincerely,
Everett Merriweather

Mother's Day 1965
IOU-
I will not hit Becca.
will feed dog and play
will not say what you sed don't say
Jeff Wishart

Lately, I wake and wonder if the people who moved into our old
house have figured out that you can't open that one cabinet if the
oven door is ajar, or that there is a hairline crack in the window over
the stairs that we chose to leave because it's the original window,

the glass thick and wavy. I forgot to tell them how they might think there's a burst pipe but it is probably only the sun hitting that one part of the roof, the snowmelt filling the gutter with a runoff so powerful no bush below has ever managed to survive. Frank begs me to stop. "Please stop," he says. "I can't think about it right now. I do not want to think about any of it right now."

Harvey

HARVEY WOULD BE scared at night if he didn't have Peggy. She is fat and warm and she snores and sometimes her paws move like she's chasing something, like she *will* chase something if she needs to, and Harvey wakes her up to tell her to do it but sometimes Harvey is the only one awake and so he whispers in Peggy's ear to *wake up*, just to make sure she will do it when he needs her to. Her ear stinks a little in a good way, like how her neck smells under her collar, kind of like the school cafeteria and those big rolls on spaghetti day. His teacher held one up to the principal and said, "Do you think we feed these children enough starch? And does this sauce really count as a vegetable? Really?"

Harvey's teacher said, "Really? Really?" when she thought you were lying. "So you already did your work," she would say. "Really? You really want me to believe that?" And they did want her to believe that, because she is the youngest teacher at the school and has a convertible and a boyfriend who makes beer. Somebody asked did her boyfriend know she always eats lunch with Mr. Stone, the man who teaches second grade and runs the summer camp Harvey's mom is making him go to. The same kid asked why didn't she dump her boyfriend and go with Mr. Stone. She already has everything anybody wants, a car and a dog—a pit bull mix named Suzy—but Mr. Stone can dance and wears cool shoes.

Harvey kisses Peggy and smells inside her big soft ear. He keeps his eyes closed and pulls Peggy tight when he hears the back door open and close. He knew it would. Peggy doesn't wake up and Harvey's mom doesn't wake up. Just Harvey knows someone's in the house and in the hall, and whoever it is stops and stands in the door, just like last time. He wants to look but is scared to, because there is some ghosts that'll blind you for looking and cut out your tongue too, so he just breathes real quiet into Peggy's soft ear and waits.

Lil

November 28, 1969
Newton, Massachusetts

It's snowing, and we're supposed to have over a foot by morning. Frank and the kids are watching something on television, one of those old monster movies I hate, but I like hearing their screams and laughter. I'm on the back porch, wrapped in a blanket and counting the minutes. Twelve short minutes, but how unbearably long they must have been to those trapped. Inside my cigarette case is a note from the children: *These will kill you.* "Yes," I say, and light one in anticipation of the 12-minute wait. "So many things will."

That night in November, my mother was going to teach a dance class, something she did more and more often at Arthur Murray, where she began by just filling in for a friend. She knew all the dances of the time, and when she couldn't convince my father to practice with her, she would let me; sometimes I saw her practicing there in the living room, right hand extended, as if to an invisible partner. She loved to dance, and she loved getting paid to do it, telling my father and me that whatever she brought home was "mad money" to go to the movies or on a vacation.

She was all bundled up in her black wool coat, a pale-pink scarf over her head and wrapped around her neck; she was wearing her favorite shoes, the black suede wedges with ankle straps. I can see her there at the top of those steep stairs, her hand on the banister. In my memory, it is as if she pauses, like someone stopping to look both ways before crossing the street. I was there in my room; my father was seated by the radio in the living room, I assume listening to the news. It was 1942, so there was a lot of news, and he was often there, eyes closed as he listened.

My mother had two different fragrances she wore: Tabu for the average day, and then on special occasions, Pavlova, a fragrance named for the great dancer. "From Paris," she whispered, and smiled and then showed me the tiny bottle, doll-sized, that she pressed against each slender wrist. She smelled wonderful (perfume, cigarettes, spearmint gum), and I recall thinking she looked like so many of the movie stars she admired and talked about as if they were friends of hers: Rita Hayworth and Jane Wyman and Joan Fontaine and Lana Turner. She loved going to the movies and often went on her own, leaving the little ticket stubs in the pockets of her coat and at the bottom of her many purses, with loose tobacco bits and gum wrappers.

It is important I remember this. No matter the weather or

whatever else is going on in life, it is important I stop and remember how it all started with the strike of a single match. I stare at the second hand on my watch while I imagine and then try not to imagine: one minute, two, a tiny flame in that dark corner of the lounge, catching and spreading, fabric and wood, walls and ceiling, fake palm trees, starry sky, hundreds of people there to have fun.

November 28, 1994

Was it planned all along that she would go to the Cocoanut Grove that night, or did something suddenly beckon her to go that way? I have looked for clues, thinking I had something a couple of times. There was the name of a man who had taken quite a few classes and danced with my mother many times—a name traced to an address and then to a daughter who had moved to Ohio and by then was middle-aged. "Did you know your father was taking dancing lessons?" I asked her. "Did he ever mention my mother's name?" Perhaps she'd had no suspicions about her father until I planted that seed, or perhaps there really was nothing to suspect. My mother had called an old friend of hers that night, someone who also taught dance classes, but the woman said her husband had answered and by the time she got to the phone, it had gone dead. "Are you sure?" I asked, and it was clear that I was suggesting she might not be telling me the truth, but the woman reached for her husband's hand and assured me that was what happened. If there was something she didn't tell me, it died with her a few years ago.

All I have are bits and pieces of a giant puzzle, like those 2,000-piece ones we used to do when we went to Gloucester. Remember, Jeff, how you would always steal a piece so you could magically produce it at the end? We should have taken better note of that. We should have had a conversation, because I think this tendency might explain what happened in your marriage and your divorce—things like withholding what's important, keeping to yourself what might benefit another, the need to always be the winner or the one who has the answer. Becca, you didn't seem to care. You just wanted to go buy some flip-flops or the latest suntan oil, or go to Virgilio's for a sandwich and then get back in the water, but, Jeff, you controlled those puzzles. And of course it feels good to find that final piece, the snug placement that completes the whole picture.

April 6, 2017
Southern Pines
It is too hot to be outside today. I breathe better in the air-conditioning, even though then I am freezing; the windows all fog over with condensation. I asked your father what if we are in a terrarium on a shelf somewhere in the twilight zone, where they are studying old age, migration, and evolution. He said he suspects we are giving them their money's worth.

I have saved some things I didn't want to save, and I'm not even sure why I did that except perhaps to remind myself what I am capable of being and doing. They remind me of times I never want to relive. Like finding that note left under my windshield wiper that time. "Leave Me Alone!" it said, among other things. You were both in your 20s, and I still look back and think that the two of you must have noticed the changes. Your father and I were like total strangers. Or were you both so caught up in all the events of your own lives (and there were many!) that you didn't even notice? I've often wondered if I would've been better off in the bliss of ignorance, emotionally unaware and somehow paralyzed, and I can't help but

wonder if people are really unaware or if they are in denial, slapping
on a pair of blinders and a muzzle, plowing the same old row until
the old ox returns to the yoke, or doesn't.

A lot of women have done that, I guess, and men, too, maybe.
Jeff, your first wife, Anna, did that, right? She waited, hoping,
though I don't see that it helped her, and I am sorry. And, what's
more, you're lucky she's not one of those vindictive ones; I have
sometimes thought she should have been, and then I remember that
I am your mother. But I really did like her. I loved her. She and I
liked many of the same things, unless she was just pretending; we
both loved spending long hours at the aquarium, and we also loved
going to all the crafty places, just wandering and touching yarns
and beads and stencils and glue guns. And she made that wonderful
dessert with all the layers in what looked like a giant brandy snifter
or goldfish bowl, I forget what you call it, begins with a "t." She
left the special bowl here one Christmas, and I never sent it back
to her. I wanted to, and you kept telling me to wait, not to interfere. "Don't bring up one more goddamned thing to argue about,"
you said.

So eventually, I bought one of those fish, the fancy Dr. Seuss–
looking thing (a red one), to live in the bowl, because I doubted I
was ever going to make a trifle. That's the name, and how ironic is
that? Trifle. And add to it that those betta fish are creatures that just
can't do well with a partner. Even if they see themselves in a reflection, they bristle up, ready for combat. "Don't trifle with me!" that
fish said. That was my joke, and one your father actually thought
was funny.

I made that joke when David was staying with us while you all
were dividing up your household. I took him to the aquarium, and
your father and I watched those vapid purple-dinosaur videos with
him until we thought we would die. We all went to a baseball game,

and somewhere in there David asked me would I rather a booger taste like candy or be filled with helium and float away. Needless to say, I voted for helium, and I suggested he remember that the next time his fingers were going toward the wall in the middle of the night and get up and get a Kleenex!

We had a lot of fun in spite of all that was happening. He only mentioned once that he was going to have two homes: two bedrooms and two Christmas trees, and maybe even two dogs. He looked so much like you, Jeff; it was good for us to feel tugged back to a happier time.

What you need to know if you don't already is that infidelity is really about immortality (note the "t" in there). You may have figured that out by now. Some people do things in order to locate a pulse, a breath, a drop of blood. Others do things for ego, the fountain of youth. Dress it up and call it lust or call it love, but really all it is is a call: You're getting old. You're going to die. You feel trapped, an animal with its leg caught in the metal teeth of time while everything young and fun is scampering past, all those things you never got to do or see or have. Such desire can be dangerous; so many of the things that brought such easy exhilaration in childhood (skates and bikes, climbing and jumping from great heights) become increasingly perilous when there is so much at stake.

I am someone who was always already old, and not by choice, certainly not by choice at all, but it was what I was given and I grew into it. I look back and, yes, I can see what I missed. But I also think that my cautiousness has served me well, even though people are rarely appreciated for the right thing at the right time. So much comes with hindsight. Look at this, these scraps of notes, a whole stack of entries where I wrote: *Something is not right. What is going on?*

I had nothing to go on but intuition; it was like that moment

when a snake comes into a yard and silence falls; the birds know. It
is a deafening silence.

How many times has your father accused me of thinking I know
everything? "Let's hear it, Lil, Miss Knower of Everything." When
he says that (and sometimes he still says that) I will say, "Not true."
I say how I have never fully understood quantum physics and a
couple of other things, like I don't speak Swahili. These days he
laughs at all of that. A joke of, what, 60 years? Still, there is so much
I don't understand in and of this world, the mind alone such a mystery. We think we will come to a place with all of the answers, but
it just doesn't work that way, even though I hope the opposite for
you two. The romantic me wants you to be the ones to defy all odds
and solve the mysteries, get all the way into that promised land. The
realistic me simply wants you to find peace with all that you will
never know.

After my mother's death, my dad and I knew we had to give each
other solid facts. Our lives depended on it. We never actually discussed this, and yet it was understood.

*I will be at the library with so-and-so, and if I am not here by 5,
you will know I stopped by Woolworth's.*

Sometimes I met my friends at the counter of Prospect Street
Drug Store, and we sat and talked about this or that (school, clothes,
boys), but I knew better than to let my dad down and leave him to
worry. Many days, I hurried along those icy streets in saddle shoes
or galoshes—oh, I could have used the tough warm boots I have
worn in these recent years—and all the while, I imagined him pacing, peeking out the window where the streetlight glowed, and my
chest ached and pulse quickened knowing the look on his face each
time I was just seconds late. "Leave a note, Lil," he said a million

times, and so I did, and he did as well. *Be right back*, we often wrote. Sometimes we just wrote *BRB*. I have saved many of his notes (the solid clear letters, his B's with a long tail like a cat). *BRB, Lil.* I tell you this because otherwise, you might spend years wondering, "Who is BRB?"

BRB was security. BRB was a promise.

Frank

∾

WHAT TO SAY? *The train has left the station. I love you because.* Though he has imagined this moment many times, Frank hesitates now, pen poised and ready. Certainly he should leave a note; it's the decent thing to do. The house is filled with Lil's notes—reminders of appointments and who people are, the day and the weather—*Remember*, the notes say. *Don't forget.*

He writes, *June 12, 2018*, and pauses.

He's forgetting, and faster with each day it seems. Her notes remind him of the little stickers in all of their windows, opaque maple leaves that are supposed to warn the birds, and yet they stubbornly keep slamming into the glass, a desperate act not unlike when he caught Lil abandoning the tubes and portable oxygen tank to wander out onto the porch to smoke. "Just one," she said. "One little puff."

Frank is tired of desperation, tired of forgetting.

Several times now he has skipped an appointment and instead driven to see his childhood home and the train tracks where his father died over seventy years ago. The last time he went, he felt guilty deceiving Lil; she had waved a Post-it note at him: *Appointment. Today. Cardiology.* Her ability to remember the present was completely eclipsed by the past—filled with the minutiae of the past—while the present was a trail of notes that resembled a board game, which took them to lunch and then to dinner, to pay a bill, watch a movie, with spurts of television news or a call from one of their kids or the knock of a neighbor he likely did not care to see in between. That particular day, he had come home to more notes: *The doctor called. You missed your appointment. Where were you? Advance two steps. Do not pass go.*

They say he needs a valve replacement. His daughter hounds him about that valve replacement, no longer willing to accept his excuses of "If it ain't broke, don't fix it," because she says it *is* broke; it *does* need to be fixed. They say it is so much better these days, that his is like an old rusty screen door, though he and Lil had grown used to hearing it years ago, the rhythmic ticking.

"We will always remember this," Lil sometimes said with a quiet, calm resolve that assured him that the two of them were in a good place. She signed her notes with the little face that made them both laugh, a face that looked like *The Scream*—round eyes and oval mouth; it was their daughter's trademark as a four-year-old, her archaeological signature, her "Kilroy was here," and she left it everywhere, crayoned behind drapes, scratched into the arm of the leather sofa, penciled inside books and on her bedroom door. Becca was the child always documenting and remembering, begging for souvenirs everywhere they went—little license plates with her name, snow globes, cheap dolls. Her drawers were filled with rocks and feathers and leaves and bottle caps. She loved to hide little pieces of Halloween candy everywhere, so she continued to eat it well into November.

Jeff had been just the opposite. Money. All he wanted was money. He set up lemonade stands and mowed yards; he filled more savings-stamps books than anyone else in their elementary school. He sold his Halloween candy or whatever else he could take to school without getting caught (firecrackers and cherry bombs), though he often did. Frank hadn't wanted to think about what that meant for Jeff's high school years, though he suspected condoms or marijuana or perhaps black-market exams. Lil praised his entrepreneurial spirit, and Frank tried not to go there, knowing he would lose his temper and make matters worse. Even now, the differences between the two are extreme: Becca, in her sleek modern home and now-happy marriage, a popular divorce lawyer, and Jeff, financially very successful doing whatever it is he does with technology but never really sinking roots, and needing his sister's legal advice way too many times. Lil said the new woman in his life is age-appropriate and very promising, but who knows; that's what they say every time. *Who knows.*

Frank draws the little face out of habit and then stares at it.

He once dared to flip open one of Lil's many notebooks, only to find dates and moods, as if she were charting the weather, page after page of her emotional forecast: *Cold and blue, but that's November—too many memories that come and pull up a chair and refuse to leave.* He flipped quickly, because he could hear her in the hall closet and knew she would return any second. He flipped, thinking surely he would read his own name, surely his presence would fill her notebook. He found *hopeful* and *grateful*, but then there was also *lonely*, *overwhelmed*, and *sad*, emotions she expressed so rarely. She had doodled little things and then x-ed them out. X marks the spot. You are *here*. And *x* equals the unknown, what is missing, a mistake, as well as a kiss.

The little face was off to the side, shocked mouth a perfect *o*.

Next to the face he's drawn, he writes the word—*their* word—and says how sorry he is to break his promise, that he's impatient and ready, that he hopes Lil is right and there's something beyond it all, but even if there isn't, it's better than just sitting around and waiting for the inevitable and feeling like a burden, fearing the disgrace and disgust that often comes with the slower route. *I'm sorry.*

"DAYLIGHT IS ONE of life's greatest gifts," his mother had told him years ago. "It is easier to accept and believe in daylight." He wonders now if this is why he has always felt a slight sinking when the sun disappears; even on the happiest of days, there is a sadness and an awareness of the shadows. Sundowning, they call it in hospitals and geriatric units, when confusion and distortion settles in. But he feels he has known some fragment of this for much of his life.

He was only ten when the train wreck took his father, but the moment divided his life as clearly and sharply as scalpel to flesh; that part of his mother that had radiated the light of day long after it passed was suddenly gone, extinguished, cut away with such exact precision that he spent the next fifty years looking for it, as if it might have been saved and frozen, like the many specimens his father had surgically removed and sent to pathology for study. It was only in the aftermath of her death that it hit him; all those hopes of a return had been futile.

As a boy, Frank was fascinated by his father's knowledge and skill, the way he could talk about the human body as if it were a machine, the way he could thread a needle and mend something

better than Frank's mother or grandmother, and the way that nothing seemed to scare or bother him, no amount of blood or trauma.
People often stopped them in public to say thank you, lifting sleeves
and pant legs, tugging shirt collars off to the side to show the excellent remnants of his work, from the faintest white lines to those
resembling a zipper or track. His father didn't look like a hero; in
fact, he was the opposite—average height and build, dark hair, and
an expression that always seemed studious, as if he were on the
verge of figuring it all out. But he had an air of confidence about him
that made others trust him, and apparently he had more than lived
up to it all in the operating room.

Frank did not inherit his father's gift or desire to be a surgeon,
and in fact was teased in high school biology for getting light-headed
when formaldehyde frogs were splayed out in front of him on a lab
table. He was much more in sync with his father's father, a general
practitioner of that earlier generation, when so much was diagnosed by clues—the eyes, the by-products, the gums, the reflexes.
His grandfather always said that what he did was not unlike someone unraveling a mystery, and he taught Frank to put all the pieces
together like a puzzle, like the blind men trying to describe an elephant and each bringing forward a different part. "The real value is
when you can put it all in context," his grandfather had said many
times, and he might've said those words when they learned Frank's
father had died, but of course that was impossible, since his grandfather had died the year before.

*The real value is when you can put it all in context, son. Decipher
it, solve the riddle.* Memory had taken two fragments of Frank's
life—both true—and lined them up to provide a story. He thinks
about it all a lot these days, the different parts of life, what he and
Lil have jokingly called the long limp to home plate, something not
as funny as it used to be. Both his father and grandfather had died
way too young—his grandfather in his early sixties, and his father

barely forty. Out at third. Out at second. Often, it had been easier to think of them that way, briefly out, but still in the dugout, just waiting for another inning.

Frank's grandfather was thin and always impeccably dressed—suspenders and bow tie and long sleeves on even the hottest of days, a wry, bemused smile that always suggested there was more to learn and understand. In 1973, when a physician with the last name Frank made the discovery of what is known as "Frank's sign"—a crease in the earlobe that might suggest cardiovascular disease or diabetes—Frank felt closer than ever to those childhood exchanges, as if he could hear his grandfather calling out to him from the grave: *Think, Frank. Look, Frank. Your job is to find the clues and put them together.* Frank was nearing retirement before it occurred to him that his grandfather's words had likely been what led him to an interest in history and archeology in the first place; so much of life was such a mystery that it was satisfying to hold a solid object for study and enlightenment, classification. How often had he stood in front of a class and held up a skull or a leg bone and asked the students to imagine the body that once housed it. Did it have scales? Feathers? Fur?

His grandfather had said, "Our job is to find the pieces and put them together, each generation getting closer to the whole." And now Frank's own earlobes bear those heavy creases, but who needs the extra proof when all else is so clear. "Just say it," Frank said at his last appointment. "I'm a walking time bomb." But the young man, barely out of school, refused to do so, just continued in that calm, steady voice talking about heart-healthy diets and surgical options, how these options don't come with guarantees, and how there are all kinds of risks anesthetizing a brain as old as his, if they would be even willing to try it, as if Frank had never heard any of it before.

Our job is to find the pieces and put them together, and, yes, Frank has always found solace in that, as well as in studying something contained by time or geography or both, contained in a way that you could imagine someday knowing all that can possibly be known. Here are the remains of a man who was born *here* and died *there* at approximately age nineteen in 1322 BC. It would drive him crazy to be in a field constantly growing and changing, to be in a lab racing for the cure, or programming computers, where the language you learned last year is dead and everything is different, like when Lil was not able to help the kids with their sixth-grade math. How frustrating to try and put together a puzzle that is constantly changing shape and size and color. No, it has been much more satisfying for him to focus, to explore the objects discovered in a particular site at a particular time. *Find the pieces and put them together.* His grandfather ended many of his case discussions this way: the symptoms, the diagnosis, the treatment. For Frank, it was the discovery, the dating and cataloging, the preservation.

"My job is to stitch up or get rid of whatever your grandfather finds that shouldn't be there," Frank's father once joked. "I'm the cleanup man." His father resembled his grandfather—the posture, the timbre of their voices—and Frank now has trouble distinguishing the physical features of one from the other, an overlapping blurred symbol of strength and knowledge. But images of his mother remain vivid—too vivid—the before and the after; the happy wife of an exemplary surgeon living in Lowell, Massachusetts, and the wife of a slow-moving tobacco farmer in rural eastern North Carolina.

A FEW MONTHS ago, he had told Lil he had an appointment at Duke, yet another checkup, and that, no, he didn't need for her to make the drive with him, she should enjoy the day, keep doing whatever it was she was doing in there surrounded by her boxes and papers, the radio tuned to classical. She said she didn't have that appointment written down. "And I always write everything down," she said. And then he lied and said he was sure he had told her. "Don't worry about it," he said. He had to look away when he saw her expression, the flush of her cheeks and the look of confusion and then irritation. He felt guilty, an old ugly pang of guilt. He had never been able to lie to her, not well anyway.

"Maybe I forgot to tell you," he said, finding a reason to turn to the window as if he had just heard something. "All routine—pee in a cup, stand on my head, recite the Pledge of Allegiance."

"That one might give you trouble."

They both laughed, but he felt the heavy weight of her studying him.

Now, he moves quickly to the front door and out into the bright morning. The humidity is already like a wet, heavy blanket as he goes to his car and slips behind the wheel. They had laughed about living on a golf course when neither had ever played. They heard someone yell, "Fore," and they called back, "Against." They tried not to complain about the humidity and ugly, scraggly pine trees, especially when Becca and some of her friends were there and working so hard to help them settle in. But they have both missed the New England weather and their home in Newton.

And, no, he hadn't missed the shoveling—not really, given all the warnings that had begun to come with it—or climbing the slick, icy steps, but they loved their house and it was hard to think about what the young couple who bought it have done—ripping out walls and the century-old radiators, blowing out the back and filling it with glass, like a huge aquarium, digging up the old hedge of lilacs to make room for a pool. Lil couldn't stop talking about it—over and over—after their old neighbor Gloria had called to report, which, for better or worse, she had done for fifty years. A hip replacement a year ago gave Gloria more time than ever before, and Lil finally had to say that it was getting hard for her to hear these things, she wasn't sleeping at night. The lilacs were difficult enough, but then her perennial beds, years of collecting and adding and tending, were plowed out for an outdoor kitchen and a big firepit.

"An outdoor kitchen?" Lil had asked, and reached for him to take her hand. "Why would you have an outdoor kitchen?"

When they had first met Gloria, Lil had despised her, a feeling that lasted for a couple of years; she called her Mrs. Kravitz, after the nosy neighbor on *Bewitched*, and did a whole little routine where she imitated her, slouched shoulders and frowning grimace as if she had just swigged vinegar: "Was Becca supposed to be with that Collins boy? Do you know he smokes? Did you know your son sometimes sneaks out his bedroom window? He's going to kill himself one of these days on the ice." They learned a lot from Gloria, whether they wanted to or not, and unfortunately the education continued after their migration south; every time Gloria called with a new installment, Lil hung up vowing to never answer again, and yet she was unable to resist the next time *not* to help herself to another round of painful news. "She's the only person I know who remembers what our house looked like when we first bought it," Lil said one day, "and the kids grew up together." And then, the recall of those memories softened even the worst effects of Gloria. "And Gloria's husband died so young," she continued, as if to convince Frank why she maintained a relationship with someone who tested her last nerve.

HE LOOKS BACK at the house, the front door painted the same shade of blue as their old one in Massachusetts. Benjamin Moore, Spectra Blue. A different name but the same formula, and no telling how many gallons he has purchased over the years, because it was often her choice for the background of sky in the many dance recitals that came each spring.

"Doors are very important to me," Lil had said when they were moving into their very first house, her hair dark and pulled up into a knot, an old paint-speckled shirt of his hanging from her shoulders as she stood and studied the door, a paintbrush in one hand and a cigarette in the other. They were barely thirty.

He brakes for two golf carts and six men dressed like Easter eggs—Tweedledees and Tweedledums—who wave broadly before disappearing over a rolling green hill. The canopy of tall, spindly pines shades his drive to the main road, the pines and humid air and blazing sun also a part of his long-ago childhood, which he spent years rejecting and trying to forget. But now he feels pulled back like never before. He needs to go back to where his father died and then where he last saw his mother. Maybe today, he will walk through that house and stand out in the yard where he played as a boy. It's where he first felt the dark waves of fear and loneliness he has run from ever since.

Shelley

SHELLEY ALWAYS HAS a to-do list much longer than she can ever finish, and she keeps it with her at all times, checking things off and then making a clean copy, putting down new things to fill the old, like those things she thinks about but never gets around to doing, like scrubbing the bathroom grout with a toothbrush dipped in Clorox or sorting that big plastic bin of Legos into colors. Those are the kinds of things she would love to do, but of course who has time? It's about all she can do to get Harvey up and dressed and moving, and then get herself to work on time.

She pulls into the parking lot of the courthouse with no idea of what to do next. Should she walk right up those granite steps and through the big doors like nothing had happened, avoiding eye contact as she always does with those lined up and waiting for some kind of sentence or judgment? Usually she feels proud that she is not among them, their eyes bloodshot and cigarettes dwindled to ash, some crime or misdemeanor heaped on their shoulders. She is sympathetic, but she is also afraid of them. She is afraid she will be told that that's where she belongs, there in the lineup of those trying to climb from a hole.

Sometimes, when she doesn't want to be home alone, Shelley comes and parks and just watches people coming and going. The Food Lion is always good, and so is the cemetery, near where she lives, and so is the courthouse. So many people and for so many different reasons: marriage licenses and restraining orders, murder trials and traffic violations. She has to keep the car running so she can stay cool in the AC, which she knows burns gas, but there's no other choice. If the wait gets to be too long, she will go across the street and wander around Food Lion and the Dollar Store, where it's cool, and if anyone ever makes eye contact, like they want to come over to her window, she studies her phone or the newspaper she always keeps in the car for this reason.

Recently, she learned about Google Maps and has been looking up places, like where she lived with Brent or where she lives now, and it's eerie to see the house there, as if she or Harvey might come out the door or peep from a window. She had looked up the name of that old man who keeps coming to the door: Frank Wishart. And now she types in his address—524 Ivy Trail—and studies the house, a neat little house like a storybook cottage with a blue front door. She zooms out and can see the golf course. Why would he ever want to come back to the house where she lives? Whitepages.com lists his family members: Lillian Wishart, Rebecca Wishart. She makes a note on the dashboard, where she has penned a lot of other information, like the phone number of Harvey's school or how many calories are in Chicken McNuggets or when her next oil change is due. Maybe she should ride over to *their* house and ask to come in. Maybe she should ask do they want to swap houses like on that TV show?

One day when Shelley was sitting like this at the cemetery—still in her bathrobe and bedroom shoes—she parked under a shade tree and watched a funeral procession. It was peaceful, and lately, she needs peaceful. But more than that, she needs to know she still has her job, and so parked here at the courthouse is the right place to be, even if it is hot as hell and scared-looking people are loitering all over the place. And she needs more sleep, uninterrupted sleep. And she needs to know there is not a person coming into her house when she isn't there or up to her car window. She locks the doors and opens the newspaper; it's a month old, but she studies it closely while the people in the car next to her get out and go up those big steps. The man stops to light a cigarette, and the woman clutches her purse close to her body. They are both painfully thin and clearly not there for something happy.

NIGHT TERRORS. THAT'S what they call it when children wake and cry and are too terrified to sleep. Shelley isn't crying, but that's how she feels all the same, maybe the fallout of being a mom with a kid who can't sleep, who often wets the bed, daily claiming he's seen a ghost, as if she didn't already have enough to worry and be afraid about without him giving her more. She looks up *night terrors*, and it says they can go on until adolescence! Harvey is only six, and the thought of seven or more years of this sounds terrible, like some of those plagues in the Bible, seven years of snakes and locusts and boils, all kinds of bad shit to mess you up.

When both of her boys were babies, the doctor talked about the Moro reflex, how infants' arms go reaching and grasping at the air as if something invisible is there to pick them up. The doctor said that it probably went way back to the beginning of time, babies reaching for the comfort of their mothers, kind of like the way Harvey always booby-traps her when she reads his story, one hand on her arm so that as soon as she tries to slip away, he wakes. The Moro reflex is the only fear humans are born with, the doctor told her; everything else is learned. The Moro is like those jerks and shivers you can't help and people say a rabbit ran over your grave, the kind of thing she would never say to Harvey these days, the way he is so scared of everything, especially ghosts, or the ghost he thinks lives in their yard and *comes in their house.*

With a cemetery practically across the street, it's all even worse. It's a pretty cemetery, some really old parts with great big trees, beautiful really, and Shelley has taken a lot of walks there since renting this house. It's peaceful in the daylight, like when she stopped to watch the funeral, but as soon as the sun starts to go down, the cemetery has a different feel to it, and so she closes the curtains and locks the doors, turns on the night-lights in the hall and in the bathrooms. "It used to be one of the best parts of town," a colleague at work had told her, not saying what was implied: *But now it's not.* But compared to some other places Shelley has known, it had seemed fine, and the rent is reasonable, and there's a big yard, and, no, it's not as big as the house they used to live in with Brent, but that was another town, another life, and now, according to Google Maps, that house doesn't look so hot either. This house will be okay once they feel settled. It takes time to feel settled, especially if you're the only adult.

"YOU'D BE SO easy to kill, Shell," Brent had told her early in their time together. "You do the exact same thing every day. Same place. Same time." They were in Atlanta then, and they'd laughed when he said this, and he'd pulled her in close. It was one of those days when she was aware of happiness; the sun was shining, the kind of golden light that makes even ugly things look good. He was teasing her, but it was true: the way she got up at the same time, made the coffee in the same way, used the same mug, parked in the same spot at work, parked in the same spot at home, sat in the same chair to watch the local news, and then circled back at ten to watch it again, to see if anything had happened or changed. He said that some nights when he came home from work, he could look in the window and see her there staring at the television, whatever was supposed to be for supper boiling or burning on the stove—teasing again.

Brent worked hard. He knew all about cars; he could fix them, and he sold them. When they first met, he even took Jason for rides in an old Mustang he had fixed up. He was someone with dreams about wanting his own dealership, and so Shelley made up some dreams, too, like she said she wanted to go to college and study plants and trees—"Botany," he told her—but the truth was, she felt like she was at the beginning of her dream when he welcomed them in. He got irritable sometimes—that vein in his forehead and flared nostrils were a sign—but he never touched her in a hurtful way.

"I'll knock you into next week," her father used to say. "I'll knock the daylights out of you." There were times when getting knocked into next week had sounded good to Shelley, one slap that maybe would be the last one, sending you way up into the sky and landing in another time and another place. When she met Brent, she felt safe.

But now, she has trouble sleeping and, yes, she hears things, too. Now that Harvey has talked about it all so much, she has started listening and she also is hearing the sounds, though sometimes it's hard to know if it is real or part of a dream. There is so much to think about and worry about that of course she might toss and turn, so she tries to relax, to think of peaceful things, like the ocean— *she sells seashells by the seashore*—or the way Brent sometimes sat and strummed a guitar, not really playing anything in particular but doing what he called "playing with playing."

That same day Shelley stopped to watch the funeral, she saw a woman standing in the newer part of the cemetery, where there is no shade from the baking sun. The woman looked middle-aged, her reddish-gray hair pulled back in a ponytail, arms crossed over her chest as she stared up at a bunch of birthday balloons tethered to a headstone. Once again, someone had gotten knocked into next week and someone who loved them was left to wonder why.

Lil

&

A FUNNY NOTE from a hundred years ago.

Dear Miss Lil,
My Girl Scout project is to help you quit smoking. If you
want too. If you don't Okay. I love to dance.
Lisa
ps) I get a badge for making people not smoke for being a
good neighbor.

"A little emphysema," your father says, "is like a little arsenic or
a little bullet in the head." We all know I need to quit smoking, but

I would argue as I have many times that the very cigarettes that are trying to kill me now might have saved me so many other times. Or that's the way I see it. I never felt alone with one between my fingers, moving back and forth, a cloud of smoke to shield my face from others, a cloak to make me invisible, like something Becca's girls were talking about from a book not too many years ago. I could hold a whole glowing fire at the tip of my fingers, and then so easily and powerfully I could put it out, under the grinding heel of my shoe or the flow of water, or into a bucket of sand.

October 24, 2016
Southern Pines
Sometimes I feel like a big antenna, circling and turning and picking up static and signals from others. Perhaps it is the result of seeking my mother, and how for years I thought I saw her, a face in the crowd, a woman at the top of an escalator or turning a corner and then gone by the time I got there. I have listened and watched for her, and now I am much older than she ever was. Isn't it odd the way my mother will always be 34, that all these times I have felt her presence, that is the person I see.

I believe in a lot of things: the calm that can come in quiet thought, the little murmurs of your intuition when you know something is awry and then gently feel your way to that weakened spot—a thin coat of ice on a river, the soft pulsing fontanel of your newborn, the whispered concern of your Jiminy Cricket. "And where has Jiminy gone?" I asked you all that so many times! "Where is Jiminy?" Remember Becca's big party when we were out of town? Or Jeff's little bouts of taking what didn't belong to him? The missing $10 bill. The gum and magazines stolen at Star Market. Or what about the crack in my mother's hand mirror, the dent in your father's new Oldsmobile. "Where is Jiminy?" Sometimes, one of you broke down

and confessed (often when you were young you did that), and then
Jiminy got old, and who knows where he went (Vietnam or a trip to
a monastery or a retirement home), and you two were left to fend
for yourselves.

"Sex, drugs, and rock and roll," you said. "A new dawn. Let
the sun shine." Who knows what you two think of all that now, all
grown, with so much of your own lives behind you. I am sure there
are many lies I never learned and that your own children have little
lies they have told you and their children will tell them. I know there
are times in both of your lives when Jiminy just went to hell. I do
know that. I do. What human doesn't know about that? And yet it
bothered me those times you didn't come to me to talk about it, to
confide, to let me help you make it better. I like to think that there
mixed with Jiminy's chirping, or whatever it is crickets do, is my
voice as well.

"Let it go, Lil," your father says. "Let go." He says, "They're
goddamn grown. They're practically middle-aged, for God's sake!"

November 28 (once again), 2005
Newton
I feel my mother's presence today. I do. It's gray and rainy, low
clouds like smoke, and I woke with her on my mind. People are so
odd about believing in spiritual encounters, as if it might be crazy
or stupid, and yet such a vast population of the world claims religious beliefs that sound like nothing more than a good ghost story,
a haunting. My religion acknowledges the power of all the dead, all
the souls. There isn't a gatekeeper or a scorekeeper. You have to do
those jobs yourself. You have to decide what it feels like at the end
of the day to rest your head and close your eyes.

I say I am not really a religious person, and yet in so many ways,
I am. Bits of this and bits of that have stuck and stayed with me; the

part of the Christmas story that I have always loved is when we are told that "Mary pondered them in her heart." I always think, yes, that's what mothers do. They ponder. They ponder in their hearts. Devoted parents never stop worrying. It's one of those things you never really know until you get there—like what it's like to have a baby, lose a parent, lose a good friend, lose many good friends.

Part of my wanting to be a dancer was all about the props, and that it made me feel close to my mother; being a dancer had been *her* dream, *her* desire, and she loved all kinds of dancing and was quick to learn. She had a natural sense of movement and rhythm, which I had to work hard to master. I was always much more comfortable with ballet—the discipline, the way that I sometimes felt I disappeared while stretching at the barre, muscles warming and lengthening. I was never able to simply cut loose on a dance floor and shake and shimmy all over. I have always admired the kind of uninhibited force that allows people to go to such places. It still makes me laugh to think of my mother breaking into song and dancing, pretending she was adorned with jewels and feathers. She once bought a pineapple (not easy to find, and quite pricey, my father noted) just to hold it up on her head like Carmen Miranda.

While I was never a natural dancer, I was a disciplined one, and I think that's what enabled me to be a good teacher. What I loved most were those years of leg warmers and classical music, the wordless stories unfolding in movement. I wanted to *teach* dance as much as anything, to create the stage for recitals, to line up the little cubbies there by the door, where they placed their street shoes and jackets. I wanted to make a difference, and I think my little school would have made my mother very proud. That's what I like to think. And at the end of the day, when all the children from the last class had been picked up and driven home, I loved to just sit there, rubbing my shoes in that box of rosin. And then I would turn the lights off and go to the center of the room, just the street light coming in, and rise on pointe, and then extend my left leg and see how long I could stay.

My mother once told me how Anna Pavlova could stand on pointe for hours at a time, frozen like a statue. The longest I ever did was 11 minutes, the big wall clock counting my time, while I stared right into the photo of my mother I kept on the side wall, near the light switch; she had drawn a little circle around her face, in a long line of women dancing the cancan, arms raised and stocking legs kicking.

I've always wondered if prayers and messages to whoever might be listening are heard as easily when they're said in our minds, or if it's better to say the words out loud. It seems the latter to me—perhaps because I like to think that what happens inside my head is mine alone. I think if I were a younger person and more the academic type like your father, that is a topic I could imagine exploring and thinking about. As is, though, the idea simply began the habit I have of talking aloud. You've laughed at it; perhaps you've even worried. For years, I had a dog there as recipient, and I miss that. I keep telling your dad how we need one more. Just one more to take us all the way home (perhaps a smaller one, a little poodle mix), and I tell your dad how it will let him off the hook when I have something to tell. But those nights, in my little dance school, there was no one there to hear me.

"Momma," I said, and sometimes still say. "You are missed."

"Momma," I said. "Please help me understand all that I don't know. Send me a sign."

One night in particular, in the studio at the end of the day, I could hear the clock ticking and the sleet against the window, and then I saw something from the corner of my eye. I knew that if I turned to look, I would lose my balance.

"I love what you've done, Lily," I imagined her saying. "It was never supposed to end that way."

"I know."

"I would never have done that to you."

"I know."

And then the streetlight outside sputtered and went dark. "Good night."

Your dad could explain it. Everyone could—it was in the paper; a car hit a pole, a teenager just learning to drive, with no business out in wintry weather, and that whole section of town was without power for hours that night. But for me it was a message: a miracle of timing, the promise that such connections are possible. I have never stopped believing.

When I look back and think of those nights alone in my school, it is hard not think of "The Steadfast Tin Soldier." It was one of those stories that made me cry as a young girl, which made me love it even more, that poor one-legged tin soldier falling in love with the ballerina he thinks has only one leg as well. I did it for the recital one year, remember? And, Jeff, I made you be the soldier because there were no boys taking class that year. You hated it, and your father told me he thought I was making a big mistake. He said if you turned out homosexual that it was all my fault, and that if I made you wear tights, he'd report me to Social Services. I can't tell you how many times over the years (the many young women calling us to ask where you were, how you could be so heartless) I told your father that if only he had let me put you in tights, perhaps to play Romeo, or even the prince in "The Nutcracker," that you might have been much kinder in the way you treated others.

There was a time I hoped you *were* gay, thinking that might explain everything, and then it could be so easy; you would just come out and find a nice man, who would also call me Mom, and live happily ever after. Because, at the risk of saying too much, I do need to tell you this—a playboy can still be relatively attractive in his 40s (where you are right now, with your young new person, who really does seem quite nice even if she could be your daughter), but once you turn 50, it begins to get dicey, son. It does. It is a fact, and who cares what those like Hugh Hefner do? An ascot and a martini will not get rid of wrinkles and crepey, scaly skin and the inability to perform without medications. Get to 70 and 80 and then it is just sad to act like a playboy. Time is always relevant. Get to 70 and 80 and the joke is how poor vision is your best friend in the bedroom. But more true is how important real love and devotion are. That is what I want for you.

The good news for you, Jeff (young you who did not want to be in the tin-soldier show), was that all the parents thought it was a sad and dark way for their little girls to end the year, and so the next recital was back to buttercups and butterflies and little rays of sunshine, and you got to do what you liked best, which was help me paint props for two months, our basement filled with our work—castles and flowers and bright-blue skies—and then you opened and closed the curtains on the night of the show. We had so much fun doing that, didn't we?

Balance. I try sometimes now to balance on one foot, and I look like a stork with vertigo, so I hold on to something and I can close my eyes and picture what I looked like the night the lights went out. I am not what I used to be. Even a series of relevés and pliés, simplest of simple, tax me. In those years when I had my school, I ended each day with a moment of balance or a series of tour jetés, or fouetté pirouettes, my eyes fixed and spotting on the photograph of my mother; and then I put on my wraparound skirt—that black knit one I had for the longest time, and probably would still, except it was what Rudolf liked to sleep with in his final years, and what I took to the vet with us the day we had to say goodbye. Too many times to count, I put on my skirt and boots and then stood there, feeling accomplished and proud in the entryway of my own business, and I smoked a cigarette, that little tiny glow on the end so contained. Powerful but contained. And I snuffed it out into a deep bucket of sand that I kept by the steps.

Thank you, Miss Lil.
Even thou you smoke like a chimbly. The general says
STOP!
Your friend, Lisa

Oh, I know I romanticize. I know there were nights I rushed, needed to hurry, nights when I was worried, one of you upset about something and not saying what, and your dad and I trying to figure out what to do, how to handle it. I ran errands for my father more and more as his health worsened. One of you had the flu or a virus or a sprained ankle, broken arm. Your dad didn't get tenure that first time, or he dreaded visiting his stepfather, or he told me he hated the drapes I had ordered or ("No offense") whatever it was I'd cooked last night. There were all those days. But now, time allows me pure silent joy. Even with (or perhaps thanks to) this awful oxygen tank, I breathe in and I breathe out. I breathe in and I breathe out. I marvel at the snow and ice, the silence there with each cold breath. I want every breath I can get.

Frank

∽

AFTER THE ACCIDENT, Frank had moved to be with his mother in eastern North Carolina, a place below sea level, with a river once known as Drowning Creek. No wonder he had begun collecting those things offering protection or luck: rabbit's feet and found pennies, horseshoes and wishbones. Although he has always professed no belief in superstition, Frank still kisses his finger and touches the windshield when going through a yellow light, doesn't walk under ladders, and on and on.

An old woman—a midwife of sorts—who checked on his mother in the aftermath of the accident and then after Frank's brother was born, told him that anyone who washed clothes on New Year's

Day would wash (she said "warsh") for the dead in the coming year. Frank's mother looked at him when the woman said this, as if intending to put his mind at ease, even though her own eyes were filled with a look of worry. "I've seen it happen many a time," the woman said, her gum bulging with snuff, and the oversized pockets of her apron filled with all kinds of rags and strings and collard leaves she said she would bind to Frank's mother's breasts "if they got heated and the milk wasn't flowing good."

His mother's face blanched with the information, or maybe it was at the rendered beef fat the woman had offered to smooth on chapped or torn skin—"A cure for what ails you," she had said—or maybe Frank's mother was wondering if she had washed clothes the New Year's before, the answer likely yes if Frank's father had worked that day or the night before and come home, as he always did, with various stains on the sleeves of his white coat.

"How's he sucking?" the woman said, and pointed to Horace, red and squirmy in Frank's mother's arms. "And how's your hurts up the leg and your shoulder?"

Frank watched and listened, thinking surely his mother would be ready to go back to Lowell soon, back to where she had a real doctor and it didn't smell like a butcher shop, back to where they had a life, but his mother assured him that there were fine doctors here and that she had seen several of them, that this woman, Mrs. Brewster, was there simply as a neighbor, trying to offer a helping hand.

Frank had told Lil this story, trying to remind both of them that people often mean well even when what they offer you is the last thing you would ever want to see. He said this after a neighbor tried to share with Lil her stash of coupons for denture gel and Depends. "No, thank you," Lil told him when he had tried to encourage her to add that extra line of politeness so many people in this part of the world do: *How sweet of you to think of me, though. So nice of you.*

"But I don't think it's sweet," Lil said. "These are *my* teeth, and my bladder is nobody's business."

He told how Mrs. Brewster once showed up at their old back door with a plate of chicken feet on rice, everything boiled to a thick, goopy white, which Frank's mother accepted graciously. "Say thank you, Frank," she had said, while the old woman was encouraging him to take a bite, but he just stared at the gelatinous bones with horror. *Surely*, he thought, *we will go home soon*, only to later watch the man who would become his stepfather gnaw on those spindly, rough bones and pronounce that he'd had better but they weren't terrible.

By then, it seemed his mother brightened whenever Preston was around, thanking him as well for his great generosity. How could she have ever managed her recovery and those early months with a newborn without him? And for him to make room for Frank to join them when school got out. "So generous, so very generous," she kept saying. Preston had stayed across town with his sister so that there was no mistaking his intentions, allowing his home to serve as a convalescent spot for several survivors in those first months after the crash, and then just Frank's mother.

"Preston was the last person to speak to your father," she whispered to Frank that night in early summer when he was shown the small cot in the corner of what Preston called the parlor, the dark floral wallpaper making it feel like a jungle, the horsehair sofa itchy on his legs if he tried to sit there to read. The window looked on to the front porch where there was a swing, and past that the street, then a dusty dirt road with a field. He had stood there many times, looking out, willing a taxi to pull up and his mother to emerge in her traveling clothes and tell him they were going home—no, not on the train, they would take the bus—but a year later, when her leg and shoulder were healed and when Horace was crawling and into everything, it became clearer and clearer that wasn't going to happen.

His mother's life seemed to dead-end like that broken track, and by then his grandmother had left Lowell and moved to Worcester to live with Frank's aunt and her husband. She missed them, but she was doing very well. She wrote to Frank that she had a little garden and cooked a lot; a black cat had taken up there, and she had decided to let him stay. She named him Midnight, after the radio show Frank liked to listen to, and she looked forward to him visiting.

PART OF HIM is afraid to go inside Preston's house, afraid he will be disappointed that none of the things he hopes to see will still be there: the nicks and cracks and clues that give proof of that long-ago life. The front yard is no longer neat and manicured, as it is in the photo with his mother. It was probably taken before his graduation or maybe a dance, because he's in a suit, his mother smiling.

In the root cellar, he had a stash of old pennies, flattened by the train, and marbles and matchbooks, and a coin his stepfather gave him from when he was in France in the war—the kinds of things Frank has spent a lifetime encouraging students to talk about, the objects that they hid or that defined them, the tokens that they felt brought good luck or protection from evil: an Eye of Horus, an ankh, a cross, a star, Saint Christopher medallions, four-leaf clovers, a mezuzah on the doorframe, a witch ball in the window.

ON DECEMBER 15, 1943, Frank was safely housed in his childhood home in Lowell, Massachusetts—632 Andover Street. He was ten years old and had spent the day, and night before, anticipating his parents' return. The window shade in his room had a bone ring he would hook his finger in and raise, once the room was dark and his eyes had adjusted, to look out over the neighborhood. His grandmother was there with him; she had stayed often after the death of his grandfather, and they were both looking forward to the next day, when his parents would pull into the station.

When darkness fell that late afternoon, his parents were already beginning their journey home, and he felt jealous of the trip that had not included him. His father had volunteered his skills and was working at a base in Miami Beach; he was coming home for the holidays and hoped he would not need to return. In every letter he wrote, he had mentioned how he felt both lucky and guilty to have not had to leave the country.

Frank's mother had gone to meet him, and to spend a couple of days in the warm sunshine before coming home to the New England winter. She said it was a good time because things were about to change. "Soon you will have a little brother or sister," she had told Frank; she was already wearing different clothes, a full blouse, like an artist's smock, with a bow at the neck. For years he had begged for a sibling but at age seven had given up and stopped asking. At ten, he found the news embarrassing, given the things he had learned—how this would have happened—and he fought hard not to let any imaginings of his parents doing anything like that enter his mind. The situation was especially complicated by his father having already been away from home so much; his visits had not been long enough to fully get beyond the awkward readjustment and go back to the way life had always been.

Before going to bed, Frank had listened to his favorite show, *Captain Midnight*. He lay on the living room floor while the sound of airplane engines filled the room. Captain Midnight could fly anything, and though Frank was drawn to the fantasy of *being* him, he was more comfortable as the young Chuck Ramsey, his charge and underling. That's what Frank had been to his grandfather, and he was missing him in ways he didn't know how to articulate.

Lil had said that maybe he had had a premonition of what was to come, but what would it have mattered anyway? What he knew was that his dad had promised to take him the next week to get his junior flight badge with the secret decoder. They were going to do that, and they were going into Boston to see the Christmas lights, like they always did, and they were going to Jordan Marsh, to get all that he needed for Boy Scouts—the canteen, compass, mess kit. But the most important was the badge, because each episode ended with a clue to decipher, and every kid with a decoder who solved the message would be entered in a special drawing. Then there was always an ad telling you to drink Ovaltine. It used to be the one about antifreeze, something Frank's dad quoted whenever he took the car to be serviced. *Kids, tell Mom and Dad to take you to Skelly Oil . . . it's time for antifreeze. Remember to remind your dad that it is cheaper to prepare than repair!*

Captain Midnight and Chuck Ramsey were once again having to battle Ivan Shark and his mean daughter, Fury; Mr. Jones, which was a code name for the president, was depending on them. During the breaks, a salesman kept begging kids to drink their Ovaltine and to get their badges, which Frank swore to the radio that he would do.

His grandmother had gone to bed soon after dinner, but she let him stay up to listen, and he lay there on the floor, hands clasped behind his head, his sock feet up on the footstool in front of his father's chair, until the last sounds of Captain Midnight's engine faded away with one final message about how to get your badge— *Don't miss out, boys and girls! Don't miss your chance!* Frank was wearing a sweater his grandmother had knit, in shades of brown and olive and tan, a sweater he dreaded outgrowing, the sleeves already too short. That was the before of his life—there he was on firm ground with so many things to look forward to—and then he was free-falling.

The radio switched to music, and he'd turned it off and walked upstairs, not noticing then what a nice home he lived in. He tiptoed past the room where his grandmother slept and stood in the cold bathroom to brush his teeth, noting with alarm, as he always did, the glass with his grandmother's teeth floating there like some kind of exotic fish. Then he looped his finger in that bone ring in his bedroom and lifted the shade to see the icy street below: an occasional car, a light here and there in windows of other houses. His sheets were turned back, warmed by the hot water bottle his grandmother had placed there, a heap of blankets on top. And then he slept. Perhaps he imagined the view from Captain Midnight's plane. Perhaps he imagined the warm sandy beaches his father had written about, or the palm trees. Maybe he just imagined himself there on the *Tamiami Champion*, seated with his parents while the dark night and all that lay beyond the tracks sped past the windows.

He had sometimes allowed himself to imagine the life that might have been if his father and mother had arrived that December morning. They would have gone to get his badge. And then they would have gone and gotten his canteen, and they would have chosen their tree at the lot where they always went—Wood Brothers, over on Bridge Street—and it would have stood there in the living room window so that he could see it as soon as he turned the corner coming home from school. He would have seen his mother laughing, hands clasped together in absolute joy when the lights were strung and the ornaments in place.

But he never saw her look that way again. There was happiness in her life in the years to follow, sure, there was goodness, and even times she laughed, but it was never the way it was before that night; that expression was another thing that got left behind in the house on Andover Street, cemented in his mind as firmly as his own initials in the concrete foundation of the porch. He once tried to explain all of this to his younger brother, but they didn't get very far, their histories so different. Horace grew up with a mother who was serious and quiet, the pensive and kind wife of a farmer in eastern North Carolina, and Frank's mother was the cheerful, bright-faced wife of a surgeon in New England. Horace was his whole brother, but only DNA could prove such a thing, because they'd grown up in two separate families.

THE FACTS WERE simple when written down, and Frank had been called upon to tell them for years. The simpler and faster the better when someone said, "Oh no, I am so sorry. What happened?" It was the middle of the night, and the southbound train derailed and landed on the northbound track between small southern towns, seemingly in the middle of nowhere, on a night when snow covered the ground, there in a part of the world where such was a rare occurrence. The people got off, only one person seriously harmed, and huddled there, waiting for help and relieved that the accident had not been worse. But it was dark and icy, and the man sent ahead to issue a warning slipped and broke the fusee he had intended to light to alert the other engineer, and on and on—one thing leading to another and another, mistakes and missteps and human error leading to the crash that shook those early morning hours, barely past midnight, jolting passengers, many of them soldiers like his father, who had managed to stay alive in the war and then were on their way home for Christmas, perhaps waking just in time to realize their lives were over.

Even now, Frank imagines the screams and the twisted steel, the cold parallel rails stretching from north to south while cars jumped and plowed forward a length of two football fields through tobacco fields and stands of pines. The sound was deafening. The thin glaze of snow that would bring a rare white Christmas was an additional hindrance to those working to find the dead and injured in the darkness. The scene was beyond comprehension to those there, devastating, while seven hundred miles north, Frank was swaddled in sleep and the anticipation of daylight and all that it would bring to his life—a Captain Midnight badge, a canteen, a Christmas tree. His greatest worry was the inevitable shy distance he would once again feel when his father got home. "Hi, Pops," he had practiced, imitating a boy in his grade, who always said that to his dad, who was a teacher in the school, but it embarrassed Frank to even try that out, not his voice at all. *Hello, Father. Daddy. Dad. Hi, Dad. Welcome home!*

A car honks. More golfers in fluorescent pants pass, and a glaring sun blinds him as he steers toward that place one more time, to stand where seventy-four years ago daylight had come not as a gift but as a glaring beacon of truth of all that had come to an end. He had read the accounts of what people saw there in the cold morning light: blood-soaked clothing and shoes strewn up and down the tracks, a wedding veil hanging from a tree, Christmas gifts and purses and luggage ripped and emptied, buttons and cigarettes and eyeglasses and watches. People would continue to find and pick up the pieces for months after, and even now, he knows that if one were to excavate beneath those tracks, there would be so much found, traces of lives that were turned over and buried, the lost meaningful detail someone had once attended, a hook on the neck of a dress or a necklace, a clasp to hold a tie, a penny returned when buying that day's paper. He needs to stand there in that place; he needs to stand and allow himself the vision—of loss and destruction and of himself, ten years old, curled under a blanket in a comfortable house, his eyes closed against the cold northern night sky while waiting for all the good things promised with his parents' return home. The canteen, the Captain Midnight badge, the Christmas tree he and his father would have dragged along the icy streets. Now it is hard to place himself back in his childhood bed and not think of how only twenty miles away, Lil had lain sleeping in her father's house. What were the odds that they would find each other?

And why does he feel so close to that part of himself now? The young boy part. That ignorant, grieving part.

Lil

❧

October 11, 2017
Southern Pines

THINGS I WANT you to know:

My father often asked where my mother got all the crazy language she used; who did she think she was?

"I read," she said. "I read a lot." And she pointed to her stack of fashion and movie magazines. She talked about "dead hoofers" and "ducky shincrackers," and told me she hoped I wasn't going to be "khaki wacky," which she then explained meant "boy crazy."

"She's only ten!" I remember my father saying, only to have her say how it's never too soon to teach a girl not to be an "able Grable" or a "sharecropper." I had no idea what she was talking about, but she said things like that often. She said of my father's sister, my aunt Cammy, whom we only saw once a year: "Mutton dressed up to look like lamb." And my father said, "It takes one to know one." She bleated and went back to what she was doing, which was teaching me to braid my own pigtails. The funny sound made my father laugh. They did laugh (sometimes at the expense of others, but they did).

You knew a different man in those later years. You two knew him as a sweet man under a crocheted lap blanket watching Walter Cronkite or old reruns of "Gunsmoke." He even liked that silly "Gong Show," remember that? But that wasn't the real him; that was just a shadow, something soft and worn.

I will always think of one afternoon in particular. My father and I were at the lunch counter in the drugstore, and the waitress asked us if everything was "lulu." It was a word my mother had used often— "That's lulu, Lily," she would say when she thought I had done something good. My father froze and stared at me as if to ask if I'd heard it, too. His first look was one of shock, and then he stared back at the woman, searching her face while ordering his sandwich. I don't recall the rest of lunch, only that when we got home, he sat in his chair and cried for a solid hour. I had never seen him cry and I wasn't sure what to do, and so I went up to my room and waited until he called up and said it was time for dinner. I remember he cooked eggs that night, my egg cooked inside a hole he'd made in a piece of bread with a drinking glass; he also toasted the little circle of bread, off to the side, just as my mother always had done. The next day he was fine, and he never mentioned it again.

I told your dad that story early in our marriage, and the conversation led us to the decision that we needed a secret word. I had heard that the Houdinis had a secret word and that they promised whichever one died first would return to communicate with the other, and I told your dad that just because the Houdinis had failed to correspond after Harry died didn't mean that we would fail. The plan is that one of us will appear on a bus or at a lunch counter in the body of someone young or foreign or living in a pasteboard box, and with that spoken word, we will recognize each other.

There was a time I read a lot of books about such connections and experiences with the spiritual realm and sought information wherever I could, my eye drawn to fortune-tellers and those who claimed that they could connect with the dead. I even went to a séance once and sat with a table of strangers. There was a sudden cold draft (I felt it), but it was also winter in Massachusetts.

I thought I heard a voice say, "Help me," but I couldn't have sworn to it. Besides, it was at a time when you children loved watching all those things on Shock Theater, and I remembered later how you both after watching "The Fly" said, "Help me, help me." I never decided if my mind was playing a trick or if I'd really heard it. I was going through a really difficult time, and I also know that "Help me" would be a reasonable thing for anyone, living or dead, to say if feeling stuck. But I told your father later that it seems to me important if you *are* going to speak to someone from the other side, it would be good to have something original or unique to say, so that there's no question or wondering about it all. We will know. We put a lot of thought into our word, and the time we spent doing so will always be some of my best time.

Our word is one I've never heard anyone else say.

We were in Florence when we chose it, and we were completely enthralled with the magic of the place, the ancient streets and buildings making us feel so hopeful and powerful in our artistic and intellectual pursuits. I was dreaming of opening my dance school and of the recitals I wanted to do—"Petrushka" and "The Sleeping Beauty," adapted to make every child feel included and important. And your father talked about the book he wanted to write; he was studying burial practices, and all the myths and history of the ages, with particular interest in Paleolithic cave art, dating and researching when humans first paid attention to the care and ritual of the dead. He talked about things like art for the sake of art, or if those drawings were there to tell a story, to reveal something specific about the death of an individual, and then he would answer all of his own questions without me saying anything at all: Doesn't *all* art communicate something? Isn't that the purpose? And I just listened, his voice going back and forth with the rhythm of an oscillating fan, the distant hills and old buildings shimmering in sunlight. I listened. The Neanderthals and the Homo sapiens—had the two been able to communicate on any level at all?

"Oh, I hope so," I said every now and then, or something like that, lit a cigarette, and poured us each a little more wine, the carafe between us nearly empty. "I really hope they all got along."

I asked: Did our sweet Margot understand when I said I didn't want to put her down but the vet said I had to? Has any child ever understood when a parent says, "This hurts me more than it hurts you"? Do people really believe what they say they believe? And I told about the experience my father and I had had at the drugstore.

That whole stretch of time in Florence has always felt removed from the rest of life; it was big and magical-feeling as we walked along, your father studying the cobblestones and every odd-shaped window, or anything etched above a doorway. I was completely transformed by the Foundling Hospital and those beautiful sculptures of swaddled infants there on a background of beautiful sky blue, like giant cameos.

I still have the notes I wrote so I would never forget the details of it all: all the names and places foreign to my tongue. It was one of those wonderful times when we spoke of two different things and yet we were able to take turns and listen and somehow complement each other. We marveled at all that remains to remind us of lost people and times, your father always noting what would have been constant—the light and length of the days, the seasons. I told how my mother once got her palm read, holding it out to me as if I could see all that had been foretold, and how I've always wished I had a photograph to go back and study.

My dad was on my mind a lot those days, there in the house on School Street, with too much time alone, so I sent a lot of postcards that arrived long after I had returned. While thinking of our word, I was reminded again of Houdini. As a young boy in 1908, my father had witnessed the great magician leaping from the Mass Avenue Bridge in shackles and locks; there was a long, silent waiting before he surfaced and swam from the river. It was a story my father liked to tell, a piece of history he had witnessed, and he spoke of the sad irony of how after all that Houdini had survived, he was felled by a sucker punch from some selfish fool who thought he could get his five minutes of fame. According to Houdini's wife, they *didn't* make contact after his death, and then on top of that, she was not allowed to be buried beside him, because she wasn't Jewish, but I like to think that they *did* make contact and kept it private, stressing that such a connection is intimate and needs to be kept that way.

Your father and I spent days thinking about it, something rarely spoken that would connect us. Remember in elementary school how we had a secret word in case of an emergency and someone you didn't know had to come get you? (Petrushka!) Thank goodness we never had to use it. But now, people need passwords just to live in this time we are in, everyone relying on old dogs and cats long dead and childhood streets and numbers, phone exchanges that belonged to people we once knew or loved, stores that no longer exist.

At the Foundling Hospital, I stared at that large wheel that rotates into the ancient building, and I tried to imagine how a mother would feel placing her newborn there and then in one half turn losing sight of her forever—almost always it *was* forever, though the hopeful ones pinned notes or little bits of jewelry, something sewn into the swaddling that the child might someday present as proof of heritage. It seems I stood there for a very long time, and it is one of those memories that comes to me so often. The light was so beautiful, like nothing I had ever seen, and as we walked through the building, I was aware of my hands pressing into the wood and stone of hallways and staircases, joining the prints of hundreds of years, the dust and oils of lives long over and yet still lingering there. You could feel them, hear them whisper.

And maybe *that* is how it all came to be—yes, I think so. I told your dad this feeling I had; I told him how sometimes I feel I am just on the verge of hearing something. "They whisper," I said, and he said that that is what he would do in the future, come back and whisper in my ear. And then we began what has been a lifelong back-and-forth argument, because neither of us wants to be the one left behind.

"I want to go first."

"No, I'm going first. Wait and see."

We were about to head back out into the light, to drink wine and talk and laugh, and then to our tiny room to make love, our young limbs wrapped and entwined like supple vines, and then sleep and wake to start life all over again. We were already thinking of you both, even though we probably couldn't have said so in the moment. But how could I not think of you when standing there in that ancient place, in front of a display of hundreds of tokens meant for the sake of remembering and reuniting, the thimbles and buttons and lockets and coins, tiny brass fish and hairpins and keys, all marked in ways that make them unique, all there to say, "I love you. I'll be back. Please don't forget me. I'll be back."

Shelley

THERE ARE SO many things Shelley wishes she could say, things that fight to get on the tongue, only to be swallowed back down in the name of composure or decency or respect. As a child, it's why she loved that book *Go, Dog. Go!* and why she has enjoyed reading it to her boys. "Do you like my hat?" one dog asks, and the other repeatedly says, "I do not!" instead of that polite girl thing so many were raised to do: *Well, it's a hat like I have never seen before*, and *What a hat that is! Oh my, that's a hat, all right*, and *Aren't you sweet to even think to ask my opinion. I am so flattered and honored that you thought of me.* Nice girls = enablers. Now there are whole libraries of books about this.

Do you like my hat? *Hell, no, it looks like shit!*

Doesn't she look just like a little doll?

Oh God, yes! A little voodoo doll, with rusty pins stuck all about the mouth.

These cases get to her this way, and she has to vent somewhere so she won't screw up and accidentally shout out in the courtroom. She likes to take shorthand the old-fashioned way, with a piece of paper and a pencil, a method that requires her alert attention and doesn't leave room for mistakes or for other thoughts to enter her mind, a problem she has had her whole life—sometimes several thoughts coming to her at one time, so that she consciously has to slow down, slow down, and she tells herself, *Slow down*, only she can't afford to do that while at work, because just that little soothing repetition could cost her a very important sentence or admission or piece of evidence. It's easy in a town without all the modern equipment to fall back on good old shorthand—stenotype or paper and pencil—and there is no one around here who comes close to her speed and accuracy on keyboard or longhand.

Her job is very stressful this way—demanding a level of vigilance almost as bad as having a newborn you're worried about, and both of her sons' births had filled her with anxiety. Jason, because she was all alone in the world, and Harvey, because of the defect. That's what they said—"the defect"—like an airbag or floor mat, or something misshapen or dented on an assembly line, only she was Harvey's assembly line, her birth canal his only way out, and so of course she feels responsible. Harvey's birth had caused so much worry she thought she would never sleep again. It was a shock to see him and a shock to see the look on the young nurse's face. It felt like blame, an accusation. *What did you do?*

This happens in court all the time, the accusation, the need to plead your innocence, even when in the back of your mind there are all those worries and fears that you might be guilty after all, that there might be bits of proof. She wasn't an older mother, but she probably *did* have a drink or two before she knew she was pregnant with Harvey; they said it all happened in those early weeks, one in seven hundred, they said, and there you are, the upper lip not fully formed. "It's such an easy repair these days," the doctor had said. "One surgery might do it." He spoke so gently she barely heard him, but she allowed herself to keep thinking, *Easy, easy. It's so easy.* But Harvey doesn't think it's easy. If he did, he wouldn't wear masks all the time, a whole series of battered Halloween masks, from an alien to a Ninja Turtle, and he wouldn't wear those fake mustaches or hold his hands up to his face whenever he laughs to hide the thin scar there.

When Shelley lived in Atlanta and had to wear that steno mask, she couldn't help but think of things like Anthony Hopkins in *Silence of the Lambs* or, and maybe even worse, that someone else had worn it, their breath trapped there. These days, it is hard enough to breathe about a lot of things, like this trial and Brent being long gone. She has to remind herself, because she has told Harvey "He'll be back" so many times, it's easy to believe it herself. But that isn't true, and someday Harvey will need to know the truth, just not today, because he is driving her nuts, and what mother says that about her son? He is only six. Harvey is *only six.* Of course it is hard to concentrate on the trial and getting every detail just right. Paper and pencil are always best, always her first choice, but the keypad is also fine. Either way, her hand or fingers moving, letters shaping. Listen to the words, only the words. If she listens to the words, she can sometimes hit 300 words a minute; her average is 250. The world record is 360, so no one else around here can even come close to what she can do. That is what she has going for her; there are others who are good, but no one is better. She writes, *I am the best.* She writes, *I can, I can, I can.*

The cases around here are not your standard domestic brawl or robbery or occasional crime of passion. There are those, too, but that's the easy stuff, all fluff compared to what she is usually taking in, the cases that cost her sleep at night and keep her looking over her shoulder at odd times. There were three heads in a freezer, right there in a normal avocado-green Kenmore—obviously old, given the color, but still running, which someone said later was certainly a fine recommendation for a Kenmore; terrible circumstances but a fine recommendation. The testimony revealed it to be a twenty-one-cubic-foot Kenmore top-freezer, even though the accused continued to call it "the Kelvinator" throughout his trial—"my momma's Kelvinator"—leaving the whole court to feel like they'd gotten spun around in a time machine and spit out somewhere eighty years ago.

The use of freezers has unfortunately been a popular thing, especially for crimes committed in the heat of summer. It seems the involvement of mothers also comes up often: Momma owned the house, Momma owned the freezer, it was Momma herself there in the chest freezer out in that garage, her legs mixed in with those of deer and rabbits—a 12.8 cubic foot Frigidaire in white; there's very little color choice in chest freezers, it seems, but Shelley did make a notation for herself, something to share with Brent, which she thought would be an interesting topic of conversation, if she ever talks to him again, that the use of freezers to hide crimes crossed all class lines. There were just as many Viking and KitchenAid freezers as there were Amana and Kenmore—murdering and freezing the body was not just a low-class crime, but it is why she had insisted they buy a Bosch refrigerator, much to Brent's impatience and obvious irritation when she said she wanted that one because it was the one brand she had *not* heard about being used.

"There's always a first," he said, and for a moment she froze, right there in Lowe's, Harvey and Jason still in her vision, sitting on a riding lawn mower. Jason was more than old enough for her to trust him with his little brother by then, which was a relief; Jason had been a boy she needed to tether to her, wrist to wrist, with what looked like a long telephone cord so she wouldn't lose him in a crowd.

"Shelley." Brent jiggled her arm. "That's a joke."

"I knew that," she said, and made herself laugh. "I really did." And she said how she was just keeping an eye on the kids; she was excited about a new refrigerator, and how Jason had told Harvey the one about is your refrigerator running? Better go catch it!

Now, they have an old refrigerator that came with the rental house, but the first thing she did was to put all the old school photos and recipes in the exact same place as when they lived with Brent in Georgia. Jason's sixth-grade school picture, cowlick sticking straight up, a grin so big his eyes are closed. A picture of Jason holding Harvey, held in place with a magnet Jason had given her around that same time, which says CHILLIN WITH MY PEEPS, because he was begging her to buy him some little chicks like they'd seen under the heat lamps at Feed and Seed.

Refrigerators are to keep your food from going bad and to hold family photos, not corpses. Bodies in freezers, *many* bodies in freezers over the course of her career, and there have also been bodies in the river, *many* bodies in the river, bodies in trash cans, bodies identified from half-decomposed tattoos, many spouses gone missing, falling down stairs, attacked by owls, dosed with arsenic by their concerned loved ones: she even read about all those things back then, Ted Bundy and what have you, and Brent always said it made him feel so much better about their—he said "their"—life to hear the stories she was reading and what she brought home from work; in fact sometimes they even laughed at the sheer horror of it all, but once she was alone again with just the kids, the terror returned and was magnified, the knowledge of how easily one human can choose to do away with another.

The latest case she has been recording is another disturbing one, and one that has the whole town focused and attentive, the least likely person accused of murder. Here's this asshole of a man, a surgeon who lives in one of the biggest houses in town, probably has Viking and Wolf appliances, and drives whatever car you might drive if you wanted to spend a lot of money, and just because he was good at taking a scalpel to someone's heart, he thought he had license to fuck anything that could fog a mirror, play head games on his wife, who since his incarceration had broken free of her dumpy-mama wardrobe and stepped back into the light of the living (part of his excuse for having affairs was that his wife had stopped taking an interest in her appearance). He sits there in his orange jumpsuit, obviously disgusted by the women who file up to testify, and not by choice, these women. Imagine getting subpoenaed into such a mess—you think you have a little secret with this prominent person in town, only to find out that not only did you screw a murderer but you are one of many, you are not so special after all. Shelley can't help but wonder what the husbands think of these wives they'd trusted who fell under the spell of this person who is not even physically attractive. And certainly there is no personality or emotion to be found in his little superficial shell; he is like those locust shells that get left behind on the pine trees.

As a child, she liked to burn those shells, hear them pop and singe, a little pile of amber cracklings, something that she never should have told Harvey about; there are little books of matches in the pockets of his pants every time she does laundry. Where does he even find those matches, with names of restaurants and hotels that haven't been around in years? She used to collect shells, *all* shells— locust and turtle and crab—because of her name; in fact, she knows that her name perhaps served as prophecy for who she would be, because she *does* have a shell, a good hard shell, and she has needed one, oh my, yes, she has needed one, growing up the way that she did. How many even survive such a thing? How many can come out of such a place and wind up with two wonderful sons and a job that comes with benefits at a time when benefits are so hard to get.

Yesterday, she was thinking of all of this and had to ask that the judge repeat herself: "Excuse me, Your Honor, too much coming in at once. Could you please repeat what you said?"

Judge: I said, "Objection overruled."

Oh no, but what was objected to? She has worked in the court with this particular judge many times, a middle-aged woman who makes Judge Judy seem like Glinda the Good Witch, and of all the judges, she is the one most people are afraid to get. They say she has had death threats, and that some lawyers do everything they can *not* to get her. They call her the Ice Queen and say she will chew nails and spit tacks, that she is known for giving the harshest sentences, especially when women and children have been harmed. She also has the best clothes that Shelley has ever seen.

Perhaps this particular case has haunted her even more than normal because the girl was not unlike who Shelley once was, a young woman raising a little boy alone, someone who had not been dealt a good hand but had still survived the childhood part and was slowly getting some traction. And on top of that, this was someone people loved, an underdog of sorts who was actually making a go of it all. In fact, that young woman was so loved by a circle of nice people that Shelley has even found herself feeling a little bit envious of the care and concern that had existed for her. And how stupid is *that*? The girl is dead, found dead right there in her own little apartment, there in a chair that had once belonged to her mother; that's what the friend of the young woman said on the witness stand. And Shelley realized she has nothing that belonged to her own mother except her blue eyes. Or did she? Maybe she has something tucked away somewhere, and she made a note that day, to look, to search, to see, or did she agree with her brother that she wanted absolutely nothing? All of that is so hard to remember sometimes, the pieces out of focus.

But imagine a chair being your prized possession even though it connects you to such a sad legacy; the young woman's mother had ended her own life, and the murderer, thinking he was so smart, had staged it all so it looked as if the young woman had simply followed the same path. The part Shelley keeps thinking about is the courage of the person who could have that chair and love it in spite of all the reminders. The woman on the witness stand described a fighter, that girl, someone determined to get beyond it all, to *not* be scarred by her mother's poor choices, to *not* raise her young son the way she had been raised. "She was so strong," the woman said. "We were all betting on her," and she looked over to a whole gathering of people, most of them really old, who were nodding and wiping their eyes.

SOMETIMES WHEN SHELLEY is on her break, she sits quietly and writes little notes to herself in shorthand. This case has made her remember things she doesn't want to remember, but it has also left her to note how lucky she is that Brent is Brent and not like the monster there in orange. Brent did not physically hurt her; he didn't even really threaten her. He just called it quits and left, so how lucky is that?

She has thought that perhaps she will someday write an exposé, or maybe even a novel or movie about all this, and so she jots down her notes about the *real* story and how she would tell it, and how she would describe people if it were a television show, because that is so much easier than thinking about herself. Then, if she has time on her break, she types it all up. She types all that comes galloping into her head, things like: *There once was an ugly, pompous asshole given a pass in society because he had money and a degree, and not even a great degree, but what do you call the worst student at the worst medical school in the world? Doctor. So, ladies, pay attention; it pays to be choosy.*

The accused withheld important information from the young woman he murdered. She trusted him, and that was her big mistake. He wanted to be in charge of everything and was capable of compartmentalizing, so he dealt with it block by simple block, his brain no more advanced than a preschooler—apologies to preschoolers everywhere. And that is why this case is so disturbing. How many have willingly trusted someone they loved? How many have wanted to believe in someone with whole heart and faith? How many hear someone has this degree or that or this job and think that means everything else lines up? The young woman made a terrible mistake and paid for it with her life. He promised her a house. He promised a future of love and devotion, the two of them raising their little boy together. But the young single woman working hard in a nursing home and living over a fast-food drive-through (Harvey calls her the Dog House Girl) couldn't have *really* liked that man in the beginning. How could she? Why would she? He's a squat pig—apologies to pigs everywhere.

Then, Shelley drew doodles of pig snouts and tails in the margin to keep herself alert while the judge called a recess. Two little things gave the man away. Two little errors. There was a scrap of paper and there was a blouse, both found by the woman who discovered the dead girl. Harvey's head is full of local kid tales about how she now haunts the little drive-in on the way to the beach. Her favorite hot dog was the Chihuahua, Harvey has said. It has salsa and guacamole on it. "She was nekked," Harvey said. "Naked," Shelley told him. Even she has never said "nekked," even though she certainly grew up with plenty of people who did. "She had matches," Harvey said. "She burned all the evidence."

But there *was* evidence, and the woman who found her also took note of the label of the blouse hanging on the chair, a blouse the woman had seen her young friend wearing earlier in the day, surprised by how out of character such a blouse was for her. And that is the kind of detail that always breaks a case: a wrapper for peanut-butter crackers in a nut-free kitchen, a cigarette butt where no one smokes, a receipt for that chest freezer that happens to coincide with someone disappearing.

And there was a note in the playpen of the young woman's apartment, in square neat print: *Go home. Dinner is waiting.* The woman who found her was smart enough to have taken photos of both the label and the note, and the handwriting expert said the bearing down of the letters showed tension and aggression. The dishonest person tries hard not to reveal something, but they always do, and you did not need to be a rocket scientist to know this if you looked over and saw the murderer there in his orange outfit. The woman on the stand said that she knew immediately that her friend would never have killed herself. "She loved her little boy more than anything on earth," the woman said, and Shelley knows that, yes, that was absolutely true. You would protect that child with every ounce of strength even if there was no father around to help you. Even if you were filled with fears that something or someone was haunting you, creeping into your life in ways that were disturbing and upsetting, you would take care of your baby. It has been impossible not to imagine herself there, naked in a chair and looking out the window, the needle in her arm thickening her thoughts of her son— her son—or perhaps she was berating herself, thinking she should have known better. *Oh, why didn't I know, why didn't I know?*

When the handwriting expert came to town, the people who worked at the courthouse all scribbled anonymously and then listened to the man explain what he saw there. When he said things like "honest" and "dependable," people jumped to claim that it was them, and so Shelley pretended one of the good ones was hers, even though hers really showed signs of someone who is "not always telling the whole truth," someone "secretive," so she worked hard to change those letters and not add those extra little loops that lock everything down, only to later hear that expert say they can *really* tell when someone is working to correct what is so obvious. The expert said it's a liar who stabs those *o*'s, and Shelley is pretty sure that she has never stabbed an *o*, perhaps punctured one a little bit from time to time, but never stabbed, and she certainly doesn't do the "felon's claw," that sharp, aggressive hook, thank God.

What she really wants to know is, What did those women see in that awful man in the first place? How did he trick them so badly? This balding narcissist with a prescription pad and a scalpel, and a head shaped like a football like in that cartoon Jason used to watch all the time? And Shelley knows she shouldn't talk about people's appearances that way; in fact, she has even wondered if Harvey's little lip was punishment for all those times she thought things like: *Good Lord, fix your hair*, or *Get some bigger pants that fit, why don't you*, or *Clean those toenails. Floss your teeth.* Still, it seems that a horrible murderer should be fair game for what anybody wants to say, and Shelley has enjoyed picking apart all those things that money couldn't help him fix—like a football head and thin lips, and eyes that are set back deep in the sockets—but women have always been more forgiving of the physical appearance, it seems, if there are the capabilities of providing what they want, or think they want, in a home. Would Shelley have fallen for him?

The woman who broke the case is a hospice volunteer who refused to let the case go cold and is raising the victim's child, the man's son, orphaned by it all. The doctor stares at that witness like he could kill her, so she rarely looks at him but instead keeps her eye on that group of elderly people who sit as if in the theater. Every day, they arrive in vans, from retirement facilities as far as two counties over; Shelley was told this is their show of support for the young woman who had spent her time washing and grooming their hair and feet. One woman sits and takes notes the whole time in a way Shelley finds impressive, especially given her age.

THE FIRST NIGHT Shelley thought she saw someone in the house, a lean figure rushing past her door, she assured herself it was a dream caused by all of Harvey's night-terror talk and drifted back into sleep, the sounds she heard—a knock, a sigh—attributed to the limbs of the maple tree grown too close to the house, their old Labrador retriever, Peggy, turning on her arthritic hips before slumping onto a cool patch of floor, Harvey tossing and turning in his lower bunk in anticipation of another morning he would fight going to school. All last year, every morning when she walked him the four blocks, he'd clung to her hips, hands gripping and squeezing, as he had done nearly every day of first grade; she had to pry his hands from her clothes and push him away, often not looking in his eyes so that she wouldn't weaken.

"It's okay," the teacher had said, a young, clear-faced woman who didn't even look old enough to be a teacher. She was always in front of the long brick building, ushering her charges from buses and cars and parents like Shelley into the main hallway, where they would line up and wait to walk together to their classroom. Once the other children were watching Harvey, he stood a little straighter, and then, with the teacher's assurance that everything would be okay, he walked into the building without looking back. Shelley would spend the rest of the day taking notes in the courtroom, imagining that someday, as a grown-up, he would do that same thing, just walk away from her and never look back. Her brother had done that, and, really, she had, too. She learned early that she was treated best when not noticed—average student, average looks, invisible, and out of the way—no one wants what the average or below-average person has, and so they leave you alone, and sometimes being left alone seems the best choice.

She'd escaped into music and videos: Nirvana, Janet Jackson, and Salt-N-Pepa. But her favorite album for a whole year was by the Red Hot Chili Peppers, and she played "Under the Bridge" a million times, because she *did* feel like she was her only friend, but who she wanted to *look* like was Mariah Carey, and she tried all kinds of ways—tiny curlers, sleeping in braids—to get her hair to do what Mariah's did. Some days, she left early so she could fix her hair and makeup on her way to school; she ducked into the Quik Pik, and then bought gum or a pack of cigarettes on the way out so they wouldn't get mad at her for being in the bathroom so long. She practiced singing "I'll Be There." If her mother had seen her—if her mother had noticed—she would have said, "What'd you do, stick your finger in a socket? You look like a clown." But as soon as the house was behind her and she started walking, she felt better, soothing herself as she had for as long as she could remember: *It's okay. You can do this. They don't know you. They have no idea who you are*. And the same words worked at school. The same words work now—*it's okay, you can do this*—though sometimes it's harder than others; sometimes there is a lot more at stake.

She feels happy those days when Harvey is able to walk away without looking back, but it also hurts a little. She would be devastated if someday he flew the coop and never looked back. But Jason hasn't ever turned away from her, and he has even more reason than Harvey might, given his early years in life when it was just the two of them moving from place to place. Her heightened sense of how terrible humans can be is the price one pays for being in the courtroom every day, an occupational hazard of one whose whole life is about recording the pounds and pounds of notes about weapons and threats and murder and guilt. How can it not invade your personal life?

"It's okay, Harvey," the teacher had said every morning. "And just think, next year you will walk in all by yourself."

"It's okay, Harvey," Shelley says when there's talk of seeing ghosts or when he comes to her in the middle of the night to say his bed is wet, always in a way as if he is surprised and has no idea how it got that way. Or when he asks the hard questions about where his dad might be. Alaska in an igloo? On a desert island? Inside a whale? The whale had caught her off guard, wondering where Harvey had learned about Jonah, since that is another ball she'd dropped in the lives of her children—no religion—or so Brent thinks, or thought, past tense; he is in past tense. But, no, not Jonah. Pinocchio. That's where it came from, Geppetto inside of the whale. The church of Disney has been a much easier church for her to attend all these years. Sure, Walt had a dark side, but doesn't everybody? Like certainly a God who smites this and that when he gets pissed off has a dark edge about him, right? Brent had been raised by people who believed that.

"Backwards," she once muttered when he quoted something his mother had said, and he pulled off the road to set her straight. That's what he said: "Let's set you straight." And then he said: "Who do you think you are anyway? Look at where you came from."

Oh God, did she have to?

Every time she vacuumed that house Brent had rented in Georgia and emptied the bag, there were some old, putrid things to discover: hair and fingernails (*whose?*) and God knows what. It reminded her of her childhood. As soon as she'd moved in, she had wanted to rip out and burn the carpet, take up the linoleum yellowed with age and depression, the very molecules screaming of sadness and abuse, and Brent had promised in the beginning that she *could* fix things up, take down the heavy old waxy drapes and let in light and air. But it had never happened, and now she's on her own in another old house, vacuuming somebody *else's* putrid remainders, like maybe that old guy and his people who died here, and why does he want to get in so bad anyway? It's creepy. She would *never* go back to where she came from.

Last Christmas, Shelley set up a wildlife camera to photograph the birds that came to her feeder. It was a gift from Jason, but now she is afraid to look and see what is recorded there. The birds looked so strange the one time she looked; she hadn't had the heart to tell him that the camera he gave her didn't show everything in color, like at the Audubon place, but in a gray fuzz, like a surveillance camera, like those eerie images of people at bank machines or convenience stores, like Princess Di and Dodi had looked in that last picture, or the young man who was murdered after getting money from the ATM; she'd worked that trial, too, his parents there in the front row.

Those pictures always look like a warning of something bad to come, perhaps because that's when we see them, after the fact. After something bad has happened and *then* people are interested, *then* people pay attention, like at the trial when they studied the screen-shots of that young man closely enough that they could see that, yes, there was a gun pressed to his head.

When Shelley looked at the footage that one time, there were squirrels, and a deer, way too thin—eerie and misshapen-looking—as it tried to eat the bulbs somebody else, maybe that old man or his dead mother, had planted.

"That was my room." The man had pointed at the back window overlooking the side yard. "And I spent a lot of time there in that strip of woods." He seemed relieved that that little bit of woods was still there, and so is she. When she moved in, her landlord said he and some others had fought to keep it; otherwise, their houses would practically be on the interstate. The woman, Lillian, had been waiting in the car that day, and she lifted her hand and waved at Shelley. She waved like she knew her, like maybe they had spoken a million times before. It gave Shelley a chill to think that; it reminded her of that old ghost story where the girl who died ages before in a car wreck keeps coming back home from the prom. But these people were real enough, because she saw the man's face up close, where he had nicked himself shaving, and she saw him trip on the under-growth and catch himself when he walked back near the tracks. They are *real* people, and she knows where they live.

Frank and Lillian Wishart. 524 Ivy Trail. She could ring *their* doorbell. She could show up and surprise *them.*

"He better be careful back there," Harvey had whispered that day, shaking his head and holding on to her leg; he was wearing a beach towel around his shoulders and holding the lid to the trash can and a broom handle. "That's where some of the bad ones stay."

The camera was aimed away from the birds and at the front

door, but Harvey said now it has Vaseline all over it and is aimed at the ground. "The ghost," Harvey had said yesterday, but she knows Harvey could have done it himself, because she has caught him playing with Vaseline, putting thick coats of the stuff on a vase and one of his Hot Wheels, and though she knows she needs to talk to him about it, there has just been too much to think and worry about. Harvey says that someday he will have a great big mustache and drive a convertible, except when he goes to Munchkinland, and then he will put the top up and lock the doors. Every day, he pretends to be a masked bandit or a surgeon, or he drapes his lip with a big fake mustache and begs her to let him wear it to camp. She taught him the Frito Bandito song, a song she associates with her mother and a time in her life when she thought things might be better than they were. Harvey loves that song and sings it over and over. Brent once asked her how she had all of that in her head, and why, and she wanted to explain the many, many mantras she'd had before she knew there was such a thing, the many repetitions and words and phrases and songs that allow her to disappear, like climbing onto a raft on the swells of the ocean and simply rolling and rolling and rolling. Not long ago, she heard a circuit judge say "the weight of fate," and the words got stuck in her head for days after. *The weight of fate, the weight of fate.*

"IT'S OKAY, HARVEY," she says a million times a day, and she tries to keep him from calling Jason. "Jason is in college now."

"He said I can always call him for any reason at any time."

"Let him enjoy summer, okay? We will, too."

"I need to tell him we have a ghost." He was wearing a thick black handlebar mustache that made it hard not to laugh, or cry—Harvey often left her feeling she didn't know which to do.

"What do you mean, we have a ghost?" She asked the question, her own skin prickling with the knowledge that she hadn't been dreaming the sounds and visions after all.

"I see it at night."

Harvey is obsessed with all the local scary or weird stories his older brother and kids at school have told him—and doesn't every town have them?—the underlying message always, *It could happen to you.* There's the Beast of Bladenboro and the Glencoe Munchkins and the maniac under the bed. "It was all just terrible," Harvey has said about the Beast of Bladenboro, sounding more like someone sixty years his senior. "It was awful, and it kilt everybody's dogs so there wouldn't be nobody to bark when it come after people." They had had this conversation more times than Shelley can count— Harvey worried that the Beast of Bladenboro would try to kill Peggy, and that it might be the maniac under the bed, because both of them killed dogs. Every time Shelley told him that the Beast of Bladenboro had attacked before she was born and had not attacked since, and that it was probably a wild bobcat or something, and the maniac under the bed is completely made up to scare people, and the Glencoe Munchkins were poor children born with terrible deformities who couldn't walk and were left to sit on the porch all day while their parents worked and people teased and mistreated them. "Something we would never do," she stressed. She told him this, and his hand instinctively went up to his mouth and lingered there. "It's not a scary story," she said. "It's a heartbreaking story. It's a story about people being cruel and hateful, and we have more than enough of those."

"People teased the Munchkins. They threw rocks at them," Harvey whispered, his own hand curled into a fist. "And I can't stop thinking about them."

"It's okay, Harvey!" Shelley tries to lead him to other topics he is interested in that will make him laugh. He loves tiny horses and Ninja Turtles and knock-knock jokes. *Orange you glad I didn't say banana again? Yes, yes, indeed I am.* Harvey is fascinated by animal droppings and has been since Brent took him to some nature hike in the mountains, where they met someone known as the Scatman Explorer who had a booth with all kinds of samples; Harvey came home and surprised her with some earrings made of petrified raccoon turds and porcupine quills; Roadkill Jewelry, it was called, and on the card there was a photo of the cute little woman named Virginia who had made them. Harvey was barely four but still talks about it all like it was yesterday.

The teacher advised her that he needed a lot of attention—even though he gets attention; he does. Shelley pays him a lot of attention, but she is also exhausted, and who wouldn't be? She blames exhaustion—worry and exhaustion—for her restless sleeping. She is on her own, and her son is obsessed with things as sweet as My Little Pony and Einstein, the tiniest horse in the world, and as dark and gross as Lizzie Borden and the Menendez brothers, and she never knows which of it he will be focused on. She could throttle Jason for introducing Harvey to all those scary, morbid things, but she's worried about Jason, too, his own sense of self so fragile. *Those are the ones who get in trouble.* She has typed or spoken that a million times. A million times, she has heard a judge say something like that. *Those are the ones who get in trouble.* She's worried about her own life and whatever truth is ahead, and she's worried about the outcome of the trial that has the whole town tuned in and waiting. Who wouldn't be worried? Who wouldn't feel frightened?

And will she lose her job? Her brain is firing odd things at odd times, unable to locate the right information when she needs it. Her brain is about to short out, and of course it is. She really needs this job, so much of life so uncertain. There are so many things to worry about and think about right now, she has to write her to-do lists in shorthand. And it was such a simple mistake when at the end of a very long and disturbing day of testimony, she also submitted her grocery list and her made-up little version of the trial, along with her additional shorthand notes for the day. *Oh God.* For twenty-four hours now, she has swung between, *Oh God, how did you do that? And Oh God, of course you did that. Who wouldn't be making mistakes and dropping balls all over the place with all that you have on your shoulders?* "The real report is all there, too, every word of it," she said. "I am the fastest in the area. Look it up. I average two hundred fifty words per minute, but I have on several occasions done three hundred. The world record is three sixty. I'm good. I'm very good. I made a mistake. Please."

The judge will get back to her, they said. There will be questions. They might, for instance, ask how she could both work on things like a grocery list and a made-up account of the trial of a horrible asshole while *also* transcribing everything that is being said on the stand, and yet she can do that, she can! Like her mind is quick to seize upon words that get used and overused; she notices when the same word is repeated, and she notices when a word becomes popular all of a sudden, like *cohort*, and *purchase*—as in "traction," and not "to buy"—words pulled from the back of the closet and then used and used, gaining *purchase* as they get used to death by the *cohorts* far and wide. She has always been able to do that. It's her gift to be able to think these things, connect the dots, while also working and taking notes on everything else, but clearly the machinery has been screwing up lately. She is alone in the world, and her son is driving her crazy, and she would almost swear that someone *did* pass by the doorway of her bedroom last night, Harvey asleep for once, Peggy too deaf to hear. Of course she made a mistake; she's human after all. She's just a human, a "human bean," as Harvey always says. She is a human who made an innocent mistake. Hasn't everyone made mistakes? Hasn't everyone needed to look away from something that was just too hard to see?

Harvey

❧

BEFORE HE LEFT for school, Jason decorated Harvey's bedroom ceiling with glow-in-the-dark stars and markers and Harvey couldn't wait for it to get dark so he could look up and see. Jason had written *Little Dude* right over the closet door and then wrote both of their names in Klingon just above the bed. Harvey's name in Klingon looks like *PEFHr* and then a bad circle, all done by somebody who can't do letters good. They do that to trick people. That's what Jason says. Jason says his *J* looks like pie, but not the kind you eat, a kind Harvey will learn about someday if he studies and can pay attention to numbers. Jason loves numbers and told a joke to their mom where he said, "Pie aren't square. Pie are round." And Harvey laughed too, even though he didn't get it, because when they all laughed together he felt like he could fly. Jason said if you know numbers you can do just about anything and he made Harvey count out loud when he stuck stars to the ceiling. They did constellations of all of Harvey's favorite things: doughnuts and turtles, including that one from China that is four hundred years old the camp teacher told about. Sometimes, Harvey pretends that he is there visiting that turtle and when he puts his hand to the glass it swims right up and stays as long as Harvey stays, and people say things like: *Look at that smart boy. He knows all about numbers and can speak Klingon, and turtles all over the world love and follow him. He's the turtle whisperer.*

The best part is what Jason called the Turdy Way. He held Harvey up on his shoulders and let him draw in all the different turds he learned from the trail where his daddy took him hiking one time. He used the sticky stars and the glow-in-the-dark marker and only he knew which was which: coyote and bear and squirrel and rabbit, fox and raccoon and possum. "Want me to do a people one?" he asked and Jason said yes and then they both laughed so hard that Jason had to lean over and flip Harvey out onto the bed, which was a game they liked to play. Instead of a moon, they did a great big mustache. A handlebar, Jason said, not a Fu Manchu, which made Harvey laugh. A mustache is the trademark of the superhero Harvey has invented and spends a lot of time drawing—Super Monkey. He has a big mustache like Harvey will have someday and he wears a baseball cap and has supersonic ears that can hear anything being said in the whole world. He just tunes his ears and can go to places everywhere in the universe, like Raleigh or Myrtle Beach or Texas, or Lake Titicaca or Uranus, which make people laugh. Jason taught him those last two and kids at school liked it when Harvey said that. They like to say Lake Titicaca and they like to hear about turds and butts and all the words you can call a butt, like *fanny* or *bum* or *tail* or *a-s-s*. And they also like knock-knock jokes, especially the ones that go on for a long time, like "Banana banana banana banana who?"

Super Monkey's specialty is that he hears murderers about to murder and he gets there just in time to make them not do that. Harvey himself wrote in teeny-tiny letters behind his bedroom door Super Monkey's message to the whole universe: *Don't get kilt*. Harvey also has left that message out in the part of the yard where he isn't supposed to go. *Don't get kilt*, he wrote in the dirt with a stick and he also put it on a piece of paper and left it near where he saw a ghost all in black crawling on the ground one night. He peeked out the window and saw that, and the next day what he wrote was gone and he found some fresh rabbit turds.

Every night before bed, his mom says the same things: "There is no such thing as ghosts, Harvey. No, we are not getting a miniature horse. Lizzie Borden never lived in this house. People cannot live without heads. That is ridiculous and has never happened. It's okay, Harvey."

"Jason?" their mom said before Jason had to move to his school. "Please tell Harvey that there's no such thing as ghosts."

Jason said, "That's right, Harvey," but he also stood behind her and shook his head no. Jason said Harvey's dad was not *his* dad, even though their mom had really, really, really wanted Jason to call him Dad.

"He's not your dad?"

"No."

"But you're my brother."

"I'm your half brother."

This made Harvey stop and think and then they both started laughing. A half brother. That's why in the corner of the ceiling is just half a boy: an arm and a leg from a stick body. Harvey said, "What if you had to choose a head or a butt. Which would you choose?"

Jason shook his head. "I can't believe you even asked that, Harvey," he said. "Of course I would want to be the butt."

"And what is Mom?"

"She's Mom."

"But is she your mom, too?"

"Yes."

"So who is your dad?"

"Dead. My dad is dead and don't ever mention him, because it will make Mom cry."

That was when Jason still lived with them. Now it's just Harvey and his mom, and old Peggy, who just wants to sleep all day. Harvey pulls Peggy close at night so he can feel her snoring. He wishes he could stay there with her every day and just draw Super Monkey and watch TV and read his comic books. Some kids stay at home for school—that's what Jason said—and their mom said those were some parents with a lot of time on their hands. Even now that it's summer, Harvey still has to go to camp while his mom is working. Summer camp, which is where a lot of kids get murdered. There are a lot of movies about that. He hasn't seen any of them yet, but he knows the killers' names, like Freddy and Jason and Chucky, and he knows what to look out for if he sees them coming.

Jason told their mom that the only way he would ever love his little brother is if he got to be the one to name him and so she let him. Jason said it had to be a comic-book name like Marvel, DC, or Harvey. Their mom had liked DC, because then she could really name him something fancy like David Charles but Jason knew what kind of trick that was and how they would have called him Dave or Charlie and it wouldn't have had anything to do with comics.

"I threw a tantrum," Jason told him (something Harvey is thinking about doing sometime). "And so you got named Harvey."

Jason used to tell Harvey jokes he didn't get and he told him all the scary stories he knew. Real stories—the Glencoe Munchkins and the Beast of Bladenboro and the Gray Man down at the beach who comes to tell you that something really terrible is about to happen, and that's just the start of it. There's that girl who worked at the Dog House killed by a killer, and Harvey's mom has even *seen* the murderer. There's a train engineer whose head got cut off and he walks around looking for it, and the statue in the cemetery who used to have ruby eyes but somebody stole them and now she haunts whoever goes there at night because she thinks they must be the ones that took her eyeballs. Jason drove Harvey by her one night and it made him shiver to look at her, even though she didn't really look scary at all. She actually kind of looked nice, like the music teacher at Harvey's school, a woman who walked with a cane and farted when she played the piano loud. If you sat right up close you could hear it and you didn't even need Super Monkey supersonic ears, but Harvey got in trouble for laughing.

Jason taught him to say, "You can tell it's Mattel. Just smell!" and everybody at school liked that. Jason had good things to say, like if somebody asked Harvey about his lip he could just say he got sliced by a killer who was hiding under his bed, like that story Jason told him about the maniac under the bed and Harvey had to ask what a *maniac* was.

"Crazy. Psycho."

"Like Lizzie Borden?"

"Who knows," Jason said. "I think she just got mad one day and let her folks have it."

At night when Harvey is being Super Monkey, he says things like: "Please, Lizzie, please don't murder people."

"I can't help it, Harvey. They make me so mad."

"Yes, you can, though, Lizzie. You can take a stick and beat on a bush or rock while you pretend it's who you're mad at. And then you can say, 'I am so sorry. I am sorry to spank you. It hurts me worse than it hurts you. Don't *ev*-er let me see you do that a-gin.'"

Lizzie Borden took an axe and gave her mother forty whacks, and when she saw what she had done, she gave her father forty-one.

"Psycho," Jason had said. This was the same day Jason gave Harvey a bunch of things as he packed to go off to school. He gave him the Klingon ring and he gave him the model of the *Enterprise* that they hung from a hook in his ceiling. He even gave him an old stuffed dog that Jason said he was pretty sure once belonged to his *real* father.

"Before he died?" Harvey said.

"Yes, before he died. Probably when he was a kid."

The dog was gray with black eyes and a little collar, and Harvey wasn't sure if he wanted something that had belonged to a dead person but he didn't want Jason to be upset.

"What's his name?"

"I have no idea," Jason said. "That's crazy, isn't it?"

Harvey shrugged. "How do you know who's psycho and who isn't?"

"You don't," Jason whispered. "And that's the scariest part of all."

Lil

❧

October 12, 2016
Southern Pines

IT'S SUNNY/WARM (WHERE is autumn?), and I'm feeling a little blue.
I think I have always felt that if I got a grip on each day, recorded
the weather and the mood, that I could hold it all in place. I wish
that every day, I had cupped my palm under my heel and raised my
leg to full extension. Would there have been a day when suddenly
I couldn't do it anymore, like that morning I woke and found I
needed reading glasses? The turn will come when you least expect
it, then the unraveling. You forget things you couldn't imagine you

could forget and, in the same moment, you remember something you haven't thought of in a hundred years, an odd little scrap that blows into your head just because the light slants across the room in a certain way or you hear a strain of music, or smell onions and peppers browning in an iron skillet. Spaghetti sauce was my mother's best dish, and it always began that way, onions and peppers in a sizzling skillet. I'm sure I have told you that before, Becca.

November (again) 2016
(Finally feels cooler)
All these years later, November comes and I can't stop thinking about that hospital lobby. All around us, people were weeping, holding torn and burned fragments of garments that had allowed them to find and know their loved ones. We were empty-handed; we didn't know where she was, and it would be many hours before we did. It was a full day before she was identified, and so there was a lot of time to imagine other ends to the story. There were a few cases where people thought to be there were not after all. Those were the happy stories, the miracles: the people who were disappointed that Boston College had lost to Holy Cross and decided to go home instead of getting a drink; a doctor who was called to deliver a baby; a young woman from Lowell too young to be served. By the end, my father and I had gone to all the places where we were told people had been taken: the hospitals, Southern Mortuary, even an empty store across the street from the club, which served as a holding place for bodies. Too many bodies. There was a place on Warren Street filled with purses that were unidentified. I paced the aisles there; so many small black clutches. There was also jewelry waiting at the mortuary, inscribed rings and bracelets.

It took 89 hours to identify all the dead. The newspaper stories told of orphans left behind, whole wedding parties lost—one couple just married at Our Lady of Pity. They wrote of blackened bodies, and those untouched by flames but dead nonetheless, their lungs filled with deadly gases. I didn't want to read the paper, but I couldn't help myself; my father threw the paper away, but I retrieved it when he wasn't looking and ran my finger along the column of names. Then one day, her name was there. We already knew by then, but it was still a shock to see it in print. I've saved all the clippings so you can read for yourself. Here's a whole folder of them, sad stories filling the Globe for weeks and weeks. I go back and read them sometimes, all of it still so shocking.

On a happier note, here is my wedding write-up and some photographs. Look at us—so young! The wedding was a happy day, but you wouldn't know it from that one photo of everyone there by the wedding cake with orange blossoms on top, a gift from Lois Starnes and her mother, who owned a bakery. There in the photo, Frank's mother and my father both look sad, and we must have been worried about them, because we aren't smiling either. Frank's mother had not been to Massachusetts in years, and she had actually ridden the train with Horace to get there, a trip she then said she would never make again, and she was good to her word. I think maybe my father was nervous; he had told me several times he wanted it to be nice for me but what did he, a man, know about any of it. I almost said what I was thinking (that I wished she were there with us, that she would have known all the right things), but I didn't.

And isn't it funny how things get layered, how my memories of your weddings are in part about the way I remember my own, as if I had a foot in two places; I was there adjusting your beautiful veil, Becca, and I was also thinking how I had not had my mother there to adjust mine. Or I watched you drive off with all kinds of things soaped onto the windows of your cars, some not repeatable, written by the fraternity brothers of your first husband, and for the life of me, I cannot recall his name, embarrassing but true (starts with an "R," I am fairly sure). Not that I need to recall it, but it's a way I challenge myself to get there, go through the alphabet, riffle those file drawers of mine, packed to maximum capacity.

Still, I watched you and him drive away, and all I could think about was how free Frank and I had felt after our wedding, there in a car he'd borrowed from an old friend, with tin cans trailing behind us, our clothes filled with rice. I felt free like I had not felt in years. I knew I would call my father along the way so he wouldn't worry; I knew I would always call and check in with him, but I also felt free. We were going to Quebec City to stay at the Château Frontenac, a place Frank had always wanted to go because his grandparents had gone right after they got married, but it was a long way, and we stopped somewhere in New Hampshire at a small motel, the Sleepytime Inn, where I shook out our clothes and collected all the grains of rice that fell, and here they are, wrapped in tissue and now in this plastic bag. But before I did that, I called my father collect from the phone in the cramped office, a quick "Here," simply to reassure him, and then I stood there in the tiniest bathroom I had ever seen—knotty pine paneling, a dim-watted bulb—and tried to see myself in my fancy pink nightgown bought just for that occasion, and what came to me was, "Once upon a time there was a girl named Lil." And years later when you called, Becca (collect, from a pay phone), to quickly say that you were in Key West, I imagined you there in that same tiny bathroom, leaning into a dark mirror to see yourself as I had done years before, thinking something like, "I'm here."

"But how could she have been there?" my father, still in shock, had asked a doctor, his white coat covered in soot as he stood there in the hospital lobby. There was an elderly couple holding each other, all of their children gone—the whole wedding party had been at the club, and the parents had left early because they were responsible for breakfast. "I should be serving the food right now," the woman said, her hands clutched to a black silk purse. "The wedding breakfast should be happening right now." My father sat with his hands clasped between his knees, his hat on top of his bundled-up coat beneath his seat. It was so crowded, the room filled with what sounded like machinery of some kind, only it was the low steady moans mixing and blending, sometimes a scream and you knew someone had gotten bad news.

My father and I told a woman with a clipboard what we remembered. I described my mother's shoes, black suede wedges with an ankle strap, a style that has circled back twice since then, and her pink scarf, lightweight, not a scarf to keep you warm, I told her, but a dress-up scarf to keep your hair from blowing, or what a dancer might tuck into her waistband. Her earrings were rhinestones, small circle clusters with screw backs, and she wore a red bangle bracelet that went with the pink and red rosebuds embroidered along the neckline of her dress. The kind woman with a clipboard wrote it all down; she took in a deep breath when I stopped talking and then asked if there was anything else we could think of. My father shook his head and then at the last minute called her back over. "She has a birthmark," he said. "A dark mole about the size of your little fingernail, way up on her thigh." He felt his own legs, maybe determining right from left. "Left, the left side," he added, and then shook his head as if to dispel whatever thought had flown in. "She hates that."

His use of present tense in that moment lifted my hopes. It's strange how that can happen, but it can. Over the years, I have read all the books, all the accounts. People either turn away and close the door on the catastrophic thing, or they turn and embrace it as I did, knowledge and understanding feeling like the rope that can pull you up and out of the pain. I felt any knowledge would inform my own life, and thus yours. I wanted to know who she was with and why she'd called her friend from the Cocoanut Grove that night a little after nine. I wanted to know why she didn't tell us where she was going. But those were things I would never know, and so I filled the void with other information—the play-by-play of how it happened, the accusations and lengthy trial, the stories of those who survived.

What I will always find amazing is the system they devised to identify people, something that I have thought of every time I've found myself in a large crowd of strangers. They separated the men from the women, then divided groups by height and weight, skin and hair color. Then, people there to claim a loved one were asked to name something (clothing, a scar, a birthmark) in hopes that those searching would need to see only two or three bodies. Sometimes there were no teeth or fingerprints to trace. One surgeon recognized his own work on an appendix scar and was able to figure out who it was. Volunteers were asked who could walk among the dead and not feel faint or get sick. These are the people who sponged faces and combed hair; they arranged jewelry and sometimes even used makeup. Your father's grandmother was one of those women, though she was ashamed to say she only lasted an hour. Still, we liked to think that his grandmother, a woman I never got to meet, had gently wiped my mother's arms and hands, her ankles and feet.

I knew my mother's hands, the pale-pink polish on her nails, and when I leaned close to her wrist, I thought I could still smell a trace of her perfume. Perhaps that sounds impossible, but I would swear it to this day. I wanted to look beneath the sheet. but the man standing there put a hand on my arm and shook his head. "Don't do it, sweetheart," he said, and held my arm, a gentle hold that put me in mind of my mother when we were crossing a street or your father when he thinks I shouldn't speak. My father had already turned and was halfway down the hall that would lead us outside.

At home, her heavy brown mixing bowl was right on the counter where she had left it, and there was a recipe she had torn from the paper on the kitchen windowsill; my father's shirts were rolled and sprinkled and ready to be ironed—all promises of her return.

There *were* happy times, and I never want to forget them. I'm on a blanket in Gloucester with my parents, my mother in a big hat, with a magazine tucked into her bag, my father in waders, gathering his fishing tackle; sometimes he tied a beer to his belt so it would stay cold in the water. I remember them talking about what we would do for supper and how even the simplest thing seemed exciting and something to look forward to. I can feel my mother's hand there on my forehead, smoothing back my hair, and I hear the surf and feel the liquid warmth of the sun.

"I can read your palm, Lily," my mother had said, and she held my hand close, her index finger tracing, arcing, circling in my hand in a way that made me want to close my eyes and drift off to sleep. She named crosses and grilles, islands and squares, the heart, the head, the Mount of Venus. "Oh my," she said, and squeezed. "Oh my, this is really something." She paused, tapping my palm with her finger. "I see roller skates. You're definitely destined for new roller skates."

Remember when Jeff got a fingerprinting kit and we all (including the dog) put our messy inked prints in the time capsule for the elementary school? It was a project you both did, the whole school participating. The assignment was to think about what your family would send to the moon. And then your children did the exact thing all over again with the turning century, and I'm sure their children will have a reason to do it again sometime before long. I have saved all of that, those time capsules. It seems, since the very beginning of time, people have been preparing for the end.

Years later, I didn't have to read your father's palm to know something was wrong. When my antenna suddenly focused on the suspicion in the air, I knew, and within minutes of knowing, I could see all the stepping stones leading there.

"A young colleague? Really?" I asked. "You're a cliché?" I said. "I've always thought so much better of you." I accused him of needing a disciple, someone who adored his lectures and explanations, someone who wanted to forge on into the promised land with him. And what was wrong with me? Hadn't I listened? I can hear you now, Becca, saying "Catch up, Mom. He's from Mars and you're from Venus." I can hear my own mother laughing with one of the women in our neighborhood, Mrs. Smythe, who was also up-to-date on cosmetics and the movies and who invited me over often and gave me my first home permanent several years after my mother died. "What can I say?" Mrs. Smythe said. "He's a man!"

After you all were out of college, your father was able to go on some digs, something he had always dreamed about doing. When he wasn't doing that, university life absorbed him, with meetings and classes and committees, and research in the library. And things can happen under those conditions. It is like the weather report when they say that all conditions are right for a tornado. It doesn't necessarily mean that one will hit and destroy your house and the rest of your life, but it does mean that there is a threat, that you should look up and pay attention. I know I sound like Mrs. Smythe, whom you never met, and wouldn't have liked if you had, since she grew old and very bitter in those later years, but still, there is truth there. Things can and do happen. And it *is* one of those things that often requires the right conditions and circumstances.

Mortality calls us all in very different ways. I was called to witness and be there for others, volunteering with the sick and dying,
maybe because their grief felt so familiar to me and when I focused
on them, I wouldn't have to think about my own hurts. What I
didn't see clearly enough back then (or for quite a few angry years
after) was that your father was also hurting, lonely and hurting,
wanting to stay young and strong and above it all.

As I said, it really comes down to the desire to be immortal.

Still, your father has lately pitched death like one of his adven-
turous trips or a romantic rendezvous. Once, he said, "Let's go
together," as if he were suggesting church, the movies, Disneyland.
He pointed to the cigarette I held burning between my fingers, as
he has done for the past 60+ years, marveling that I still smoke in
an age when so few do, that I don't seem to care the way people
look at me with shock as if I were stupid not to care more about my
health, the way I have gotten used to the frowning and social rejec-
tion reserved for people who have contagious diseases and cough
out into the open air, the way some people even stare in disbelief
when they learn about my history with fire and the power of a single
match. Frank reminded me that I have emphysema, in case I had forgotten (!!). He said that my lungs are shriveled and drowning, and
his heart is about to explode, and both of us have brains that aren't
what they are supposed to be. He said even if he wanted surgery,
he's too old to be put under and have his chest cracked open, and he
refuses to give up *living* for some pale imitation of living.

"Let's go," he said. "We can find a better word for it all."

"A better word."

"A hastening," he said. "How about a hastening?"

Hastening time, hastening the inevitable while it's all still in our
control.

Control. It's always been about control, and don't we all know that control would not even exist if not for the truth that when things go *out* of control there is no getting it back: the match catches, the tons of steel slip from the track, a loved one forgets to look back or says something that can never be erased.

Ever since he proposed it, I am left to wonder every time he leaves the house what is on his mind. There are things he says he has to do first. He needs to go back to his boyhood home just once more to see if what he hid there still remains. We have ridden by the place several times, always driving by the site of the train wreck first. He has pointed to the room where he slept and described what he calls "the lucky jar"; he always laughs, as if embarrassed, and yet it clearly is still very important to him. The last time we rode by, there was a child out in the yard wearing a big fake mustache, with a rope sticking out of the back of his pants and dragging behind him like a tail. I waved to the young mother half hidden behind the door.

"I'm ready to go soon," Frank said, and I told him that I wasn't. I told him that I have always loved him more than life itself, but now I am thinking that might not be true; I love my life. "I don't want to leave."

"But we are anyway, and you can't change that."

"Not the way you suggest."

I know where he keeps his gun. It belonged to his stepfather, and I have always hated having it in the house. I put it in a lockbox, which I then hid away.

"I won't do it today," Frank said, and now the words hang in the air, whether spoken or not. Is this the day? Do I trust him? There was a time early in life when I would have trusted him with everything I owned, but no longer, not in the same way. It's like an electrical cord that gets chewed or frayed; it still works, all taped and bandaged, but the damage leaves you handling it with caution and a little uncertainty, a little fear, and when he sensed my fear, he said, "Have I ever lied?" And I said, "Yes. Yes, you have."

"If I choose to do this," he whispered late one night; perhaps he thought I was still sleeping. "If I choose this, will you still love and respect me? Will you spin it for the kids so they will understand and forgive?"

I waited a long minute, his arm barely brushing mine, and then I said, "Haven't I always?"

Frank

"IF YOU'RE GOING to walk out there, please take the phone," Lil had said the first time he went. They had just moved in, and Lil was unpacking, Becca and her girls there to help. She handed him that awful thing Becca had bought and given to them, the Jitterbug—an oversized phone with gigantic numbers, like they might be stupid—and he pulled Lil off to the side where Becca couldn't hear and said, "Absolutely not." He said, "I'd rather die on the tracks," and he said if their children really wanted to talk to them, then let them call on the real phone or write a letter or keep coming over; he said if he needed a phone, he'd do what he had always done, find a pay phone, or stop at a gas station and ask to borrow one.

Now Frank has an iPhone like everyone else, and for him that's all it is, a *phone*, just like the computer is nothing more than a type-writer. He believes totally in history, and the endless cycle of those civilizations that advance so far out on the limb that it snaps and sends them right back down to the dirt that birthed them. Study the graves and the caves and what was most necessary in life and you will find that it was the simplest things: utensils and tools for eating and drinking and staying warm; the occasional object there in the skeletal hand—totem, toy, relic.

He pulls off the highway and inches up into the pines, where the car is shaded from the heat. The air is heavy and humid, starlings screaming from the trees. It's very different from where he and Lil live, with their house tucked into that golf course that could be anywhere or a part of a movie set. But here, there is something primal, which strikes him every time he comes, the heavy rails stretching in either direction, the dusty fields, and the hot cloudless sky. So much about being there feels like a time warp, like he might turn around and see his stepfather standing there in an awkward attempt at having a conversation. But of course there are all the differences, too: litter in the roadside ditches, beer and soda cans, scraps of fast-food meals, cigarette wrappers and butts. He has even seen on these recent visits syringes and condoms tossed to the ground and finds himself wonder-ing what on earth these tall, scraggly pines have witnessed at night. He doesn't even want to imagine. A car roars past, muffler in need of repair, and someone yells something unintelligible, which makes him feel vulnerable and old, as well as ashamed that he is so aware of his privilege, and of his instinct to run to the safety of his car.

"PLEASE DON'T GO stand on the tracks, Frank." The tone in Lil's voice, her worried frown, was so familiar to him. His own mother had said the same thing. "Please, Frank," she had said, "don't stand on the tracks," and by then, he could drive a car, he could do any damn thing he wanted to, except he wasn't yet legal age, so he couldn't leave. He couldn't join the service yet; he couldn't go off to college. He was a sophomore in high school, dating a girl who had lived in that town her whole life, and so had her parents before her, in a house on Elm Street. He liked her. Truth is, he liked a lot of the people there, even though he didn't always let on to his mother. It was easier, if unkind, to make her listen to him wondering about all the friends he had known in their other home, his *real* home, he said, his *real* life, and watch her turn away in sadness.

"You're the one who brought me here!" he finally told her, raising his voice in a way he had never done.

His father had been a relatively soft-spoken man—there were never any arguments that he could recall—and his stepfather was silent much of the time, though when he did talk, it was often with a kind of humor Frank had never before witnessed. He was the sort of man who if nervous would do things like pull a quarter from behind your ear or pretend to steal your nose. Horace, ten years younger than Frank, had never known any other father *but* Preston, with his kind, dark eyes and solemn expression, clothes dusty from his tobacco fields. "Got your nose, son," Preston would say, and Horace would laugh and laugh, their mother smiling that sweet, weak smile Frank had always associated with the way she looked at people with some infirmity that led her to express pity.

"Here's a nickel. Oops, no, there's a nickel," Preston had said, his beefy, tan hand rustling behind Horace's dark, curly hair—their father's hair.

"Just give him the goddamned nickel," Frank said, and he knew his mother wanted to slap him; he could see her jaw go tight before she turned and rushed forward in a loud, overly cheerful way to make something of that simple stupid magic trick.

"Please don't go stand on the tracks, Frank," his mother would say, and he finally asked her why. Wasn't that her reason for staying down here? He asked why she had made such an awful choice to leave their home, the only home they had ever known.

"I stayed because I couldn't leave," she said. "And because your dad was here."

"He was dead!"

Frank will never forget the look of shock on her face when he said this; it was if she was hearing the news for the first time.

He was about to walk and meet Millie Rogers to go to the movies. It was 1949, and they were going to go see a movie called *A Letter to Three Wives*, which he wasn't big on but his date was. Millie was the kind of girl everyone noticed, because she was pretty and smart, and her father owned a department store, and it felt good to be with a girl like that. It gave him clout without him having to do a thing, and it also left him there in the shadows while she glowed in the spotlight. Millie Rogers could twirl a fire baton, and when he put his hand on her thigh during the movie, she didn't move it.

He was thinking of all this but not breaking eye contact with his mother. "Dad was dead. We could have had a funeral at *our* church in *our* town, and we could be visiting *that* cemetery. That's where we would be right now."

"We couldn't find him," she said. "I couldn't find him."

She began to cry, and Frank lost all thoughts of Millie Rogers then. Part of him wanted to lash out at his mother, and the other part wanted to hug her. He was almost afraid to breathe, and so he did nothing.

"And I was pregnant. I was pregnant and I was afraid I might lose the baby, and that was all we had left of him, and I had broken bones, a shoulder and an ankle. They said I was so lucky." She wiped her eyes and looked at him until he had to look away, over at the mantel clock. Millie would be on her porch waiting; they would surely miss the cartoons if he didn't hurry. "Lucky," she said, "because the baby was okay, and because I still had you, Frank."

He doesn't remember what else was said, just that when he got to Millie's, she was out on the sidewalk, waiting, and silent through the whole brisk walk to the theater, though by the end of the movie she had leaned her shoulder in close to his, and all was forgiven. And, of course, he always thought of the unspoken, the way that he had wished himself onto that train, there between his parents, a wish that had it been granted, could have been his last wish.

AFTER THE CRASH, the waiting period to get news had been unbearable. When his mother was finally able to call, she said that she had waited until she knew for certain. "No one could have survived where he was," his grandmother told him in quiet, clipped words. She was at the kitchen table, and she stared at the cut glass saltshaker, moved it in a small circle, as she spoke. "Your mother isn't able to travel," she told him. "I'll go and take you to her when the time is right."

It had all come back to him those first times he and Lil talked about it, and it was back now with full impact, given Lil's obsession to document and remember. Perhaps that was part of his connection to Lil in the beginning; maybe he needed someone to *make* him think about it all. She was the only person he had told everything to, and she was solid and attentive, as strong-seeming as his grandmother had been, there at the kitchen table. He was grown before he was able to imagine what his grandmother had gone through. "Oh, that poor woman," Lil had said, and shaken her head, both hands holding her cup of coffee. "How old was she?"

Sixty-four. Frank mouths the number now, way too young to have lost a husband and then a son. His grandmother, who seemed an ancient ruin at that point in his life, was more than twenty years younger than he is now.

"I'll take you to her," his grandmother had said, as if for a visit, something temporary, which is what it was, since school was still in session.

There were two other people recovering there in Preston's house: an older woman from Connecticut, her pelvis crushed and her shoulder broken, who also lost her husband; and the woman's niece, who, they whispered, would be lucky if she ever walked again. A nurse came and went daily, and so did Preston, bringing food and whatever they needed. He had given over his house and was staying down the road with his sister.

Frank and his grandmother stayed in a nearby town at the Lorraine Hotel, a big brick building that looked out onto the small bus station and large tobacco warehouses. The railroad tracks were right there, running alongside the river, and the sound of the passing trains was a constant reminder. The crash was the reason so many were there, and had been for months, first to identify and claim bodies, and then to attend to those like his mother, too badly hurt to travel. The small two-story hospital in town was filled to capacity with those injured, and remained so for months.

They believed, in those early days, that Frank's mother would go home just as soon as the baby was born and she was able to travel. But by the end of the summer, when the tobacco warehouses were filled with the sweet-smelling leaves, and wagons and trucks rumbled past the Lorraine Hotel, and Frank's little brother, Horace, was already sitting, his mother was still saying that she wasn't quite ready to travel, she needed more time, and because it was summer, Frank stayed there with her, his life shifting in tiny increments. "You really need to attend school," his mother had said, "and your work will all transfer when we go back."

By then, the women from Connecticut had left. There was the occasional letter with hopeful reports about the niece walking again, but as far as Frank knows, that never happened. They always asked when Frank's mother would be returning to her home, and just the question being asked had felt encouraging, even though, months into the school year, he had begun to feel the dull edge of false hope. He and his mother and Horace lived tucked away in the back rooms of Preston's modest house. The one bathroom was theirs, and Preston never went near it, as far as Frank knew; he said he bathed at his sister's, and Frank suspected he did all else he had to do there as well, except peeing into the darkness off the porch, which he did late at night, when he didn't know Frank was looking.

"We need to pay rent," his mother had announced to Preston one night, also saying that she was happy to do all the cooking and cleaning and laundry. His mother and Preston had begun sitting on the porch together after Horace got quiet and when they thought Frank was asleep. Frank continued to ask—others did as well—when they would be returning to Massachusetts, and one of those times, he saw fear in Preston's eyes, something he noticed every time that followed. It was not long after when his mother began talking about how much a baby needs a father, and how though no one would ever—*could ever*—replace Frank's father, that Frank also needed a man in his life, someone who could teach him things.

The first ten years of his life were encased back on Andover Street, as if in a museum, his own personal excavation: here is the good life, here is the ideal life, that once-in-a-blue-moon perfect life. But then he was in *this* place, and the strange, rare winter weather that occurred the night of the crash was long gone and replaced with the mild warmth that brought early springs and hot, humid summers.

And even though his grandmother shipped boxes of things—linens and dishes and photographs—from Worcester, when she went to live with Frank's aunt, he continued to picture her right where he had left her, in the house on Andover. Even after she died and they all went to the funeral—a long bus ride—he still pictured her there in that old kitchen.

Most of the letters she sent mentioned the kitchen, probably because she was sitting there at that same white table, or because she was baking or she had just cooked or was about to cook. She once wrote that she was knitting a sweater to replace the one he loved, but if she ever finished it, he never knew. Even now, he pictures his grandmother that way, just as his strongest memories of his mother are in the kitchen of that house near here, the place he wants to visit—if only that frazzled-looking big-eyed young woman would let him in for a few minutes instead of saying that it's not a good time, her face appearing there in the opening of the chain lock.

THE FIRST TIME he ever stood at the site of the crash was in the spring after it happened. Most of the twisted metal and debris had been cleaned up by then, but the land still bore the scars. He had seen photographs of the wreck, read accounts and names of those dead. It had been on the front page of major newspapers: one of the worst train wrecks the country had seen, many of the fatalities soldiers who had survived the war on their way home for Christmas. Seventy-two dead, his father among them, and at least that many injured, his mother one of them, and the news so slow to reach anyone. There were people unaccounted for, and there were people who stepped from the wreckage unharmed.

His father had been in one of those sections where they had to use acetylene torches to cut through the metal, and if his mother had not had to use the bathroom, she and his unborn brother would have been with him. Most of the deaths were in the second and third cars; the people who survived described the sounds there in the darkness: the screams and cries and moans on into daybreak. His mother was someone they were trying to get to the hospital in a town down the road, but she refused to leave, because she said she could hear his father screaming out that she not leave him. And that's how she met Preston, one of many volunteers sent to carry people to safety.

Preston told Frank much later how there were bits of gift wrap and ribbons, and scraps of clothing, in the pine trees on either side of the tracks. He said there were bodies everywhere, and he didn't want Frank's mother to see those things, he didn't want to upset her anymore, because she was clearly in shock, and so he did his best to keep her safe and calm until the shot given to her made her sleep and they were able to take her over to the hospital. She had given him all of her information, begging that he find her husband and that he please get word to her mother-in-law and son that they were fine. "Tell them we are fine," she said, "but we won't be home in the morning like we said." Preston never made that call; he continued to work through darkness and on into the next day, but then he *was* the one who finally, when there was no hope of finding Frank's father alive, got her to a phone so she could call herself.

Preston had also spent seven hours with a young soldier pinned from his hips down until the crew could get him released and sent on for the medical attention he needed. Frank had heard the story every Christmas, because each year the man would send a big box of oranges, giving Preston credit for saving his life. "All I did was talk," Preston said, and he smiled at Frank's mother, but she never participated in those conversations, finding something to do in the kitchen instead.

• • •

FRANK HAD LOOKED it all up again not long before he and
Lil moved back, the information published in newspapers spanning
the East Coast:

- Unidentified woman: unrecognizable
- Middle-aged woman, appears Jewish
- Woman: brown corduroy dress labeled Oppenheimer, NY,
  size 5 brown oxfords
- Stout lady: brown hair, tan suit, laundry ticket 5-158
- Wedding ring: K to LK 7-26-42
- Lady between 20-30, 110 lbs.; has had Cesarean operation;
  suntan, so appears to be from Florida; plaid dress, large
  diamond ring
- Baby, 18 months

The lists went on and on and on.

"YOUR PARENTS WERE in the second car," Preston had said,
looking up from his feet only once before continuing. "The ninety-
one train—it was snowing that night, so rare for these parts. There
was ice. Most people were killed instantly, but your mother swears
your dad's voice was the one she heard calling from within the
wreckage. I can't swear to you one way or another, just that she
believes it was him."

"What did he say?"

There was a long pause, and Frank stopped swinging the tobacco
tie he was holding, while he waited. They were taking a break under
a large oak tree at the edge of the field.

"He said, 'Don't leave me.'"

"You heard him?"

"I heard someone say, 'Don't leave me.'"

Frank recalls the great clarity of Preston's statement that second time—no hesitation, "Don't leave me"—and he recalls the heavy, sweet smell of tobacco and the way his shirt was sticky and drenched in sweat.

"But you never saw him."

"No. Those four cars were compressed into the size of one. There was no way to see those trapped."

"But he was calling."

"*Someone* was calling." Preston looked up then and motioned in the direction of the field. By then, the hard work had grown on Frank, and it showed in the muscles of his arms and back; he liked the way he slept so hard at night, too, but he never would have admitted it.

He had said *someone* was calling.

PRESTON ANSWERED FRANK'S questions during those breaks from the midday sun, his slow soft voice careful with the descriptions and information, as if worried he might give too much at once, the same concentrated look his mother had when measuring out castor oil or whatever was prescribed for Horace and his constant croup. "More is not better or faster," Frank's grandfather had always said. "The right amount is key. Measure."

Preston's voice was measured just that way, doling out inoculations of facts and memories; he told how photographers and news reporters came from far away, cars parked all up and down along the highway, with a steady stream of onlookers, some there to help, others just curious to see the disaster for themselves. He said you could see where the train had plowed through the earth. There were people picking things up, sifting and searching.

When Frank came that very first time with his grandmother, Horace newly born and his mother still unable to get around, he

had combed through sticks and pine straw along the tracks and
on into the woods, digging a little, as others had done, kicking and
turning the dirt. He found what looked like a money clip with the
initial *B*. He found some coins and brass buttons. He found the
Captain Midnight decoder badge that he had been hearing about
on the radio for years, and it had felt like magic, like his father or
God or something out in the universe had given him the very thing
that he was supposed to have next in his life. *Hey, kids, tell Mom
and Dad to take you down to your local Skelly Oil Company and
get your Secret Squadron badge. And, remember, tell Dad it is easier
to prepare than repair.*

He was so shocked when he saw it that he quickly put it in his
pocket, for fear someone would take it or that it would disappear.
He wondered the whole ride back if it was really in his pocket, had
that really happened? And yet there it was, cupped in his hand when
he entered the kitchen, to find his mother cutting up vegetables for
soup, Horace asleep in a little basket in the corner of the room.

Dad, it is so much easier to prepare than to repair. That's what
he wished he could have said. But no one could repair this. No one
could have prepared for this.

THEN, AND IN all the years since, he has tried to script the
story behind that badge he found. Perhaps it was going to be a
Christmas present, or maybe someone had mailed it in a letter to
one of the servicemen. Captain Midnight's Secret Squadron. Perhaps
it was someone's way of connecting to a husband or a brother or a
friend.

The badge is still in his pocket. He once, probably thirty years
ago, thought he had lost it, and he tore through every drawer in the
house, only to find it safely tucked in the upper breast pocket in a
suit.

"What was the last thing you said to him?" he asked his mother years later; he had tried to ask before, but the look on her face had kept him pushed away.

"I said how odd to see ice and snow this far south," she said. "I told him how when I woke just minutes before, the baby pressing so hard on my bladder I knew I couldn't make it until morning, that I saw the white glaze on the ground and thought surely we were getting close to home. But we were still seven hundred miles away. And then I kissed him—he was still half-asleep, stubble on his cheek, a tiny scratch from shaving that morning—and I made my way to the Pullman car to find a restroom.

"The cars rocked back and forth, and I had to hold to the many seats I passed. People were sleeping, snoring, shifting, servicemen with duffels tossed up overhead or at their feet, and outside the windows the world was like a winter wonderland, the trees and ground coated in white. I had to use the bathroom so bad I was afraid I wouldn't make it. I was carrying your little brother so low. I was so relieved to finally get there. That's where I was, a tiny cubicle with a cracked mirror and barely room to stretch my legs and attempt to straighten my stockings. Everything made me uncomfortable then. And that's where I was. One minute, I was watching the dark, glistening trees fly past, and the next, there was a terrible sound and I was thrown into the wall.

"I lost my breath when I landed on the floor," his mother told him, "and it took what seemed forever to breathe, forever for the screeching sounds and screams to subside. But then there was just a second of jolted silence before the screams began again, screams from every direction, and my thought was so foolish: there I was carrying a baby, there I was with what I knew were broken bones, but all I could think about was my clean hair and clothes on that dirty bathroom floor, where so many strangers had been before me.

Then after what seemed an eternity, I was pulled out and out and out, into the cold, and I couldn't see anything. By then, I was calling your dad's name as loud as I could scream."

She stopped then and reached for Frank's hand. "I'm so sorry I took you from your home." It was something she said many times before she died, but that was the first time. "But he begged me," she said. "He said, 'Don't leave. Don't leave.'"

Toward the end of her life, she talked more and more about his father, when it was just the two of them, things like: *Do you remember that hill where your father and I took you sledding? Do you remember how your father had written phone exchanges right there on the kitchen wall in a pencil he sharpened with my paring knife? Do you remember how dark his eyes were, and that he had a little dark mole on his left cheek?*

"I saved you," his brother, Horace, liked to say to their mother as a child, and he continued on into adulthood, especially when he became a nephrologist. "Mom's kidneys saved her life, and I was the reason for all that pressure on her bladder," he said. Frank tired of the joke, but their mother never seemed to; she would smile, a hand pressed to her abdomen, as if it were all happening again, as if for just a second her husband was still sleeping comfortably in his darkened seat.

Horace was named for a young sweet-faced Eagle Scout who ran telegrams and helped Frank's mother make contact in the days following the wreck. That's how they got the news: a telegram.

His mother ran into that Horace—Frank called him the *real* Horace—a few times over the years; he grew up to become a lawyer, like his father before him, a well-loved pillar of the community, which Frank's mother always said did not surprise her one bit. She said that night, December 16, had pulled all the communities together in a way that would warm your heart if it weren't so badly broken. His mother always quoted his dad about sleep, work, kindness—such power to quote the dead! But if Preston was nearby, she never really talked about their private life, the days sledding and the things that had made them laugh; that was a part of herself she let only Frank see, and then just in brief glimpses, which usually led to her getting very quiet and turning away.

IT IS HARD now, on this hot June day, to conjure that night, to pull the ghosts in around him. The tracks extend as far as Frank can see, the sun glaring. This has been a place of comfort; in those early years, he kept digging and finding things, never as good as the Captain Midnight badge, but things nonetheless, all in a jar and stashed in the old hiding place of that childhood home. And maybe it's long gone, but maybe it's not. Maybe it waits, like treasures in a tomb, and that's why it's important for him to go there and see. And Lil has encouraged that part of it all; she said she wanted to see everything that he stashed away.

"How romantic," their children often said. "Grave artifacts and a match made in tragedy." Their grandson, David, now college age, had joked that his dad talked about how depressing they were all through his childhood, that maybe there should be a dating site called Morbidity Match, and Frank had laughed along; it was clever—what else can you do? But he would dare them all to find the kind of glue he and Lil had because of it all.

When they first met, they had both felt so alone with their grief. There wasn't an internet or therapy sessions about anything. A lot of people didn't even talk about anything emotional. And, no, Lil was not who he would have picked out at first glance around a dance hall, but in no time, he found a sense of comfort he had not even known he was missing, and she said she felt that way, too.

She worked at Filene's then, and her dream was to open a dance school. Frank was in graduate school. At one time, he had wanted to be a minister, but he feared his beliefs changed too often to fit into that role. He *did* believe and he *wanted* to believe. But he also thought that surely a great power who knows everything would also know you had doubts and sometimes were faking it. Still, for the most part, he *did* believe, and he thought of that Captain Midnight badge he found there in a heap of steel and ash and scorched earth, a sign, a miracle of a message to remind him that there *is* something out there; there *is* a greater power.

"It's why you're interested in history and religion," Lil had said on an early date. He could tell she was annoyed when he put ketchup on his mashed potatoes, but big deal, because he found her looks to be bland, her lips bare of color. "She's nice," people said about her. *Nice.* The necessary word when trying to convince others of someone's worth. But then they had stumbled on all they had in common, and the many times they might have been in the same places at the same time.

"So tell me about yourself," she had said, her hair tucked behind one ear, a beige scarf wrapped around her neck and fastened there with a little pin—an ivory Scottie dog with little rhinestone eyes, something he later learned had belonged to her mother.

How romantic. A match made in tragedy.

Yes, sixty-five years. And, yes, lots of digging and searching, for both of them, and both literally and figuratively. Burial practices became a focus of his, the beliefs and rituals in preparation for the afterlife. He was especially drawn to the graves of children, that premature closure, some ancient graves containing a keepsake, a toy to take along into the next life.

Lil liked to say maybe it *was* a match made in tragedy, but they had built a beautiful and happy life on top of it. The knowledge and experience of tragedy groaned and heaved like an old furnace in the basement—and ultimately, sent waves of warmth that radiated and lit the good parts. Now, fragments of memory course through his veins like the pieces of plaque that threaten to seize his heart.

FRANK OFTEN THINKS of the man whose responsibility was to walk ahead to warn any approaching train—all of those people, their lives in his hands—and then he slipped on the ice and broke the fusee flare he carried. Maybe the man woke early that day and he chose the wrong shoes, he didn't *prepare*; he slipped on the ice, and down he went. The snow was falling, and perhaps the sight had made him think things he rarely thought. He might have even looked out and beyond the ice-glazed trees and thought how beautiful it was, how excited his children would be, how good it would feel to get home and slip beneath the heavy pile of quilts where his warm wife was already sleeping. But he slipped and he went down, and how easy to make a mistake. And then one mistake begat another mistake: Doesn't every human make mistakes?

Hadn't Frank made a mistake those times, slipped and fell when Lil was so preoccupied, first with the kids, perfect mother, having lost hers, and then later, drawn to the sick and dying, while ignoring the living; it was like she chose to stand there by the exit door and see everyone off, bid them farewell, like some modern-day Charon paddling the Acheron. As if it was her calling, a kind of obsession, either to punish herself or to feel closer to her mother. At the time, she was lost to him, in a place he had no desire to visit.

He wanted to forget what he'd done, and who wouldn't? Who wouldn't want to get beyond the turbulence into calmer waters. Of course he wanted to forget, and in fact, he had succeeded in doing just that until Lil brought it up again, as if referencing something they had been meaning to get around to, like cleaning out the garage or shredding old tax returns. How could he know what was on her mind? How could he know what was bothering her unless she just came right out and said it in clear spoken syllables?

But things don't always get resolved; people don't always get to see it coming and prepare. War, catastrophic accidents, the betrayal of a body shutting down all of a sudden without warning—the number of those who have had no time to get ready is too large to count. Frank's own mother had been so consumed by her grief, and then with her concerns about a new baby, that nothing else seemed to matter to her, and then Lil did that exact same thing. She carried her big sack of grief like a badge of honor as she catered to first her father and then whomever from the outside world needed catering to. And of course she was there for the children, and she was a good mother, but then they were gone and off at school, and instead of giving him that time, she filled up even *more* spaces with those in need, and so of course it was easy for Frank, to fall, to slip—and of course he looked like the bad guy! He fell into something he had never seen or noticed before, like snow in southern climates where it is so rare.

At first, it was just letters, little friendly back-and-forth exchanges that allowed his mind to wander away from whatever was bothering him at the time, and there's no crime in that, no crime in communicating with a like-minded creature, and yet what about the way he chose not to mention it, the way he hid the letters away in files of schoolwork that appeared so boring and messy, who would want to look? And then there were those times in the empty-nest years—Lil so strange and distracted—that the conversations happened in person; it was certainly nothing he ever would have planned.

He can't even recall the young woman's face, just the kind of energy that comes with such a connection or flirtation, call it what you will, attention, a secret, that feeling of being invited in,

everything easy and no strings to tie or alarms going off. He slipped
and then floundered, and found himself wanting to be near the
young woman in blousy Indian cotton tops and faded jeans and
flip-flops, long hair yanked back, and not a trace of makeup on
her young, smooth skin, a body tanned and untouched by childbirth cool beneath him. She lay there, arms raised over her head,
wispy auburn hair there under her arms, something he found arous-
ing, which surprised him, and he had to shut off that part of his
brain where he could hear Lil telling their daughter how she really
hoped she would shave under her arms: Lil had called Becca "Fuzzy
Wuzzy" and said that rhyme—"Fuzzy Wuzzy was a bear," like Becca
might've been six and not a grown woman in her twenties, and a
woman in her twenties is every bit a woman, or can be, which had
surprised him—and then Becca had said, "Mom, please," as she had
said a million times before, and Frank slammed the door of his mind
on them. He slammed the door because he was drawn into the warm
smell of citrus and earth, and he had never been kissed or touched
that way, or so it seemed, and what were years after all? Lines etched
in a tree or a shell or a face.

They passed notes in department meetings and lectures—how
innocent was that? Little slips of paper that he threw into the sewer
on his way to his car, except then he wanted to save a couple and
he couldn't help but reread them, couldn't help but study the letters
and the word choice: Was there more meaning there?

One day, she drew the Eye of Horus, and he thought of it for days
after. Was she suggesting safe travel for them together? Warding off
anything that might interfere with what seemed a tender connection? Or was it just fun? A doodle: an eye with the curl below, what
could be a tear. It seemed a secret message, and with it came a rush
of power and energy he had not felt in years. It was the same kind of
sudden excitement that comes when you spot something shining in

the earth or the flash of silver with a fish on the line, the tug and pull that exhilarates and, for just that little bit of time, erases all else. He once wrote an article on the earliest known fishhook, carved from a snail shell twenty-three thousand years ago and found in a cave in Okinawa—rustic and primitive, and yet its purpose the same as modern hooks, the need behind the purpose the same.

He sent back a drawing, big nose and eyes peering over a wall—*Kilroy was here*—which he realized dated him, so he said how much the Kilroy drawing resembles the sign for omega and wondered if that went into the creation.

She had read it and smiled and immediately sent back an alpha. A beginning? Dominance? And why did he allow his mind to see what was conjured by that, and why did he want to enter that imagined space, like a quiet, dark room, footsteps silenced, drapes drawn to the harsh glare of day, a place of secret rest and release? He was a married man, with children out on their own as well, and she was on the fast track: an appointment for further doctoral work at Harvard, a piece all about an excavation in Peru about to be published, a boyfriend off somewhere in the Peace Corps.

He realized his mind had wandered; he had no idea what was being discussed in the meeting, and he tried to appear indifferent to her new scribbling. She wrote: *What's the Maat-er? Truth? Justice?* Maybe she was letting him know she had a sense of humor, by playing with the Egyptian goddess's name in that way, not taking it all seriously, perhaps telling him she was someone to be trusted.

He wanted to return something witty but felt himself going blank. Something playful about Ba, how he felt he was moving between the living and the dead, his outward appearance and interactions with the world half-hearted and unfulfilled, his empty soul hoping to find the physical manifestation that would allow him rest.

The idea was hers first, after all. One day in his office, when she

began the habit of stopping by after lunch, she had asked how crazy
it is to imagine being in one of the ancient tombs, to be one of the
humans placed there to service the waking king. "You would have
food and riches," she said. "I think you would hope he would wake,
right?" She was watching him so closely he had to look out the window. "I mean, you would know it couldn't last forever. The wine and
food would run out. The air." It was raining outside, and he watched
students rushing along the brick paths, heads down, books cradled,
colorful umbrellas, and when he turned back, she was still watching
him, smiling. "But it could be pretty good for a night or two."

"Yes," he said. "Yes, I think that's probably right." He laughed
and then spent days wondering what message he had sent. A yes?
A no?

What's the Maat-er?

Ba can't find his body, he wrote, and passed the little piece of
paper before he could talk himself out of it, and then he got up and
left early. Such an elemental response; if only it were all so simple.
It was autumn, gray skies and damp leaves under his feet; it would
be dark in an hour.

He was almost to his car when she ran up and slipped the piece
of paper back into his hand; she held it there, pressing hard before
disappearing into the crowd at the crosswalk, waiting for the light
to change. *Ba needs to let me help*, it said.

Things can happen so suddenly, and now he hates remembering
all of this, hates that it was Lil who always reminded him.

THE MAN FROM the train was on his way to do the right
thing, just doing his job and going to warn the northbound train,
but he slipped and fell, and he later took his own life, the burden
too great to bear, too much darkness to see. And the older you get,
the more there is to see, and the signs are everywhere: the teeth and

bones and heart and brain, creases in the lobes, capillaries in eyes and cheeks, bubbles of cholesterol, and moles too dark not to fear. Or what about little slips of memory? Or a bit of plaque, part of a crumbling wall breaking off and racing along a river of blood straight to the heart, a rusty old valve creaking on its hinges. His grandfather had described the human body like an adventure trip, and now the rivers of Frank's body are struggling to keep flowing, the source is all dammed up, and it's too painful to wait for the break. Why wait to be felled by what you know is coming anyway?

"I hate surprises," Lil told him right after they got married. "Please, never surprise me beyond a little something of note on my birthday or our anniversary."

He didn't say it then, but he hates surprises as well, and the best way to *not* be surprised is to head things off, take control: put down the suffering dog, pop the goddamn balloon, and pull the trigger.

Harvey

Jason told Harvey that there's a place not far from where he goes to school called Munchkinland and if you ride through there after dark a whole bunch of mad little people will come and flip your car and try to kill you, that there are people who went there and never came back. People said to stay away, because bad and crazy things will happen to you. Harvey asked the teacher and, sure enough, it was in a book about all the ghosts and bad things that have happened. His mom has heard of it too, but she said it was very, very sad, little children picked on by mean bullies.

"They were people with problems," his mom said. "I looked it up. They couldn't walk and were left to sit on a porch all day, and cruel people called them names and they defended themselves the best they could. And now they are all dead. End of story." Then she drove him through the cemetery and they both sat on the lap of the dead woman who looked like the music teacher. Harvey told her how they say if you kiss her you will die, and she said that was why they were there. To prove to him that that was nonsense.

"See?" his mama said, and before Harvey could stop her, she kissed the woman's hard face and he really wishes she had not done that.

Then they drove out to the Dog House but Harvey didn't feel like eating. His mama said it seemed wrong that the place was still open, even though the people who owned the business couldn't help that a bad person had gone in there and murdered that girl. Harvey watched the upstairs window the whole time, because if her ghost was there, he knew that was where she would be. And if only Super Monkey had been there that night the mean doctor came. "Please, Mr. Doctor, don't kill her," he would have said. "She has a little boy. She makes people happy with hot dogs. She can make you a hot dog, like a Chihuahua or a Collie. She won't tell nobody you were about to do a bad thing and then you can maybe do a good thing instead."

Harvey's mama says, "It's okay, Harvey," and he wants to believe her, especially when it's just the two of them and he hears their ghost coming in the back door. He knows the ghost has been in his room too and he wants to open his eyes but is afraid to, because what if it got mad? Then what?

"It's okay, Harvey," she said, but when he asked her to explain what he'd heard about a woman's head that was found in a freezer and those children murdered by their daddy and left in the river, his mother took in a great big breath like the Big Bad Wolf and then put her head down. "Jason didn't tell me that," he said and that was true. He heard those stories at school. One kid saw it on the news and another has an uncle who is a fireman and went there to help those children. Kids listen to stories like that so Harvey told everyone at school what Jason told him, about a boy in a long black coat killing kids at school, and then the teacher said she needed Harvey's help with something. She had over a thousand paper clips that needed to be divided up into colors and if he did all that quietly, he would get a page of stickers to take home, either Ninja Turtle ones or puppies. He took the Turtles. He can make a picture for his mom, because she likes things with shells, and he can put something in Klingon. Something good, like *Cowabunga* or *Roses is red.*

Lil

∾

TODAY, BECCA ASKED what I remember about that last night with my mother:

That night, my mother called out, "Good night, Lilliput," and then she said something to my dad that left me puzzled. Had she known what was up ahead, she would have chosen her last words with great care, but of course, had she known, she wouldn't have gone at all. A premonition would have kept her there with us and perhaps her last words to me, "Good night, Lilliput," could have lingered there on my scalp, her warm breath in my hair. She would have curled there beside me. If she had been angry with my father, they would have resolved it and been sitting together at the kitchen table when I woke up.

It would have been so much easier if she had been diagnosed with something. We would have treated her illness like Gladys Fitzhue's visit, when she came to town and wouldn't leave. It was awful, but the visit pulled the three of us closer than we had ever been; they let me climb in their bed with them as we told the despicable things she had said and done that day, the way she insisted on cloth napkins and a china cup and extended her pinkie to bite into her toast but then chewed with her mouth open and also belched as loud as a man when she thought we couldn't hear. She gossiped and even admitted she sometimes told people she liked their hair or clothes when she didn't so she would look better.

We huddled there laughing. All it took was for one of us to offer a fake belch and lift a pinkie in the air. Lying there between them, the room was so dark I could barely trace the lines of my mother's dresser and the rack where my father hung his coat, Gladys Fitzhue down the hall, snoring and burping away, with no knowledge of all we had whispered about her, my father's arm curled up and over his pillow, my mother's warm backside safely tucking me in, their breath in the rhythm of sleep. I had no idea how hard life could be. I lay there safe and pretending we were on a boat far out at sea—my father's snores, the ocean, my mother's sighs, the wind.

She said, "Good night, Lilliput," using the pet name she had called me as long as I remember. When I was in high school and had to read "Gulliver's Travels," I was shocked to find my name there, a name I thought she had made up herself. She was not a reader, and so I suspect it was something my father had probably said first and then she'd claimed for her own; in fact, I'm sure of it, because later he told me how she should have called me "Lilliputian": a person and not a place. Had they aged together, she would have grown to love the bits and pieces of knowledge he housed in his mind, the mechanics of which were not unlike the many watches he worked on there at Waltham Watch. He was precise and constant, and she was anything but; what brought me a great sense of security in life (his steady sameness) probably bored her. In fact, I sometimes have worried that my steady sameness bores your father.

My mother said dance is making something from nothing, that you use your body to stir the molecules, paint a picture on the air that then only lasts in memory. It was like when she once gave me a paint-brush and can of water and told me I could paint anything I wanted anywhere in the house. I painted the front porch, and then I painted the front door. I painted my name, and I painted a bird, wispy wings like a swan, like the many photos my mother had shown me of dancers, feathery circles moving in unison, like the ghostly ones all in white—the wilis, those restless creatures in "Giselle." My mother told me the story before we saw a performance, and I cried for days thinking of her, a girl dead from a broken heart, and then all of the other girls, an epidemic of them rising from their graves to torment the men who had hurt them. We agreed that was the good part, they at least got a turn, but how tragic that they had to die to get there. I didn't want to be one of them, these angry girls with their unrequited loves. I wanted to be Swanhilda in "Coppélia"; I wanted laughter and comedy and happily ever after.

My mother once told me Anna Pavlova's dying request was to hold her swan costume and that her last words were "Play that measure very softly." In a performance right after her death, a single spotlight marked the stage where she should have been dancing.

My father asked why she was always filling my head with such sad things. We were in their bedroom, sitting on the bed, my mother trying once again to teach me how to make a French knot in the pillowcase she was letting me embroider, and she just shook her head, a needle threaded with pale-pink floss in her hand, and she told him he knew nothing about romance, that ballet is full of the heartbreak of romance: "Giselle" and "Petrushka" and "Swan Lake."

"Good night, Lilliput," my mother said, and then she said something to my father, who was seated in his chair, listening to the radio, as he usually was that time of day. And then she was gone from our lives.

My mother had said she was teaching a dance lesson that night, something she had been doing for a couple of years. She didn't say a private client; she didn't say in a nightclub. She said, "Good night, Lilliput." Then she said, "See ya, dope," or did she say, "I can't cope," or, "I have no hope," or, "Not me, nope"? I once asked my father what she'd said to him, and he said he couldn't recall, that he didn't remember her saying anything other than "Leave the light on," which was what she always said.

Then, all we knew in that early morning light was that the hall lamp was still on and she had not come home.

She had told me about the Cocoanut Grove one night when I sat on the bed and watched her getting ready for sleep. She put big white circles of cold cream around her eyes and then tissued off the mascara, the eyeliner, saving a corner to dab all around her lips. She tied her hair in a turban, something she had seen Rita Hayworth do in a movie.

"Stars are painted on the ceiling," she said. "It can be a blizzard outdoors or pouring rain, but inside, it's always warm, and the palms are swaying and the stars are shining and the music is playing. On a beautiful night, they can even open the ceiling to the real night sky." There were zebra-skin couches, she told me, and palm trees that looked so real you needed to go up and touch them, and famous people were always surrounding the bandstand and the long shiny bar.

My father had taken her there for her birthday, and it was all she'd talked about for weeks after. There were leather walls and a rolling stage: She had seen Jimmy Durante. She had seen Rudy Vallee. She turned then and looked at me, her whole body animated with the descriptions of what people were wearing. One woman wore a floor-length sable with matching hat, and another was in leopard. She said that was the kind of place where people got discovered; she had even heard about a young woman who got noticed just because she looked like Claudette Colbert.

Just a couple of weeks before I lost my mother, she called me into the kitchen to explain menstruation and to tell me where she kept her pads. I was horrified at the time, and even cried and asked why she was doing that to me. I thought she had called me in there to taste what she was cooking or to tell me something funny. Why, on that beautiful afternoon, was she telling me those things? And now, I feel so lucky that she was the one to tell me. and that I remember it all so clearly.

"Used to be mothers would slap their daughters when this happened." My mother laughed. "But I would never do that to you," she said, and waited for me to look up. "It's a good thing. It is. It's how I have you."

Sometimes, I close my eyes and work hard to hear that again: "It's how I have you." The limbs on the tree outside the kitchen window were bare, the sky gray and promising snow. She had just cut up a chicken and the pimply-skinned parts lay sprawled there on the counter, her damp hands warm on my back. Sometimes, I stay there as long as I can.

So many times, I have followed what I assume was her path. My mother would have taken the train and gotten off at Tremont Street. I have gone and stood on that corner of Piedmont Street. Now, it is hard to even find, or it was the last time Frank indulged me and went along, because it was icy and because he said I was way too old to be out walking around the city like that. There's a parking garage and a hotel (the old Radisson, now something like the Revere). It's the same geography, the same earth below all the glass and metal and concrete; it's as close as I could get.

I always thought that if I stood very still and turned my ear just right that I might be able to hear it: the music, the clink of glasses and laughter, the screams slow at first and then rising, the roar of fire. There are people who claim to have seen ghosts there, and I have always wished I would. There is a pull more powerful than anything I can describe; it is not unlike the pull of homesickness, and the way that you can feel homesick for a time and a place even when you know that life was not good then. You might miss a particular tree outside your window or a sweater you owned at the time, or the place you liked to sit at the end of the day. You might miss the wave of hope that years stretching ahead of you lends even in the darkest of times. I think I will always think of that place, to get as close as life might allow.

That Sunday morning was cold and gray, and I remember going with my father from place to place and then finally sitting there in the lobby of Massachusetts General Hospital, the sky still misting while we waited there with all the others to eventually be sent across town. I overheard someone say that he wasn't sure what to hope for, what was best to hope for in such a situation. There were many stories of those burned beyond recognition. There were people with the letter M on their foreheads, lipsticked in the frenzy and haste of the night before, marking who had been given morphine and who had not.

Perhaps the best we could have hoped for is that she had left us: that sometime in the night she had made a decision and ridden away to a brand-new life, that somewhere, perhaps in a car with someone we didn't know, perhaps in a bed with someone we didn't know, she was feeling heartbroken, knowing all that she would miss about my father and me. She would miss that chestnut tree at the end of our street and the Christmas decorations she had collected. She would miss going to the Embassy Theatre, where she had just seen "To Be or Not to Be," a comedy that was not so funny when you knew that Carole Lombard had died in a plane crash just before the movie came out. That's what she had said at the time, and that is the kind of irony she would have seized on if she had had the power to send a message from the grave, to rise up like the wilis and circle round me: "I had a premonition, Lily."

But that afternoon, I was still clinging to the possibility that maybe she had run away from home, gone to become the great dancer she thought she was destined to be, gone to walk someone else's stairs in a home where I would one day find her and reconcile. She was in a car, the cold wind in her face, her scarf tied around her hair; she was in a warm bed, curled on her side in the way she always slept, eyes closed, hair mussed, her heart still beating.

Shelley

HOW CAN YOU *possibly work on a grocery list while speculating about the case and still do your job?* That's probably what the judge will ask her, and she is still working on what to say: how it is like walking through a house where there are many televisions on and you tease out little threads from each, just enough to know what is going on even as you stay fixed and focused on the one in front of you. *Come on down!* She hears game-show applause and laughter and jingles. Then she hears: *But I don't understand. How can you carry the child of a man who was dead before you got pregnant?* And then the soap opera music gets louder and louder, because it's getting near the end of the hour and the end of the week.

Her mother watched *One Life to Live* and *All My Children*. Her grandmother, who'd sometimes lived with them, watched the game shows. Her older brother watched reruns of old westerns—"Saddle up, Hoss. Find Little Joe"—which was totally out of character for somebody who stayed stoned all the time and loved Black Sabbath and the Sex Pistols, but he did. He said he liked those simpler times, when you just shot whoever was fucking with you and then rode off into the sunset. She wishes she could tell him that is exactly what is going on in the world today, only there are no horses or sunsets or somebody like Ben Cartwright pontificating on whatever bit of a moral there might be. Shelley had loved *Dawson's Creek* and MTV, but good luck getting time all by yourself with a television in that house.

And now she does have time to herself, sometimes too much time, especially at night when Harvey is asleep and she starts to hear things. She certainly had not planned to add losing a job to her long to-do list, but there it is, or at least the possibility if they don't find a way to forgive her for doodling and writing all kinds of other weird shit in the midst of a murder trial. She knew better. Of course she knew better, but this particular trial bothers her more than all the others, and that is saying a lot, because there have been some really terrifying ones!

But still, she can explain how she is able to transcribe everything that is being said on the stand while thinking of a couple of other things, too. It's no different than knowing the commercial break was about to bring her mother out into daylight ("Yes, I bought your cigarettes and took out the trash," Shelley had said, instead of what she'd wanted to say, which is, *Who in the fuck do you think you are watching television on your fat ass with no food in the house and then judging me?*), or when the Ponderosa was signing off and her brother said, "Please leave me alone. I hate them as much as you do, so don't take it out on me!" She can do that and still solve the word puzzles on *Wheel of Fortune* before her old grandmother (LET SLEEPING DOGS LIE, you old idiot). She can do that, and it is actually a soothing kind of thing to do when disturbing things are introduced into the world.

And maybe, if the judge shows any signs of understanding, she will then say, *I am alone*, or *Harvey is driving me crazy with all of his fears*, or *Now I am terrified at night, too*. Or maybe she could show how sometimes she doodles while the judge pauses or someone takes a long time to answer a question. She could show how it looks like she just drew a little picture, when really it says: *I am, I am, I can, I can*. Marks, curves, horizontal, perpendicular. She learned Teeline, which some think is faster, but it looks so loud and harsh to her; she prefers Gregg, enough loops to soften and lower the volume. *I can be good. I am good. Fuck whoever doesn't think so.*

If Shelley were in a movie, she would pay attention to that old man appearing out of nowhere and saying he wants to see inside her house. There would be creepy music every time he rides by. A lot of the people she has seen convicted have at first seemed nice and normal. There was a serial killer who was also a religious grandmother. A special ed teacher teaching things that should never be taught. A preacher with purification rituals that involved children taking off their clothes. The last time the old man showed up at the door was when school was still in session and she was having to battle every day to make Harvey go. The man said he understood and he would keep trying; he gave her his phone number, and then he disappeared for a while and she thought maybe he'd forgotten, but lately she has seen his car again. He says he just wants to see inside once more and to wander around the yard, but the whole thing unnerves her. If she really thought he would look once and go away forever, she might, but there's almost always a string attached. Nothing is that easy. He might be trying to buy that house back from her landlord, and where would that leave her?

At least, now it's summer, and the day camp she forces Harvey to attend is a much easier situation. The camp is at the small children's museum downtown and is run by a teacher in the elementary school, the man all the kids want for second grade, because he wears purple high-top sneakers and dances on his desk when all the children get one hundred on the spelling test. He seems like a nice guy, too, but Shelley's job has taught her to question everyone. "We talk about dinosaurs, pirates," he had said, trying to assure her. "Mummies. What children aren't interested in those topics?" Two days in a row, Harvey has done all of his clinging and begging in the car and then walked off without looking back once, and even though she feels so proud of him, it also breaks her heart, because she fears there could be a day when he or Jason might do that for good. *People do that*, she thinks yet again. *People sometimes leave and you don't know why, or if they will ever come back; you don't know if they are alive or dead.*

She misses Jason and the way he has always been such a help with Harvey, but she is also thrilled, finally, to get cheerful messages or texts from him. He is doing fine. He loves school. Loves numbers. Calculus. Coding. She'd told him that he didn't have her brain, and he'd immediately said his skills must come from his dad, something he always circles back to.

"Thanks, Mom," Jason has said. If he has thanked her once, he has done so thousands of times by now. "I know it's a lot of money." All through his life, he has thanked her, and there is some part of her that breaks every time; she knows he felt slightly on the outside when Brent was in their lives. Before that, it had been just the two of them, with Harvey on the way, and making ends meet was really hard then. He loved, as all children do, to hear stories about himself, and so she told him how he had once refused to play with a child who'd intentionally killed a granddaddy longlegs, or how he only ate orange food for a couple of years—goldfish, cantaloupe, Kraft macaroni and cheese—how there was a period of time when he cried to see the sun set, fearful it would not come back.

She has told him stories about his dad and what a huge loss to the world it was when he died. "We were so in love," she has told Jason many times. And she has painted the things she remembers, as well as things she wishes she remembered, and still he had questions: *Did he like cantaloupe, too? Did he ever jump from a plane? Or kill somebody?* She tells Jason that his father watches over him and will bring him great luck and strength. She tells it so well that she believes it, too.

She tells Harvey that he is also special, that often something happens at birth to make sure everyone is aware of how important that person is. "So smile, honey," she says, and he does, but it is always with his hand raised to cover his mouth, the scar that splits his top lip, the tiny white line up to his nose. He loves the kit of fake mustaches Jason gave him, especially the big bushy handlebar one. He says that is what he will grow when he's a teenager, that he bets his daddy will have a big mustache when he gets home from building an igloo and from hiking on the Appalachian Trail. He says when he is a man his mustache will be put in *Ripley's Believe It or Not* for being the longest mustache ever. He is sure his lost turtle will come back home any day now, and he says he has seen a murderer at least once—maybe in a parked car when they are leaving a store or on the highway. He has also seen a ghost in their house.

PEOPLE LEAVING AND never returning is as common as someone getting a gun, going into a public place, and blowing people away. During many trials, Shelley has heard people say: "And we never saw him again." Or they say: "Yet another angry white man with a gun." The shootings happen so often, people ask: *Terrorist or sick white dude? Pass the salt. How was your day?* Just like in that song Shelley's mama used to sing, "Ode to Billie Joe," where all the people sit at the table eating like no big deal when this boy has killed himself, and nobody ever even knows what the girl had to do with it all in the first place. It's clear she was involved, but how? She was seen with him up on the bridge—*pass the biscuits*—and then he was dead, gone, like all those poor people just going about their lives before the crazy person showed up. That's what she has heard a judge say: "One minute they were where they were supposed to be—school, work, worship—and the next minute they were not."

Death is never easy to explain. When their cat went missing in Georgia, she told the kids she was sure he had found a new home. "Of course he did. Who wouldn't want that sweet little kitty cat? Or he might come right back here," she had told Jason. "Cats do that all the time."

"Why do you tell such lies?" Brent had asked, certain the cat was long gone. "Coyote chow," he said. But she said the cat was lost, missing—missing like the piece of luggage she once lost. She owned so little, and then that, too, was gone, and maybe *that* is why this trial is so important to her. She is a lot like that young woman who was murdered, one of the people who could so easily be lifted from the Earth with barely a footnote—*pass the gravy, please.*

Shelley never got her luggage back, left on a Greyhound bus, and yet she has never stopped thinking about the life of her things; she likes to think they were found by someone homeless, the fancy nightgown she loved—nylon, but it felt like silk—finding a home with someone who, like her, had never had something so impractical, the scent of fabric softener and the sachets she kept with it giving an added sense of comfort. The same with her favorite sweater, its fibers carrying her smell onto the body of the person who found it. To them, her loss was their luck, a stroke of good fortune, the sort of thing that might help change an attitude or turn a life around. To think otherwise, to think of her things pissed on or burned, bloodied beyond recognition, was too painful to even imagine, as was picturing the slender calico running for her life, ears tucked back and a guttural scream emitted with the swift tear of a coyote or the speeding tire of a car. Shelley's eye is always drawn to the side of the road—so much loss there in the ditches and wooded areas.

Brent had said it was over and he was going his own way.

What about us? she wanted to ask, but she didn't. Her brother had told her, "Don't ever beg, Shelley." But now she's thinking she might have to beg a little to keep her job. He would probably say that in this case, begging might be a good thing.

WHEN THE LAWYERS looked over the other day and realized she was listening to their conversation, she studied the shorthand pad in her lap, where she had recorded their jokes; they were always telling little jokes. A couple of their jokes were racist, even though the judge was black, and Shelley had notated all of that as well—*oh God, that was there, too, with the grocery list, not my joke,* their *joke*—and she'd also put in her own two cents about how the judge would've made Judge Judy melt like sugar. Shelley had once seen the woman in Pinehurst buying shoes—and really expensive shoes, too—but Shelley didn't make eye contact, because there is no way that woman would remember her, but still, she took note of those shoes, beautiful ostrich-skin pumps in a kind of burgundy color, and she has seen the judge come into the courtroom wearing them, too, and it's hard not to feel a little connected since she herself witnessed her buying them.

Now, she cringes with the idea that someone so fiercely intelligent has by now probably read all that Shelley wrote about the trial and would know that she sometimes buys inferior products, that in fact her list is filled with places where it says *buy whichever is cheapest*. It would be so much better, make such a better impression, if she had written a particular brand: Crest, Colgate, Tom's of Maine (that would have really made a good impression probably—all natural). And there was a time when that would have been true, like in high school when she'd wanted to use Vibrance shampoo because of the commercials and the way it showed the girl's hair go from straight and stringy to a wild wavy mass like Mariah's. *Hair so full of life!* And she liked Aquafresh—the cool, freshening stripes—ski slopes, and happy families. *That's the way I like it.*

But the list Shelley accidentally turned in really doesn't represent her well, and, even worse than that, she'd described the judge as having angry eyes and hair that all but leapt from her head as if it might burst into flame, the way the pirate Blackbeard's beard supposedly used to do. She had learned that from Harvey, that he put candles in the beard so it looked like he was on fire when he invaded ships. "Harvey, do not ever let me catch you putting candles in one of those fake beards," she had said, and Harvey asked how she knew he was thinking that. But she knew. She did know. She later found a box of birthday-cake candles tucked under the stuffed turtle on his bed.

Shelley's job has always kept her feeling better about herself. Sometimes the worse the case, the happier her life can feel, because, yes, it may be difficult to not know where someone is, but at least no one has put a cigarette out in your eye while you slept or a broomstick up your vagina, no one has shaken your baby to death or drugged you and then shot heroin into your arm to make it look like you killed yourself in a sad little apartment above a hot-dog drive-in, while your sweet little baby was staying with a friend just so you could have a *date*. That's the story of the trial, and she can't get it out of her head. It all feels so close to her life—Brent could have killed *her* when she showed up at his house and told him about Harvey—and so she actively seeks ways to distract herself so she won't feel afraid, something she learned to do a long time ago when the sounds of all those televisions and voices in her childhood home joined together in one loud vacuum-like hum.

Since childhood, Shelley's mind has wandered, and so she is especially sympathetic to Harvey and the way the teacher described his staring out the window. This is why her job is so good for her—taking notes, word after word, stroke after stroke—such a healthy way to stay focused and productive, to contribute to the good of society while also taking care of herself and her children. She practices begging while walking the aisles of Food Lion. *Please let me keep my job.* She shakes her head against the thought of the judge's eyes, that piercing stare that demands truth from all the lowlifes. "I will need to speak to you," the judge had said, and Shelley practices begging one more time while she spins the rack of L'eggs and No Nonsense. Gentlemen might prefer Hanes, but she hates pantyhose and always has. How can it even be healthy to be all bound up that way like a Jimmy Dean sausage; a pair of pantyhose was the weapon of choice in a trial just six months ago: mask and strangulation tool, all for under five dollars.

I tend to wear nice pants instead of skirts, she imagines telling the judge. *I take my work very seriously. Every aspect of it.*

Harvey

◦≈◦

A LOT OF what Jason has told Harvey is funny in the daytime but not in the dark, like about cave fish that go blind because they don't need eyes. "If you don't use it, you lose it," Jason always said and that's why Harvey tries to use his eyes and ears every day. Jason told him about the Beast of Bladenboro and the Munchkin people and the maniac under the bed. Jason said don't tell their mom all that stuff, because it would frighten her. But Harvey has told her. He had to, especially in the middle of the night when it was just the two of them.

Harvey thinks a lot about the Dog House Girl too and the way they found her naked and dead like that. He imagines that he is in that room with her. He tiptoes in. First, he goes and gets himself a Chihuahua hot dog dripping with chili and salsa, and there she is, waving and saying, *Aren't you the cutest! That's my favorite too, Harvey.* She says, *Only you can see me. You know that, right?* Thinking about this in the day is okay.

But Lizzie is never good to think about. He might try to imagine being friends with her and getting her to act good and be kind to others but as soon as he says that, she reaches for her axe and says she has to give somebody forty whacks, and that always wakes him up and he feels like he needs to go stand by his mother's bed.

Come see me, Harvey, Dog House Girl says. *You don't need to be afraid.* And what she meant was in the cemetery. Come see her in the cemetery. Come see where people leave little flowers above where she is, down there in the dirt, where it is as dark as where the cave fish are, which is why they don't have eyes.

Super Monkey can keep the bad people from doing what is bad and mean so people like that girl can keep her eyes and keep on living there at the Dog House with her little boy. Harvey's a little like a superhero or a Ninja Turtle, like Leonardo, but more like Michelangelo, telling jokes and making everybody laugh. He uses nunchakus—that's like his specialty. Jason says Harvey loves the Turtles as much as Jason used to love Power Rangers. "The good ones stay forever," Jason said. "Look at Superman. He's like eighty."

"Eighty?"

"Yes, or a hundred," Jason said. "One time they said he died."

"He can't do that," Harvey said. And now that's another thing that Super Monkey is having to try to fix. Don't get Superman killed or hurt or old.

"But then they let him come back," Jason said. "Like Jesus or E.T." Jason loved that movie and he would sometimes reach his fingertip out to Harvey and say, "Phone home," and that's what Harvey said when Jason left to go to school—"Phone home"—and Jason took a pen and wrote his number inside Harvey's closet and drew a picture of E.T. so Harvey could call whenever he wanted to, but lately he just gets Jason saying he can't talk, leave a message. Harvey says, "Phone home. There's ghosts in the yard."

Now, Harvey spends a lot of time watching the blackberry thicket between their yard and the new house, because this is where the ghosts go. "Don't go out there," Jason said. "Not without me." Jason is like Leonardo. The fearless leader, serious and smart. Jason's number is also written on the kitchen wall, right beside the phone. It is there beside everything else important to remember for when Harvey gets a ride and might be home too early: 911, never call unless an emergency; 411 will give you someone's number if you know their name. He once got them mixed up and was trying to figure out how to call his mother at the courthouse and the person kept saying, "Where are you? Where are you?" And he knew not to tell about himself to a stranger and he didn't know that person. His mother told him that. They said that at school. And the woman said, "Don't go anywhere, little boy. Stay on the line." And then in no time there were sirens and several policemen and of course there wasn't an adult at home, which he was never supposed to say. He was supposed to say that his mother was in the shower and she will have to call right back. His mom said the best answer was to say his daddy was in the garage working on the car, could he call back soon, because people act different if a man is there, like working on a car or chopping wood.

He left Jason a message about the Dog House Girl and how he can't stop thinking about her even though their mom tells him not to worry and then he told Jason how their mom cries sometimes and puts her head on the table like they make you do at school during quiet time. He told him how he's having trouble eating hot dogs, and he loves hot dogs. Last time he told Jason that, Jason said, "Then eat pizza—that's what Michelangelo would do. Pizza with lots of good junk on it."

The only good thing about when it gets dark is story time. Not whatever his mother tells or reads to him, even though he likes that part too. He loves how she smells like the bathtub and the way she is so warm; her bathrobe is like a real soft towel. Sometimes he closes his eyes and pretends that she is a mini horse there beside him, his horse, the first horse to ever be housebroken. This horse stands over the commode and then flushes. His mom says "commode" but the first-grade teacher said "toilet."

Harvey likes his story time, when he tells his own story to himself with his eyes closed and it's a like a movie going, and the problem lately is that the other stories are interrupted, like when the TV goes out when they say that something needs to be told right now and it's really, really bad stuff like a tornado is coming or something else scary. So last night when Harvey was in his own story time and living in that hollowed-out tree with the Runaway Bunny, waiting for their mother to come and get them, some of the others tried to get in instead. He was in there curled up and nice and warm and he knows people would tease him for being in a book that is written for babies but what they don't know is that this tree is different. The others closed the book and didn't know what came after, that they got a big television in this tree and they eat lots of good food and there is a mama and a daddy and they all curl up and watch things like *Finding Nemo* on the TV and the mama and daddy say I love you—"I love you"—and Bunny and Harvey pretend to sleep so that the mom and dad will keep staying there in the dark tree but then sometimes something shakes the tree hard and claws at the windows and the mom and dad aren't there anymore, because Lizzie got them, and even though he was so tired and even though all that shaking made him pee, he had to get up and put on his outfit to go out there and tell Lizzie that he is Super Monkey, whose specialty is to tell everyone in the universe, "Don't get killed," and she has to go back and start over and not do bad things.

Make me, Lizzie said. *You can't stop me.* And then he felt so bad and scared he went and got in bed with his mom and stayed real quiet so she wouldn't know, and he pretended he was back inside the tree with the bunny family. Jason said sometimes daddies go places and never come back and that's just how it is. Jason said that's why brothers are important. He said, "Don't ask Mom about it," and Harvey hasn't, because if he starts to, Lizzie will pick up her axe and stare. If he asks, then she might start murdering again and it would be all his fault, so he thinks about all the things he *can* ask his mom about. There is the Maco Light, about the train engineer that lost his head and goes looking for it down near the beach, and there are the Munchkins throwing rocks, and the Dog House Girl, who wasn't wearing any clothes at all, and Harvey hates that part of the story. He hates that part as much as he does to think about a needle stuck in her arm by that terrible man Super Monkey has not been able to make quit.

When they rode by one time, Harvey thought he saw her in the window looking out with a finger up to her lips—*shhhhhhhh*—just like the teacher in first grade, Mrs. Theresa Morgan. "Oh, no, you don't, mister!" She was big up top with a puff of blond hair like cotton candy that everybody wanted to touch. "Don't misbehave, you hear? I don't want to have to tell your mother." In story circle, she talked about how they should sow seeds of kindness and then she ended by saying, "So go and sow, you so-and-so," and everybody laughed. She liked to use the same word spelled different and she liked to make cards of *to*, *too*, and *two*, and *blue* and *blew*, and *new* and *knew*. Harvey asked was it like *but* and *butt*, which Jason had taught him. *I could hit your butt but Mom would get mad.* Jason taught him that the same time he taught him *You can tell it's Mattel—just smell.*

The blackberry patch is not far from where Harvey has the fish cemetery. Goldfish and guppies, and there's a hamster in there: Skippy. Jason's hamster, Kong, killed and ate part of Skippy. And that's the day Harvey got in trouble for writing on the wall. *Shit*, he wrote. *Dam.* And then he threw some rocks as hard as he could at a tree and then he got a trash-can lid and marched in a circle with a big, sharp stick, like a sword fighter, and then Jason taught him how to say things in Klingon. He can write *shit* in Klingon and kids really like that a lot.

Harvey was playing in his mom's closet one day when she got in her bed and started crying so loud he held his ears. He wasn't supposed to be in her closet, because it was where she kept good things like sparkly shoes and stuff she had when she was little, like a naked Barbie doll and an old smelly quilt. There's an old bowling ball in there too. Jason showed it to him and told him it was like the Magic 8 Ball, only bigger, and Jason could read messages in the black and red swirlies: *It is certain. Yes.* In the closet, Harvey held on to the ball while he sat real quiet and watched his mom's dirty white socks kicking back and forth.

Michelangelo would have popped out and scared her. Michelangelo would have told a joke, like he might've said, *Hey, dude, does your nose run? Do your feet smell? Or why does your crack go thisaway and not thataway?* And then he would have made that funny sound with his lips that a butt would do on a sliding board if it was cracked the other way, like Jason taught him, and his mom would have thought that was funny. She would have laughed instead of crying and he wouldn't have needed to hold his breath, like he was waiting for something or like he was way deep underwater with that old turtle with the nice eyes. He isn't supposed to touch the bowling ball but sometimes he does, because he misses Jason telling him what it says—*Let's eat* or *Burp loud*—and throwing him high in the air. *Be good.*

Lil

Christmas 2014
Newton

YOU TWO ALWAYS shook your heads and got impatient when I said
I had to have a huge tree and spent way too long (your father said)
there on the lot studying them all. I wanted big trees, beautiful trees.
The whole process of it was a joy, from buying and getting it home
to dealing with the hateful old stands, greeting each curse and slam
of your father's hammer, or whatever he was using to make it stand
upright, with the expression of how beautiful it was all going to be,
how it was worth every minute of trouble.

I loved pulling out the ornaments, and you loved hearing the stories that went with each: the ones that were gifts from teachers; the old fragile glass balls with your names in glue and glitter; and all those snowflakes you cut out yourself; the photos on the lap of Santa; and those little elves with the bendy legs that sat on top of boxes of chocolates. Other than the ones you two had made, my favorites were the little pine-cone elves with their different instruments, maybe because they had been my mother's favorites, those and the little cardboard houses, with the snow on the roof and the places for a bulb to glow within. I loved the silver icicles and the way we could toss the strings up and let them land as they pleased, sweep the strays up from the floor and throw them back on. I even liked when it was all over and I'd carefully tucked everything back into its little bed for the year, recycling the icicles by using them to shield and protect the fragile decorations.

Now, you have your own trees and your share of all those early ornaments; this year, we bought a four-foot one, and it's on a table in the front window. We have the same star and colored lights and, of course, icicles. From the street, it looks like a full-sized tree.

The year my mother died, there was no Christmas tree, and the one time I mentioned it, my father's look let me know it wasn't going to happen. But still, I pretended. I decorated the coatrack and called it a tree. I paid special attention to the tree in the window of a house near ours, one I passed each day walking to school. At first, it made me feel left out, but then it became my focus, it became *my* tree and was a bright spot in my day. And then January passed and it still stood, and then February, too, and I began to wonder if the people had died. But, no, I saw them, coming and going. Still, it was a lesson to me how hanging on to something long after the fact can diminish the power of what *was*. It's where memory comes in, I guess, the abstract strength of what is no longer there to see and touch. I don't even recall if I got a gift that year, but I must have; my father's sister visited, and she cooked for several days and left the icebox full of food.

My mother had become the past. And the effects on my father were like that forgotten old Christmas tree.

"But she loved Christmas," I told him, and he said, "Exactly."

At the time, his response seemed harsh, but I grew to see it as protective, part of the scaffolding he constructed to hold himself upright through those long, dark winter weeks as our numbness and shock slowly thawed with the muddy earth and green of spring into this new way of living. He dreaded winter and all the memories it brought, and I loved it; I felt closer to her when I felt close to those final days. I still do. November weather reports always fill me with anticipation.

A few months later, I overheard my father talking to my mother's friend Janie, a woman he had once thought was a bad influence (he'd said she aspired to too much), but there he was inviting her into our living room and talking to her, saying things that he had not said to me, revealing things about my mother's clothes and what he had discovered in her drawer, like a receipt for money she still owed the local dress shop where Janie worked (for a new coat on layaway). They didn't know that I was in the hallway, holding my breath so that I could hear. "Why was she hiding things from me?" he asked. "There were things in her drawer I had never seen before. A lacy slip, some handkerchiefs."

"Just because someone is dead doesn't mean you should tell their secrets," I was thinking.

"Do you know who she was with?" he asked, and Janie said, no, she didn't, but she had her suspicions. Then the two sat there for what felt like an unbearable amount of time. It seemed Janie was about to explain more, but before she could say it, I came into the room.

I said that maybe my mother was helping to plan a surprise. "For you," I said, and turned to Janie, her shell left cracked and vulnerable. "Or maybe something nice for *you*." I turned back to my father, who was not as easily cracked. "Or maybe she was earning extra money so she could have those nice things without having to ask you; maybe she was afraid you would say no, because you usually say no." That one got him, and so I kept going, about how maybe just maybe she was earning extra money so they would have a big Christmas. "So I would have a big Christmas! Maybe, she was doing it all for me."

"Let it stop," I thought. "Let her just be my mother."

They were quiet, and finally they both nodded, as if to say I could be right, and then, in a strange distant way, they simply closed the door on it all.

Janie came over often after that; she was a solid placeholder. She didn't smoke nearly as much as my mother had, and she didn't drink at all. She had a nice singing voice and was an excellent cook. She filled a chair and performed many tasks. She helped my father go through and sort my mother's things. She cooked and cleaned and sometimes even spent the night, though I never saw her any way other than fully dressed. For a long time, I simply thought she had returned bright and early to cook our breakfast, and then I realized she was in the same dress from the day before, her hair down around her shoulders instead of pulled up the way she usually wore it. In the spring, she even made an Easter dress for me and embroidered the yoke with tiny roses, but by summer something seemed to have happened, and the stretches of time when we did not see her lengthened. Eventually, we heard that she'd married a man from Texas, and to my knowledge, we never heard from her again.

"It's just as well," my father had said. "She deserves someone who wants to marry," something I would learn he was not interested in thinking about until I had graduated and left home.

Though our house was a quiet one and the food questionable much of the time, I took great pride in my father's position, unsure if it was for my benefit or for his own; it occurred to me that the wilis, those grieving ghostly virgins in "Giselle," did not have a monopoly on broken hearts. His weighed the same.

I wanted to ask who Janie had suspected my mother was with, but there never seemed a good time to interrupt the rhythm and security of the life we came to know. When he was sad or worried, I didn't want to add to the burden; and when he was happy, I just wanted the good time to last. Then, before I knew it, he was an old man, and together we carried those fragile memories of my mother as gingerly as I do that brittle silver star on top of the tree. I bought it at Woolworth's before either of you were born.

Shelley

THE FEW TIMES Shelley has been able to afford good therapy, she has learned that on occasion she *disassociates*—that she might realize she has heard nothing coming out of the mouth of the person standing in front of her because the tightening of her own throat has forced her to think only of the click, click, click of a distant ceiling fan while she wonders, *What next? What next? What next?* And apparently it isn't a legitimate excuse that someone is boring and eating up all the oxygen around you in a way you find offensive. The spoken word is overrated, and if there is a hell like what Brent's parents taught him to believe and she is forced to go there, she will have to sit in a doorless room and listen on and on and on.

Her job has been a lesson in focus and vigilance as she records every word and gesture and mannerism but as objectively as possible, which is another lesson in discipline, such amazing discipline, and focusing on the concrete without analyzing, a nearly impossible exercise to pull off in real life, and in fact it has been quite difficult in this particular case, because the young murdered woman's face is so familiar. Shelley knows that she probably passed her a million times, in the grocery store, in the post office, the makeup masking the very young face of someone nearly invisible in society, and so in light of that—the murder and abuse—how can you possibly listen to someone talking about the young woman's weight or the way she wore her hair as if that is significant? And it is hard for Shelley to listen to all of that because she's heard it her whole life. *Have you gained a little weight? What made your skin break out? Do you think if you had a job that forced you to walk around you wouldn't gain weight? Do you think if you just gave up anything that has ever given you pleasure that maybe you would look better, behave better, do better in school? I'd take you to a dermatologist if I could afford it—try some Clearasil, scrub harder.* The alternative to criticism was no attention at all, which would have been the better choice had she had any power to choose.

Her dad had said things like: "If those people really wanted money, they'd get up off their lazy asses and work like everybody else." He said people like being in prison, because they get three meals a day and endless television, all at the hardworking taxpayer's expense. He said nobody ever gave him anything. He said, "So if you don't like it, get the hell out," and that's what her brother did, and in many ways that is what her mother did, hidden there behind a wall of magazines and ashtrays, and laundry that never got hung up. "How-ma-ny-times-do-I-have-to-tell-you," he would say, a belt crack with each syllable, and Shelley's mother would say how doing that hurt him worse than it hurt Shelley and her brother, but her mother never did anything to stop it. "Well, that's a fucking load of shit," her brother told Shelley. He told her they were on their own. "It was an accident," he said the last time she saw him. "An accident."

In yoga, once she bought her own props and could stop worrying about whose butt had been on the bolster or blanket her face was on, she discovered that the kind of repetition that accompanied her steps and passages all through the day was a kind of meditation. All this time, she'd been meditating and didn't even know it: rhythm and rhyme, fragments of songs repeated in ways that blanked and swaddled her mind and thoughts. *"Meditating" sounds better than "disassociating,"* she thought. Words and rhythm lifting her from the scene before her, whatever it might be—escaping boredom in the midst of chatter, seeking safety in the midst of fear. But now, these recent days, the simple *I am, I am, I am,* calm or strong or peaceful, has turned to *Terrified, terrified, paralyzed, paralyzed,* and *slick red satin damp with fatigue.*

"Why don't you tell me about your childhood," Brent had said to her, and if he ever came back, maybe she would tell him. She would tell what had really happened with her family, and she would tell about the old man who'd once lived here, and how he keeps circling back like a lost cat wanting in, and how, now that she has had time to think about it, she *hated* those things Brent said to her—they weren't funny at all—like that she'd be so easy to kill. She would say she thinks that was mean, and so was the way he sometimes stared at Harvey's mouth and then at her, like it was her fault, when the doctor had been so kind and reassuring to say no one was to blame; besides, it could have been much worse, much more complicated. The nurse had told her it would not affect his speech, and she was right about that, and the scar in the center of his lip—what they call Cupid's bow—will fade. *We are doing fine*, she would say. *I take good care of us*. She would say this and then repeat it; she would say it until she believed it herself.

SHELLEY REMEMBERS THE case where the man said, "I'll take care of you." It was a crime of passion, and the arguments went round and round, the man testifying that he'd said those words in love, in his attempt to reassure his wife how much he loved her and wanted to take good care of her, but the prosecution seeing it as a threat—*I'll take care of* you—the way it was spoken suggesting the man had a twisty villain mustache and a maniacal laugh. The weight fell on the word *you*, a threat more than a promise. I'll take care of *you*—that is the line she hears the times she wakes to a sound that is unfamiliar, a shadow that races past her eyes, when what she wishes for is the comfort of laying her head down and closing her eyes and feeling someone really is there to take care of her, to love and watch over her.

SHELLEY DIDN'T BELIEVE in making children lick soap for saying bad words or physically spanking or yanking or switching. She and Brent were different this way. He believed the previous generation sometimes knew best and that she was spoiling Jason and Harvey; she thought whipping and all that "spare the rod" shit was barbaric behavior, abominable and sadistic, and did nothing but perpetuate fear and anger and all those terrible weaknesses that feed everything bad in society, and she told him so. Brent had looked surprised, and she wasn't sure if it was because she had stood up to him or that she had used *barbaric, abominable, sadistic*, and *perpetuate* all in one sentence. She usually just said things like "I think that's fucked-up," but there had been a recent trial with some people being accused of embezzlement, and she had picked up some powerful vocabulary.

"You are calling someone fucked-up? You?" he asked incredulously, which is another word popular among the lawyers. "Let's talk about you, Shelley," he said. "Let's talk about the way you have lived."

Who wouldn't want to cuss? That's what she said when Harvey was standing beside her bed for the third time the other night. He said he'd had a bad thought and he needed to tell her, that he was worried and he needed to tell her. He'd seen a ghost all dressed in black, and he couldn't stop thinking about the bad things bad people do. He told her how the Glencoe Munchkins threw rocks and cussed at the people who passed by.

"Of course they did," she said. "Like I keep telling you, people made fun of them and were mean about things they couldn't help. They were born with problems, a lot of sad problems." She sat up and turned on the light. He was bare-legged, his Nemo nightshirt barely reaching his briefs, and she knew she would find wet pajama pants in the sink and a towel over the wet spot in his bed.

"So that made it okay to cuss?" he said.

She turned back the covers and moved over so Harvey could get in. "It made it understandable," she said. "I understand why they did what they did." She knew there was probably something he still wanted to tell her and hadn't, but before she could ask, he was fast asleep, his hand holding her arm. She had to help him get over this problem, but for the moment she allowed herself the comfort of his warm little body beside her and the rhythmic breaths. When he was younger, he liked to pretend they were bears in a cave or the three bears in their little house, and at nap time he would ask to hibernate, a word Jason taught him, and pull the blanket up over his head.

Lately, Shelley feels like someone who's been hibernating, the way she knows she has taken on the mom look—the tug and longing of motherhood pulling you toward a kind of domestic hibernation, comfort food and easy clothes, hair pulled into ponytails, and face cleaned of makeup. As in nature—birds and beasts blending to hide and protect their nest or den—a warm, soft mama spreads her wings or paws to comfort and protect. "You don't even try to look attractive," Brent had said, or was that what the murderer had said? Yes, that is what the murderer had said of his wife: "She stopped trying to look attractive. She stopped being there for me as a partner. What man wouldn't look elsewhere? Does that make me a murderer?"

What man wouldn't look elsewhere? That was the line that got stuck in her head, playing the same part again and again. *What man wouldn't look elsewhere?* A line that seemed to repeat itself as she watched all the women who had to take the stand during the trial—all of them preened and ready, wedding rings in full view, and diamond or pearl earrings, trails of perfume. They all were thin and tanned, with ropy muscles in their arms and calves, even though the skin of more than one was showing the sagginess of age. Linen sheaths, tailored suits, conservative colors. Shelley once heard a lawyer say that people on the witness stand should wear navy blue, because it suggests truth and dependability, only to go home that night and realize she owned nothing navy other than blue jeans and one pair of underwear. Shelley has seen a lot of these women elsewhere in town, and they looked very different when sporting clothes made for teenagers, short skirts and leotards, leopard and zebra prints—all those things that seem to say, *Look at me, look at me.* And such flamboyance is not a crime, and it certainly doesn't invite violence, but Shelley has always been aware of how the louder one is, the more color visible, the easier the target. The picture of the young woman who was murdered was the opposite of these: she was well camouflaged, with dark rings of eye makeup—what Jason calls "goth"—and hair dyed and pulled up in a messy knot. That last night, there was no eye makeup at all, just a little bit of lip gloss, and she wore something very different, something more in keeping with the parade of women who had taken the stand, an expensive, conservative-looking silk blouse.

"I can swear on that Bible a hundred times," the murdered woman's friend said, "that she never would have bought that for herself. Not her style and not her budget." She then told how the young woman wore only black and kept a low profile, which made her an exception to Shelley's idea about what might keep you safe, proof that sometimes there is no way out. That's what Shelley's brother had said to her. He said there was "no way out." He'd said he was sorry he wouldn't be there to help her clean up the mess.

Harvey told her he has also seen the Dog House Girl in their yard, moving from tree to tree. He says it is hard to sleep when you know things like about her, and about Lyle and Erik and what they did, and Lizzie Borden and what she did, the Beast of Bladenboro, right down the road, and the statue in the cemetery that will chase you at night. He says he tries to think about happy things, to have a party in his head for just nice people who are still alive, but the others all keep coming anyway. He'd asked her if she thought the Dog House Girl knew she was being killed, and Shelley said she hoped not.

Marva, Shelley's only friend at work, said Harvey might need a little counseling, and she gave her a name of someone, but Shelley hasn't had a chance to call yet. She and Marva—everybody calls her Marvy Marva—bonded when they discovered they both had always loved tiny little dolls they could keep in their pockets. Shelley had had a Polly Pocket and one of the newer versions of Liddle Kiddles, one with pink hair, like strawberries, but Marva is older, and so she has one of the original ones, a little cowgirl with white boots and a spotted orange rocking horse. Marva is the kind of person who makes Shelley feel safe, because she's confident and does that southern thing where she pats your arm and blesses your heart, and Shelley's heart cannot possibly be blessed enough these days. But what would Marva say if she saw what Shelley wrote that has the judge so upset? *Fuck this monster. Send his ass up the river.* She would probably chew on those pearls she always wears and then snap her fingers with some words of wisdom that would again lead her to bless Shelley's heart, which is sometimes a kind way to say you feel sorry for someone or that you think they're stupid. *Bless your heart.* She doesn't say that to Harvey, because she shares his feeling that there is something there—a ghost?—that someone *might* be watching them. Brent? Someone from her past? That old man? Surely not the old man. She has his address, and Google says he used to be a teacher in college somewhere in the north; he isn't steady enough on his feet to be that quiet. She is not ready to tell Marva or anyone else, who might think she's losing it. Not yet. Last night, in the time it took her eyes to adjust and her heart to slow, whatever she thought she saw was gone, surely just a dream, a bad dream because of all the stress.

I made a bad mistake, she will tell the judge, *even though you should know that I am capable of holding a lot of words in my head at one time.* All she wanted was to get all the language crowding her head *out* so she wouldn't be tempted to say any of it. She wants it all behind her and forgotten. She wants to go to work and pretend nothing happened, to pick up a pencil or sit at a keyboard and let the words come tumbling out in a way that finds order on the page.

Call. Please call and give me another chance.

The more she thinks it—*chance, chance*—the more foreign the sound and the more desperate she feels. *I made a bad mistake*, she will say. Or she could say that she didn't write any of that at work but that it was in her satchel and she accidentally got it mixed in. She could say that she is taking a writing class at the community college, something that she really has thought about doing, or maybe she could say that she is *teaching* a little writing group, because that would sound even more responsible.

"When will you ever learn, Shelley?" Brent had asked as he packed his stuff. "When will you ever learn to just tell the truth?"

Lil

September 7, 1969 (a keeper!)
Newton

BACK TO SCHOOL! And already it is feeling like fall, my favorite
time of year. I have all the windows open, and it is glorious, but I
know by the time Frank gets home from work, I will need to close
them and maybe even think about turning on the heat. Everyone is
still talking about Chappaquiddick (and how do you explain such
a thing to children?), such a horrifying story, and one that nearly
eclipsed the moon landing. Jeff mimics the giant leap for mankind
at every opportunity, often offering his sister one small step (or

cookie, or whatever he is supposed to be sharing) and "one giant one for Jeff."

The back-to-school project for all the grades (even kindergarten) is to prepare a time capsule. What would you tell about your life and this world? What are your wishes? Becca wishes for world peace, and peace with the Martians if that is who finds it. She wants the world to know about her summer camp in Sturbridge and that she hopes to be an actress, and at the last minute she added a little troll doll from her collection but then took it back. Jeff, at Frank's urging, said he wants the Red Sox to win the World Series, and he put in a photo of Carl Yastrzemski he cut from the paper and an old Duncan yo-yo and those clacker balls that are no longer allowed in school because somewhere (Ohio, maybe?) one broke and blinded a child. (Glad to send it to the moon!) Together, the children took a Polaroid of Margot and the new puppy, Rudolf, and added another photo of the four of us we had our neighbor take. Jeff touched it before it was dry, so there's a big smudge on me, and I said that was just as well. I wrote that I hope my father's good health and happiness will continue, that we will have a nice Christmas this year, and that I hope my dance school can survive, and I included a program from last year's recital (yet another woodland forest free-for-all with bunnies and sunbeams). We put in a copy of the latest Billboard hits, and I added the front page of the Globe. I'm not sure what Frank wrote; he took his time, sealed his envelope, and handed it over to Becca, who is in charge of collecting and wrapping it all up airtight. The whole process reminded me of that old cartoon, where that frog is stuck in the cornerstone of a building and leaps out singing and dancing with a top hat and cane. That song has been stuck in my head ever since.

Now we are into the routine of homework and early bedtimes. The kids get to choose one night a week to sit up a little bit later and watch a show. Usually they pick "Bewitched," and I enjoy that one, too. Wish I could twitch my nose and get everything done in the kitchen! Becca is also obsessed with that spooky afternoon show "Dark Shadows," and there's all this talk of vampires and drinking blood. These girls act it out, silly and carrying on in ways I don't remember ever doing. I take great vicarious pleasure! And I am about to do what I do every year and buy up all the cheap discarded perennials that have been marked down to nothing at the nursery, just empty pots with roots in dirt. But come spring, what a bounty. I have yet to be disappointed.

Becca's back to school list:
  Blue Horse notebook/Fat Boy paper/#2 pencils/Crayolas
  New booksack—(the red one we saw)
  Dark Shadows lunchbox—PLEASE!
  Milk money—5¢/day (teacher prefers nickels to pennies)
  Snacks (teacher prefers things without crumbs)

All accomplished, and she is fast asleep with tomorrow's clothes on the chair by her bed! Jeff wanted to sleep in his clothes so he'd be ready early, and I gave in and let him.

The entries in this envelope are all from the same year in our Newton house. Can't decide if I should keep or burn. I am inclined to burn. What is there to gain?

May 13, 1981
It's a clear, beautiful day (at last), and I am finally seeing green in the garden. I love the cleanup, pulling away all the old, rotted dead to make room for the new. I added four peonies in the fall, those reduced for final sale, 50¢ for a pot of roots, because who knows

what color they will be. Something to look forward to, because
Frank is so agitated these days. He gets agitated over little things
(maybe I forget to turn down the thermostat or to buy milk). And
he jingles whatever is in his pocket (maybe that old badge from his
childhood or one of his flattened pennies). "So sue me," I say.

He may not think it's a lot to direct a stageful of children, but I
have bad days, too. If one dancer vomits, three more will follow, or
if somebody whines about not getting the part she wanted. I'm doing
"The Four Seasons," and they all wanted to be Spring or Summer,
because they love the bright colors, so now I also have pink snowflakes and purple leaves.

I certainly don't bite *his* head off if I find his socks beside his
chair or little shaved hairs all over the sink. I'm the one planning
Becca's graduation party, and I'm the one helping Jeff move out of
his dorm; freshman year barely behind him and he's already saying
he wants to transfer somewhere warmer. It's just the two of us, so
shouldn't that make life easier? People say "empty nest," and I for
one am sick of hearing it. Everything has a name now—a label or
diagnosis or definition or little slot to get filed away. As if I don't
hear enough about labels and classifications for anything that gets
dug up. Frank is obsessed with the plans for the upcoming Big Dig,
which they say might take years of construction, bridges and tunnels
that will help city traffic but might also send rats looking for new
homes. I listen to it all. I listen, and I don't jingle my pockets and
huff and puff. I listen, but let's just say, my mind is occupied with
other things.

October 18, 1981
Dad is not doing well these days. He forgets things and is not steady
on his feet. I feel I need to check on him more and more often. It was
a hectic summer; it seemed to fly, and I'm not even sure why, and

now the back-to-school rush with kids signing up for dance keeps me busy. I have someone coming in once a week to teach tap and gymnastics, and the kids are flocking to her classes. I love ordering all those little pink shoes and tights. Always have. But now, the fall feels settled, Frank's semester up and running, overloaded as always, and today I fully realized the shift in light—a quick venture into Star Market in the late afternoon and by the time I got home, it was dark. People complain about the early darkness (they order special lights and so on), but I love it.

Everyone says I come through the house at dusk, clicking first the hall lamp and then the one by the green chair, in the exact same order, stopping and lighting the candles on the dining room table, adjusting the door to the hallway just so. "Clockwork," Becca said. "Obsessive." And I said, "What about dependable? What about reliable?" Clockwork, that was my father, and how interesting the importance of time to the men in my life—one whose work was all about precision and trying to keep it moving forward second by second, and one whose career is all about reaching back and digging (except when personal). Some days, I feel like I am like that tiny screw in the center, holding the hands in place.

October 23, 1981
Even though we occupy the same space, Frank and I politely excuse ourselves if we bump in the hallway or when lying side by side in the bed we have shared for years. It is October, my favorite kind of breezy, sharp day, the kind that makes even an old dog like Rudolf frisk about and nuzzle into the fallen leaves. I walked him while all of the little things that have bothered me lately were building in my brain. By the time we had made our big loop and I turned the corner to see our house, it all came together. The ringing of the phone and no one there. Odd errands at odd times. The agitated jingling of his

pocket on top of my doing nothing right. The kiss good night barely a brush against my cheek, if that. The name of a colleague that comes up a little too often, and then suddenly, not at all.

October 31, 1981
It's Halloween, my favorite holiday, but I am not up to the task. Frank has a "meeting"; he said he was sorry to miss the trick-or-treaters, and then he laughed and said I never let him answer the door anyway, so I would probably enjoy the solitude. I have left a big basket of candy on the porch with an electric jack-o'-lantern, to give enough light for their coming and going, and have chosen to sit here with just the street light coming in the window. It's easier than putting on my usual witch garb and cackling through the night, oohing and aahing over the various costumes, especially the little ones'. But it's easier to just drink a glass of wine or two, and have a cigarette or three or four, and listen to the laughter, the mothers admonishing not to take too much, those who are regulars wondering where I am this year.

Not only did Frank suddenly forget that he had a "meeting"—on a Saturday night, no less—but I also got a note from Jeff today. It seems I am not the only one having trouble communicating with their father. He wrote:

He talks about the Titanic when I want to talk about school
and what is happening in MY life. Who gives a shit? It sank.
That was then and this is now. He is the iceberg. He is an
asshole in the middle of an ice cold sea and it would take
more than a cruise liner to chip the surface. You say you'll
talk to him but you haven't yet, so just forget it. Okay? Just
forget it, Mom.

I read his note, and I felt sick, like such a failure, and I thought immediately of a saying about taking an axe to the ice. Something I heard at one of those awful faculty parties I attended with Frank one year or another. One of those where I smiled and was polite and tried to hear something that interested me without drinking too much too fast or chain-smoking, while secretly wishing I could find an escape hatch. I recall that the person who wrote about the axe also wrote about being a cockroach, which is what I feel like tonight, hunkered down in the dark here and dreading the bright light of truth. What breaks the ice?

I want to tell Jeff I can't forget how he is feeling, because there is nothing more important to me, that I also want to break the ice, but I also hope to spare him whatever ugly facts I might find; I want him and Becca to be okay. When Jeff was seven and ran away, I saved his note, written in red crayon on a paper towel: *I'm GONE and you will miss me.* I found him within 10 minutes, in the toolshed, with a bag of Cheetos and a packet of Pop-Tarts; he said he was never coming back, but as soon as it started getting cold and dark, he did. He came in just in time for Huckleberry Hound and Quick Draw McGraw. This time, it might not be as easy to get him back. Like father, like son.

The trick-or-treaters are dwindling—many adults this year dressed as Ronald Reagan with his big grin and his pompadour, tagging along with the witches and ninjas and devils—and when I last peeped out, the candy was almost gone. My favorite was a little swaybacked, flare-footed guy dressed as Hulk Hogan with a long blond wig, pulled along by his sister, Tinker Bell, and it has left me completely weepy and nostalgic for days that now seem so easy, even though I know they weren't. Still, I'd give anything right this minute to be out there trudging through the thick, damp leaves with my two, the only worry being how many more doorbells we might ring before the houses go dark.

November 4, 1985
This was left on my windshield while I was inside teaching dance this afternoon, there where a parent or one of my little students might have seen it:

> Leave me alone! I know it's you calling every day. You are pitiful and he deserves better. Blame yourself and leave me alone!

I saw the glances. I felt the shift in the air as clear as Rudolf knows a storm is coming and starts drooling and panting and scratching and digging into the floor. That's how I feel right now—panicked and panting and needing a cave. Leave her alone? Leave *her* alone? What about me? That's what I plan to ask Frank. I blame him for not thinking of *me*. What about me? And all this time he has continued to do all the normal things: brief hugs hello and goodbye, getting the snow tires, putting in a supply of salt, and telling me about his classes or what he has read in the paper. He'll talk about holiday plans and what the kids will do, but he won't look me in the eye anymore.

I also keep thinking about Jeff's note and trying to figure out what to say or do. He asked who cares about the Titanic, but clearly many people do. I can't stop thinking about how it is 370 miles from land and far below the ocean's surface. It is so hard for my mind to go there, like driving from here to Delaware or beyond, and then taking a straight turn downward into the cold and dark. How quiet it must be. I keep thinking that. How quiet it must be.

November 5, 1985

A day as dark and dreary as I feel. A day where the bed beckons me to crawl back in and disappear, but I know that is the wrong answer. If the kids were coming home from high school, there would be no chance of that, but they are off in their own lives, so I have given in, sinking and sinking.

I ask Frank how he can do what he is doing to me, and he responds with what I have done to *him*, as if the two are equal, as if one didn't come before the other. And, yes, I may have had a drink or two too many at that faculty gathering. Guilty as charged. It was boring, for one thing, but more important (because I have withstood boring many times before) were those glances between them, that feeling I got that confirmed what I have been thinking for a while now. I only know that I was there in a crowded room and people seemed to ask how I was and then look over my shoulder as if searching for a better conversation. Just "How are you?" and before I could even formulate a thought, they were gone. And there I was, alone in a corner, surrounded by strangers as my husband expounded on the merits of something or other dead a million trillion years ago to eager listeners with no awareness of me. I did hear someone talking about the Ice Age or the Stone Age or some age when things were living that no longer are. "Who recalls the Sinclair dinosaur?" I called out. And that's when I noticed that I had lost sight of Frank, and I panicked. I felt like a dinosaur myself, nearing extinction; my time was up, a newer and more interesting shape of life was already slipping into my footsteps.

I remember crying. I remember crying and telling someone how my dad always went to Sinclair for gas and how he got out of the car and watched everything the man in his little cap did there under the hood of our old Pontiac, and I told about the night my mother died, and by then several people were listening, and they asked me to sit on the sofa and drink coffee. I remember suggesting that their department put up a sign that said DIG THIS, and a couple of people thought that was funny, except this one man who raised his voice louder, so that everyone would listen to him explain whatever it was he was doing or had done or was going to do.

Frank later told me that was the guest lecturer, there to talk about a recent discovery of a mammoth that had been written about in all the major papers. Apparently, I said, "That's mammoth, all right, but can you do this?" And I proceeded to do an arabesque and a partial tour jeté, and that's when we left.

We left, and Frank's young colleague was watching the whole time. I saw the glare. She looked at me with pure hatred, as if she wished me dead, and I wanted to tell her that there are worse things. There really are worse things. If I had had my wits, I might very well have said that I'd rather be dead than to be a selfish, self-centered liar. Even here, stone sober on this cold gray day, I do maintain that. And just writing it down, looking at it here in daylight, makes me feel better. I am sorry for the embarrassment I might have caused Frank. I truly am. But what is he sorry for? Didn't we promise to be honest? Didn't we agree about the damage that secrets can bring?

Shelley

SHELLEY HAS FELT invisible for so much of her life, with bodies around but none capable of responding, like those dreams where no one can hear you. *Hello? Anyone home? I'm bleeding. Yes, looks like I need to go the emergency room. Hello? Yoo-hoo! I just won the school spelling bee, going to the state championship. I'm falling apart here; can anyone hear me? The guidance counselor says I need to go to college. The guidance counselor says I am someone capable of success and an advanced degree.*

Brent had heard her, and he saw her, at least for a little while. He'd opened up his world and invited her in, and so what more could she do but come in and curl up near that promised fire of comfort. He even encouraged her to apply to college, but soon she recognized how foolish to really think magic could happen to someone like her. How does the fish feel when it grabs a shiny bit of lunch and finds itself hooked and dragged into a place it can't breathe?

Still, it was good in the beginning, and she was hopeful. She took a course at the community college and really sharpened her shorthand skills, discovering how easily it all came to her, as if this was her first language and she just never knew. But now, the tribe speaking her language, those quiet people tucked away in offices and courtrooms, are dying out, replaced by recording equipment, keyboards, and masks. Some might say it's a dying language, but she thinks it's an art like cursive; she and Brent often wrote things in cursive so Jason couldn't read their love notes. Now it's Harvey who studies the loops and swirls of things that come in the mail and asks her to read them. Harvey says her shorthand looks like a little bird got ink on its feet and did a dance.

Shelley once met a woman whose first language was American Sign Language; the child of two deaf parents, this woman grew up watching her parents' fingers—*I love you, sweetie pie, beddy-bye time*—those were the examples the woman had used, phrases that Shelley had later used with Jason and Harvey, so lovely and sweet and lyrical, that had never been called out to her.

Sometimes Shelley traces things like *I love you, sweetie pie* and *beddy-bye time* on Harvey's back as she waits for him to fall asleep. *Sweetie pie*. Sometimes in cursive and sometimes in print. So he can try and feel the letters, get the message.

The first time Shelley ever saw Brent, he reminded her a little of Jason's dad, though of course she never would have said that, and how strange to even figure out how to say it or why it was, one man white and one man dark, one man middle-aged and one man young. One beefy and one painfully thin. Still there was something in the eyes that pulled her in. It really came down to kindness in their eyes, at least in the beginning. No one ever wants to be compared, even though it seems people are often attracted to similarities—voices, gestures—some part responding to something, maybe something really old, the same way they say a baby hears things before it's born.

In childbirth class, she'd heard a woman say how beautiful it is to imagine all that the baby hears, that she had been giving her baby a steady diet of Mozart and traditional African folk music. Shelley just smiled at her and did not say what she was thinking, how she couldn't stop thinking about all those babies who have to hear things like screams and threats and slams and shots before they ever even enter the world. She didn't want to tell her that with Jason, she had listened to all of her old favorites like Nirvana and Mariah and Janet Jackson, even though what would have been wrong with that? The night that Harvey was conceived, Brent was playing Miles Davis. They hadn't known each other long; they had met in a bar. "A nice bar," she always added when Brent told that. He once said, "Who knew a one-night stand would stretch into years," and then, when she didn't say anything back, added that he was glad it had, shook her shoulder as if to say, *A joke! That's a joke!* It took so long for him to say the second part that it didn't feel good to hear, but by then there *were* good things to hear, things like Harvey in his little bouncy chair, his breath against her cheek, and the sounds of Jason's Game Boy, something Brent took him to buy, an outing that had made her feel hopeful, even though it didn't last.

Still that kind of memory is such a good distraction, and these days, she is actively seeking distraction. The other day, Harvey's camp teacher, Mr. Stone—"Call me Ned"—told her how Harvey has such a vivid imagination, and that he will do his best to help the little guy get through this difficult time. That's what he said:

"this difficult time." And she said, yes, she knows that Harvey has a vivid imagination. The ghost stories, the Ninja Turtles, how the one named Michelangelo lived in his closet for years and they had to put a glass of milk in there for him every night. Oh, and that mini horse, Einstein. Harvey has built little trails and stables all over the yard for his toy horse.

But Ned said that a lot of what Harvey was talking about was darker than that. "He's been talking about that murder trial," he said. "And he knows all the details. You work at the courthouse, right?"

"Oh dear," Shelley said. *Such a stupid response*, she thinks—as she continues to think about it—especially since it felt like Ned was accusing *her* of telling Harvey things. "He must have heard me talking to his big brother, who used to tell him lots of scary things but has stopped now; he really has. We're working on all that now. In fact, the Ninja Turtles are really good, and I try to keep him interested in them."

"He knows a lot, Mrs. . . . . I'm sorry, is your last name the same as Harvey's?"

She nodded—she likes matching Harvey—but told him, since he told her to call him Ned, that he could call her Shelley.

Twice, the teacher has called her to talk about Harvey, and camp only started a week ago. Twice, he has told her something she didn't know—he knows the names of a lot of serial killers, for instance—and maybe didn't want to know. Both times he has lingered as if he had more to say.

"What?" she asked. "What?"

"He's a nice kid—really he is," he said, but then there was that pause everyone recognizes, that pause like screwing the lid tight on something about to explode.

"Why do you indulge him with all this bedtime routine?" Brent had asked when Harvey was three. "We have to help him grow up. You won't always be there to hold his hand." The worried expression on Brent's face seemed more about her than about Harvey. The underlying message was about how she had raised Jason. Jason was spoiled. Jason was a mama's boy. Jason needed to buck up. Jason needed to keep scary stories to himself.

"Michelangelo gets thirsty in the middle of the night," she said, and proceeded to put the milk in the closet, her chest tight with the anxiety of doing what was so hard for her to do, which was say what she really meant. But you have to defend your children. You do. Children without a defender don't get shit. At the time, all she wanted was that milk inside of Harvey's closet, the door left cracked just enough that he could see it, so she could get him to fall asleep.

And about Einstein, the world's smallest horse, Ned said when he called. Did she know Harvey had told all the kids that he was *getting* a miniature horse?

No. No, she didn't know that.

Did she know that he'd promised a party for everyone in the class to come over and meet the horse? That he said his dad is bringing the horse when he comes back home from his hike in Alaska. And did she know Harvey leaves messages for the ghosts out in their yard, and sometimes leaves food out there?

No, she didn't know that either.

Did she know he was in her closet that last night before his dad left? That in fact, one of the Ninja Turtles—he believes the one who says "Cowabunga" all the time, Michelangelo maybe—had slept in *her* closet?

No, no, she didn't know that. But he was only four then; how could he remember?

And she didn't know that he had memorized a lot of really disturbing facts about murders and keeps a list to share with kids who pick on him, that he had successfully scared the hell out of several of them, that the teacher had gotten phone calls from parents.

No, no, she didn't know.

"So it's just the two of you?" he said.

She gets asked that a lot, it seems, and it bothers her. It happened in the grocery store when a man in army fatigues, maybe from Fort Bragg, asked her, and was he trying to meet her? Did he know something about her, or did they know someone in common? But Harvey was spinning a rack, spinning a rack, spinning a rack, and it was hard not to think about spinning, about time spinning and the way Jason's dad had done his time in the Gulf War. She learned all of that the first night she met him. That was back when war first became something to watch on television, the first reality show starring a very young Wolf Blitzer; yes, there's the war—bombs and lights, and they say people might be dying—and now a word from our sponsors—*Show 'em your Crest best*—and it's a good time to go to the bathroom or to the kitchen to get something to drink before the war comes back on. That's what she remembers people saying: "I'm gonna watch a little of the war before I go to bed." Why didn't anyone see something wrong with that? She was going to ask that man what he thought about that, but when she'd looked up, he was in the checkout line talking to someone else, a woman in exercise pants, with pink hair and a tattoo that said FEELIN GROOVY.

"He has an older brother," she told him now.

"Harvey also mentions the Smile Train a lot," Ned said, his voice lowered to a kind whisper.

"Oh."

"He said he's saving money for it." He paused. "And a couple of times, he has talked about wishing his dad would come back or that he could go see him."

She waited, not responding

Lil

∽

ALL THESE YEARS later, in spite of the difficult times we had, I can still remember the details around meeting your dad like it was yesterday. It was 1952, and I had never been to a more lackluster party, hosted by a woman I worked with at Filene's, whose name I can't even recall; we really had nothing in common except that we were both about 20 and we both worked there, she in hosiery and me in cosmetics. She was nice enough, bubbly and self-centered in that way I sometimes find annoying, always checking herself in the mirror, always asking for an opinion about her hair or skirt or shoes. Still, it was somewhere to go on a night I otherwise would have been sitting at home with my father, and so I went. I probably only remember it at all because I met your father there, and whenever we had awkward moments of silence in the beginning of our relationship, we often turned the conversation back to the details of that night.

She lived in a tiny fourth-floor walk-up on Commonwealth, once the maid's quarters for the larger space below, where her elderly aunt and uncle lived, and there were 12 of us squeezed into an array of uncomfortable chairs. It was uncomfortable enough, but then she had a whole list of games for us to play, things like passing a Life Saver from person to person on toothpicks we were supposed to hold between our teeth; then it was passing an orange under the chin. Obviously, the whole point of her silly games (she insisted the circle be boy, girl, boy, girl) was physical closeness. I don't remember her name, and yet I can see the small round table in the corner of that room so clearly, where there was a cut glass punch bowl with her mix of ginger ale and pineapple juice, and little wedding cookies and a vase with a single red rose. The window shade was raised, and I could see the trees lining Commonwealth, below, my eyes fixed there as I nuzzled an orange under the chin of a cousin of hers who worked packing fish and, in fact, continued talking about fish and fishing the whole while that we were up close and personal with an orange between us.

"He was trying to hook you," your father said later as we walked to catch our separate trains. By then, we were laughing about the awkwardness of the night, and before we knew it, we began talking about ourselves and our families.

What were the odds? We were walking along, probably both

thinking that we might never see each other again, and then I said something—I can't tell you what, but it led to me telling about my mother and her untimely death, and then he told about his father, and it was like we couldn't say or hear enough. We ended up going to get a cup of coffee and sat for over an hour, heavy white mugs in our hands, and he wrote my phone number on the inside of the matchbook on the table.

Needless to say, I didn't know at the time that he collected them and that as a young man, your father kept a lot of important phone numbers and information inside those little matchbooks. In fact, he still has a little book from the Lorraine Hotel, where he and his grandmother stayed when he first came to North Carolina as a boy. If you ever find it there on his dresser top, you will know those old dull matches have traveled many miles with him. And speaking of old dull matches, that's us.

It was December, and there were trees and lights everywhere. Your father was wearing a dark-green wool scarf that I later learned had once belonged to his father, and when his train approached, he hastily asked what I was doing the next day, and we made plans to meet there in that same place after work.

"It would take more than that to hook me," I had said in a moment of great confidence. For a long time after, we joked about bait and lures; he wrote me a little note that said I was "so a-luring." In fact, our very first Christmas tree was decorated with the lures and tackle we'd bought for each other in those earliest days. I still have them all (bits of silver and feathers like exotic jewelry), and I often think how you might one day find them and wonder, "What is this old rusty junk?" Some look a lot like the earrings Becca once wore during her poncho, Indian beads, and moccasin days. "So alluring." You might have heard us say that.

September 1, 1964

I love the dance school. It's slow going but a work in progress. We had fun thinking of a name: My Turn, or That's the Pointe, or simply Lil's School of Dance, which is what I ultimately went with, if for no other reason than it suits me (it's not cute or witty, just straight-forward). The squat cinder-block building was once a tire store but, with paint and new floors, has now been transformed into a sanctu-ary: barres, wall-length mirrors, a tiny dressing room with cubbies, a shelf filled with items ordered for these first students (lamb's wool and leg warmers, Capezio shoes and Danskin tights). I love when I am there all alone.

I look at Margot some days and think if my mother returned as a dog, that would be her, paws in first position, graceful and alert, refined one moment and silly the next. "Is that you?" I whispered the other day, and Margot cocked her head and returned my stare. "Are you here?"

February 1974

If I put my foot behind my head every single day, do an arabesque on pointe, and hold it there, can I trick time? I like to think that and, in fact, am going to hold myself to a schedule. Every day, same time, like a clock. Will it work? We will see, but first I have to get Becca to the orthodontist; we're all hoping she can stop wear-ing "the strap," and Jeff has hockey, and there is a PTA meeting I can't skip since I'm one of the officers (what was I thinking?!), so my plans to put my foot behind my head and then stand on pointe indefinitely might have to wait until tomorrow. BRB.

Spring 1980

I love recitals. I love preparing the dancers for their parts. Sometimes I read stories aloud; sometimes we watch films that match the ballet.

The story of Romeo and Juliet was one we watched when you were
a student, Becca; a circle of 15-year-old girls at the theater for the
Zeffirelli version shrieking in delight to see Romeo's bare butt. You
all knew the story (you had read it in English class), but you watched
faithfully, all hoping for the very best and happiest of endings. And
yet Romeo still died. Don't we all harbor the hope, the wish, that
something magnificent will happen? Don't we all marvel at how
easily we can get lost within a work of art? That's what dance has
always meant to me. I can get as lost watching as I can in my own
movement to music, feet gliding as if on autopilot.

The recital of "Romeo and Juliet" was not one of the best given.
That boy from Wellesley who'd volunteered to help since we had so
few boys in class overplayed the comic appeal of Mercutio's character and kept springing back to life for one more little dance. I
wanted to slap him for getting in the way of what should have been
a poignant part, but in the end it didn't matter. Parents did not like
how few parts there were for the little ones, and more than one said
that there was way too much death for the children to understand.
Such is my occupational hazard, and so back to woodland fairies
and "The Nutcracker" I go, bribing little Polichinelles to stay under
Mother Ginger's skirt until the right moment, and explaining why
we all can't be Clara.

(Shred?)
"What did you tell her about *me*?" I asked Frank when it was
clear to me that something had happened and he was avoiding the
conversation. More than what they might have done physically
was the sickening thought that he had shared any intimate details
about my life, my mother's death, our children, our dogs; it was
the era of Margot and Rudolf, Margot winding down, cloudy eyes

and gray streaks in her muzzle, her apricot coat laced with white
as well. I felt threatened and protective of anything linked to our
home.

"Oh, come on, Lily."

"Don't call me that!" I nearly spat in his face. "Only my mother
calls me that." I said how there is nothing cheaper and more superficial than someone unauthorized stealing and using another's pet
name.

"Did you tell her our word?" I said.

"Of course not!"

I had found little traces and pieces: a note in his pocket—a
phone number, a street address on the fringes of Cambridge, which
I later drove past—a pink office memo slip like the secretaries in his
department used to fill out and leave in his mailbox ("While you
were out . . ."). One remained rolled up there near the matchbooks
on his dresser: a call at 3 on a Wednesday afternoon; the message:
"Tomb Time." Book title? Lecture idea?

I asked myself: "Can you spell stupid? Can you spell b-l-i-n-d?"

March 2017
Southern Pines
Have I ever told you two how often in the dull waking of morning I sometimes have the sensation that I am there walking our old
neighborhood? I pass your elementary school, I pass the yard with
that strange sculpture we never figured out (you two called it the
Giant Egg; the neighbors called it an eyesore), and I pass the mailbox I always used, that beautiful chestnut tree on the corner, and the
house with the beautiful rose garden, and I can't help but wonder if
there isn't someone walking along Aspen Avenue or Grove Street in
these moments who thinks she glimpses someone she's never seen

wandering there, that dogs and babies stop and stare out into the nothingness of me as I pass through my old life. My feet and hands are never cold, as they always were, and I am never worried about my little dance school, which was almost always in the red, or what to prepare for dinner or if I have called to check on my father. The thoughts are just about walking, about one foot in front of the other, about making my way around our neighborhood and anticipating you two coming home from school. Sometimes, I wake with a vivid recall of a certain sweater or a pair of shoes, or with my fingers pinched, as if I am holding a feather or a rock or a leaf or a penny, all those things I have always collected.

If you've ever wondered where I keep my my stash of little treasures, I will tell you now. The wooden box high on the shelf in my closet. My father's hat, the Kleenex my mother kissed, the lipstick barely there now, an eyelash I once wished on right before I met your father, carefully taped to a piece of paper (wishing on an eyelash was a belief held by the coworker at Filene's whose name I can't recall!). The beads that were on your perfect little wrists right after you were born, the cards that said your name and gender there in the nursery viewing room. Letters. Notes. My father's scribbles: BRB.

I've always known that I am not the kind of woman your father is naturally attracted to. I think his eye is drawn to my opposite: the brightly plumed strutters. His young colleague was of the plumed sort; Becca, think Carla Robinson in your high school class (remember? the girl who, like an ill-trained dog or toddler, always wanted what someone else had), except that this young woman was the high-voltage of a Carla coupled with a scholarly pedigree and some genuine academic success, which perhaps was just the right combination (or wrong, from my point of view). She was (perhaps still is)

the kind of person who makes you want to cross yourself when you
see them coming.

"Harsh," I can hear your father say. "You are so harsh."

I say truthful.

I love the memory of your father watching me as I passed a silly
orange under my chin, onto the throat of a handsome young man
in banking, originally from Chicago, Juicy Fruit gum and tobacco
and that awful pineapple punch on his breath. That's the memory
I should give you. I didn't even know your father, and on the walk
home he seemed jealous of that total stranger I had stood so close
to, a man I could have just as easily walked with that night. Now,
that is *not* bigheaded of me to say; trust me that the competition
was slim, but I did appreciate how attentive your father was as it
neared time to leave. The walk to the train with him that night is still
a place I like to go in my mind. I go there, and I wait outside your
elementary school. I lie in my childhood bed and watch my mother
descend the stairs.

People say hearts get broken all the time. They say people die all
the time. But what does that help? What does that even do, other
than attempt to diminish the emotions at hand. I hope I haven't
done that to you, though I suspect in all these years that I have,
that there have been times in my attempt to make you feel better
you might have felt I was slighting your pain. Such a tricky balance.
The key word is always balance. I cannot hear that word without
picturing the little windup seal that was always in your toy box.
Becca, you were barely the size of a grain of rice when your father
bought it. I was vomiting several times a day, and whenever I came
out of the bathroom of that old tiny apartment there in Cambridge,
the tile of the bathroom so cold, your father would have the seal
wound up so that the little red ball spun on the tip of its nose. We

lost the seal somewhere along the way, but the ball is still there in the box.

My mother read "The Red Shoes" to me many times in childhood. That poor girl punished for wanting those shoes and wanting to dance. I remember sitting, the book on my lap, my mother beside me on the bed. I read "The Red Shoes" to you as well, and it always made you beg for "The Elves and the Shoemaker," a much happier story for sure. A girl punished for her desires and sentenced to amputation or death, or a man rewarded for his acts of generous charity? My mother loved all the sad ones: "The Little Match Girl" and "The Little Mermaid" (the real version). She would have loved the movie "The Red Shoes," which came out six years after she died. It was 1948, and I was 15 years old. Moira Shearer had to choose between her true love and being a famous dancer. I could imagine my mother in that high whine of hers: "Why did they make her choose?" And actually, I wondered the same thing. I didn't sleep for weeks after, haunted by the harrowing final scene, where she goes after her true love only to go sailing out in front of a train.

In fact, I thought of that scene the first night I met your father and we stood there on the platform, and of course was so glad later that I had not mentioned it. I saw the movie a second time when I was in college, and it all held up for me; I was studying bookkeeping, which is what most girls did then. I loved psychology, and I loved literature, too.

For many years when I thought of my mother, I had to walk through the Cocoanut Grove to get to any other memories. I had to imagine where she might have been, what part of the building, what table, when she realized that her life was in danger. Then I had to traverse the lobby of Mass General, the large clock ticking, my

father's hands clasped, and then Southern Mortuary, to those terrible moments staring at her blackened hand exposed there on the
white sheet.

I wanted to be like my mother, but I recognize our differences. I
am someone interested in shoes that blend in—the feathered plumes
of a more cautious bird, one safely sheltered in a nest; I like black
leather or the pale pink of ballet slippers, soft as skin. I like shoes
that blend, protect, comfort. Even now, I see young women clomp-
ing along in their boots or stilettos, heels so high their knees often
bow out like someone just off of a horse, or about to have a gyneco-
logical procedure. I have seen Polly and Lindsey, in fact; Becca, you
know it is true. I feel a pain in my lower back to watch, jarred by the
clip-clopping that counteracts what is meant to appear smooth and
sophisticated and sexy. You yourself wore those way-up platforms
in high school, and I was amazed you never broke something. Those
shoes are for sitting, legs crossed, perhaps with a sign that says "I am
exotic, like an animal in the zoo." My mother liked being noticed.
She liked the flamboyant accessories: the flamingo, the peacock.

In my fantasies, I often wear peacock blue or Moroccan red.
And whenever I imagine confronting people, I am always dressed
vibrantly, in clothes I never would really wear in life. I remain the
colors of soft earth; I am sandalwood, buff. I am careful. That's why
I stretched out beside you all those nights, my head leaned close
enough to smell the milky scent of your sighs, to see your chests rise
and fall, feel your breath. "I'm here. Mommy's here," I whispered if
you shifted in your sleep.

Lately, I don't trust what your father says, and what a shock that has
been after these many good years that restored my faith. Every time
he leaves the house, I question if he is really going where he says he
is going. One day, he said he was going to have his car serviced, but

later when I called, that wasn't true. I almost confronted him when he came home, but then something about the way he acted, something so fragile, made me keep the questions to myself.

"A hastening," he had said. He has never been a very good liar, and I love this about him, though these days it concerns me. Sometimes, when I am there walking the old neighborhood, I see his car pull into the driveway, and then I follow his steps into the house.

Shelley

THE JURY WILL return later today, and she is still wandering Food
Lion, waiting for the judge to call. The manager has asked her twice
if she needs help, and so now she has a cart and is slowly filling it
and then putting things back to kill time. She is ready. She wants to
hear the verdict. She wants to see that awful man's face and hear
the news she is hoping will come. *All rise for the judge.* All rise for
the judge, and in her mind, she can see the whole room, the dark
wood and the brass rail, the dirty windows and the cobwebs she has
been studying for several weeks now. *Guilty.* People from all over
the community will be there—the grand finale of this long-running
show. And the judge will probably be so relieved to have it all end;

this case has aged her there in her expensive burgundy pumps and those gold knot earrings she wears every day, but that is the last thing that Shelley would *ever* say—even to Marva—for fear of getting in trouble, and it reminds her again how alone she is.

The surgeon who repaired Harvey's lip was very kind, and she'd stared at his clean, agile brown hands as he spoke and explained everything to her. All during the trial, she has had to remind herself of this so she won't throw out the whole of a profession based on one rotten egg. It isn't fair to judge that way even though it is so easy to look at a whole group and point to the one they resemble or remind you of. But people could do that to her, too, and it wouldn't be fair. People could do that to Jason or to Harvey. People did it to that young girl who got murdered, seeing only the mess of her life, a needle in her arm, and not the love she felt for her young son, not all that she had endured that had led her to such a dark and frightening place. And did she hear Brent say "harelip," or did she imagine that, too? "No one says that anymore," she told him. "No one is perfect."

Brent had grown up with parents who believed that bad things happened to people who had not lived right, and he said their affection for Harvey would have been compromised by that, and Shelley said, well, then she was glad they were dead, and he looked like he wanted to slap her. Even though he agreed with her, his impulse was to defend them and their old backward ways. She and Brent disagreed on so many things, like he liked that creepy Elf on the Shelf and wanted to get one so Harvey would behave better, but she said everybody needs privacy and that kind of spying is just wrong. Now the memory leaves her cold, leaves her studying the house for signs of someone watching *her*. She hated the way people say God is always watching you and remembers asking, "Even when I pee?" And being sent from a classroom. She is sure what she felt then is what Harvey is feeling all those times he is standing there beside the bed waiting for her to wake. "Mom? Mom?" His breath like old chocolate milk and Starburst candies.

Shelley has not always told the truth, and now it is all coming and filling her head as she watches people holding up their right hands and swearing to tell the truth, the whole truth, nothing but the truth, and sometimes a word will fly in and get stuck, like fly to flypaper, lint on an album; like the way the word *purchase* keeps flying in, the word perhaps having a little surge in popularity, as words often do. Lately it has gotten traction. If you were someone hearing voices or reading signs, you might think this has meaning, you might think it is a sign. And she does. She does think that. Harvey has put a note in the pocket of her sweater, and it is in his little code, but she can't take the time to study it now. Klingon. He keeps begging her to teach him shorthand. Jason told him computer coding would be much more lucrative, and she felt so proud to hear her son use such words: *lucrative, coding*.

Waiting is hard. When she was a child, she used that time to clean; she liked to go through things and organize, to find a little bit of order. Each doll had its own place on the shelf; each stuffed animal was assigned the right spot on her bed. Once, when she was in sixth grade, she saved her money to buy Hefty trash bags—the giant heavy plastic ones like they have at hardware stores, for removing debris from construction sites; her brother drove her to buy them and said, "Good luck with that," but he didn't really think she could change anything. He said their mother and grandmother would still sit there in their bathrobes, surrounded by stacks of paper, and their dad would still pile up burned-out appliances—toasters, electric razors, hair dryers, blown lamps, radios—out on the back porch, where Shelley thought there should be a hammock with a quilt on it and little pillows. She thought if she surprised them and started cleaning that everyone would pitch in, like all the little birds and mice in *Cinderella*.

"Sorry to tell you, kid," her brother said, the pupils of his eyes like pinpricks, "but we live in shit, and the only way out is what I'm fixing to do." She didn't think much of it until late that night when he hadn't returned home and, while their mother slept, she filled those bags with all the trash and all the shit, all the *detritus*—a word that makes her think of the word *viscera* more than it should.

Surely, the judge will forgive her; surely, the judge won't judge. She is hoping that the story she wrote comes true. She wrote:

The judge, angry as hell but looking very sophisticated in expensive shoes, slammed her gavel and shouted, "He's the white Bill Cosby, only worse, because he has never said anything funny," while the ugly murderer stood in his ugly orange jumpsuit, wet where he had pissed himself, and cursed everyone who had made this decision, but the people laughed and sang and danced and said they would have a huge party and everyone would pee on his grave like dogs to cover up his scent. "Don't you agree?" the judge asked the young stenographer, whose shoes weren't so bad, given her salary. The judge told the court that she relied heavily on the opinion of this young woman, who could take notes faster than anyone on the East Coast. "She's brilliant," the judge said. The stenographer gave the judge a high five and was applauded by everyone, and then the judge went on to explain how all the women who had fucked the ugly guy would have to go home and work out their own marriages. They'd be doing favors and chores forevermore, and happily so, and the old people would go back and pull out bottles of

champagne for those not on heavy meds and raise a toast to
"their girl," her murder finally vindicated. They would laugh
and say, "Good riddance, asshole," but then, when alone in
their beds, would cry for the young woman and the life that
was stolen from her, and they would think up something
new to distract them from what is just up and around the
corner—game over.

It made Shelley cry to write that, though now she imagines the
judge reading it and looking at her and thinking, *You have the audac-
ity to call others ugly? You? Who do you think you are? Meeting
men in bars and growing up in racist squalor? You? The mother of a
young man born with a birth defect that could render him the butt
of teasing and cruelty, and yet you have spent your words talking
about how physically ugly the man is?*

Not long ago, she read how people have to learn how to reject
others. That in fact learning to be rejected and learning how to reject
is as important as any other skill you might have. But she didn't
learn it. Secure people have that skill, and she never learned it. She
was intimidated by waitresses and salesclerks; beauticians, especially
beauticians. She got to the place she was afraid to make friends,
in case she couldn't stand them and then wouldn't know how to
politely get rid of them.

And now, Harvey's teacher says he wants to meet with her *again*
to continue the conversation, and she isn't sure if he is asking her
out or feeling sorry for her and thinking Harvey's situation needs
some really serious one-on-one face-to-face time. But she has been
afraid to go, because what if he has something else on his mind,
and she knows that she can't reject him even if she decides she
wants to.

That time with the giant Hefty trash bags, she found abandoned nests of all kinds on their porch with the appliances—squirrel and mouse and bird. And she found empty toilet-paper rolls and hot-water bottles and loads of nail clippers and old rolls of duct tape, which together made a horrible story if that's all you had to go on. She was afraid to reach her hand in drawers without shining a flashlight to make sure there wasn't a snake or a rat or a black widow or a brown recluse spider, something that would multiply and you would never get rid of, like in that movie *Gremlins* that Jason loved to watch, and they looked so cute, like those Furbies that everybody had to have that one Christmas, but they weren't cute at all. They were really, really scary! And destructive.

Jason sent a text last week that was indecipherable. Butt-dialed. An accident. Rushing to class. She wrote back: *I love you. Come see us soon.*

OK, Mom. Soon.

Any nice girls?

He didn't answer, and she knows she shouldn't have done that; he needs his space. He had told her he didn't have a lot of spare time, that he has a heavy schedule, all kinds of projects and research going on.

"So, are you alone now?" She gets asked that question a lot these days, a question she was asked back when no one knew where her brother had gone. Just recently in the grocery store, Harvey was spinning a rack and she was thinking about how a head of cauliflower looks like a brain, like those growths you sometimes see on a tree; there was a tree in her hometown, not far from here, that looked like that, a giant cyst or tumor on its trunk, its limbs reaching upward to get away from it. And why did she even move back this close to where she started, anyway, except thinking her brother might be there, that she might suddenly find him. "It was an accident," he'd told her. "I swear it was."

"What do you remember?" people asked, and all she could come up with was a number and the words *do not remove*.

Jason has asked her to tell him all that she remembers about his father, and she plans to. Someday she will tell him all that he needs to know. But right now, she needs to get her job back so she can find out how it all ends, this trial that has distracted her for months now. Shelley feels so sorry for the wife and the children of this awful man, who have already moved away, and who can blame them? People often forget about the lives of those who are tied to such a person, and that *their* innocent lives are fucked up by it all when they are not responsible for any of it.

At one point in the trial, the murderer had told how heavy his wife had gotten, as if people needed to feel sorry for *him*, and then on a break, Shelley overheard one of the old people there to watch the show saying how that *monster* killed *our girl*. They called her "our girl"—such a nice endearment for someone who must have felt so estranged and lonely most of her life. Our girl.

"That's a girl," Shelley's brother had said when he let go of the back of that small rusty bike, and thinking he was still right there beside her, she went pedaling down Cobb Road at full speed. *That's a girl*, she sometimes tells herself. *That's a girl*. And when that doesn't work, she sings "I Have Confidence" and does her very best to channel Julie Andrews channeling Maria Von Trapp, though in her imagination she does *not* wear that really bad hat. She is going to get her job back, and she'll get a letter from her brother and learn that he is just fine and has been all these years, that he's right down the road, and everything is so much better now. *Can't wait to see you, Baby Sis. Please come see me!* and Brent will come to see Harvey and realize what a mistake he made—*What was I thinking?* he'll say—and Harvey and Jason will be happy and they will all settle in for a good supper and to watch a movie, and then they will all live happily ever after. *Do you like my hat? No, no, I do not like your hat, but I really, really love you.* And she is repeating that aloud—"I really, really love you"—when the phone rings and the person on the other end tells her to get to the courthouse as quickly as she can. They need her to come back to work, but the judge wants to speak to her first.

She breathes a sigh and once again finds the promise of that voice from long ago: *You will be fine. You will be fine.* And since she is already there, across the street from the courthouse waiting, she has plenty of time. She goes and looks in the mirror over the produce to check her hair and then leaves her cart in the paper products aisle. It can't be helped; she's in a hurry. She will switch to Lowes Foods in the future, or she will tell the Food Lion people it was an emergency. And it is.

Lil

❧

THE WALL PHONE rang once that long-ago day: a signal. "That is so annoying," I said, and your father agreed; he was reading the paper and talking about how they feared rats might infest the city because of the Big Dig, or that they might once again uncover graves, as they had years before when building the subway, long-buried bones of undocumented dead, and wondering how such a thing can even happen, and yet it has, and it does.

Your father was wearing my favorite shirt of his, a soft pinwale corduroy in forest green that I'd given him one Christmas. He said sometimes the phone rings when the phone company is working on the lines. We talked about that a little. We talked about the mouse problem we had had years before in our tiny first apartment, and the way it was not uncommon for squirrels to get stuck in the walls and slam around for a couple of days. And then the phone rang again, a shrill ring there from the kitchen, and then we talked about you, Becca, and how you and Alan seemed very happy together, and we talked about you, Jeff, and how relieved we were that you had really found your strength there in those business courses. And then your father stood suddenly, and in a voice I had heard only when he was rounding you kids up for some outing years before, he said: "I know what!" He clapped his hands. "I am going to get us takeout Chinese."

It was out of character, but in the moment, I thought it was just a nice thing. I had everything I needed for a meatloaf, but that would keep. I could just sit and watch the news, read the paper. And I planned that the next time the phone rang, I would grab it fast and give whoever an earful. But it didn't ring again, and it took longer than it should have for him to get the food. He said there was traffic, and a miscommunication about the order of the person in front of him, but I have never eaten an egg roll since when I don't remember the overly cheerful, exuberant tone of your father's voice, and the way he avoided eye contact, so focused he was on the food on his plate, saying how he really had to watch out for those hot red peppers, and then later carefully cracking the thin cookie to extract his fortune, something stupid and common ("There is a bend in the road" or "Seek and ye shall find," something like that), but I pretended I saw great and deep meaning there. Then I said, "But of course, now I understand," and I looked at him until he had to look away.

• • •

How odd the way an obsession that has blinded and trapped you can suddenly lift like a heavy fog. It dissipates, dissolves. When in the thick of it, you can't imagine that it could happen, that the help-less panic you feel will shift back into something safe and solid, but it can. It was an afternoon several years later when it hit me just that way (perhaps because I was seated there on that olive sofa and your father in his chair, just as we had been that day in October), and the phone rang, but we let it go to the machine and listened as we were told that the coat I had taken to the cleaners was ready for pickup. It was winter, and we couldn't fill the bird feeders fast enough, a bright-red cardinal and a host of chickadees constantly outside the window. We resisted turning on the lights and instead built a fire and let the blue dusk fill the room. We could hear the popping of the wood and the cars passing as people made their way home.

"It's all good, isn't it?" your father asked, and I knew exactly what he meant. I said, "Absolutely." I said, "It's all very good." And fearing the phone would once again disrupt our silence, I went and unplugged it from the wall. I said that I would never want to go back. Though I do wonder if we aren't tested from time to time, my vision now so much clearer than it might have been.

And how complicated it must be for people these days, with all those devices and chatter—the way you can see where the call comes from, trace it, even tape it. And yet people still find ways to cheat and creep and bury their bones. I am glad I grew up with a rotary phone. I am glad I grew up with silence. I'm glad Frank and I found our way back.

Sometimes lately, here in the blurry buzz of air-conditioning, the soft, cushioned peach-colored carpet under my feet, the Easter egg men and the stark ugly pine trees out the window in the glaring heat,

I find my mind takes me home. My first home. I am in Waltham, with the drip, drip, drip of the bathroom sink. My father had tied a cloth around the pipe to muffle the sound until it could be fixed, and yet I could still hear it. And on another night, barely spring outside, he took a hammer to the faucet and then stood back, an arching spray of water covering him and all of the bathroom. He stood there, hammer in hand, and I couldn't tell if the water on his face was coming from without or within.

I worry about Frank. Every day, I feel him slipping from me; I imagine each day takes him a little bit closer to that place, pulling him like the Sirens calling him into the rocks. Hastening. I look for messages. I look for signs. Every day I think, "It could be today." I look out and see the bright sunlight and think, "Yes, he would choose a day like today," a happy, bright day, a day and time opposite from that long-ago accident that changed his whole life. Or I look out in the dark of winter and think: "No, this is it." He will choose a day to match that of that December night so very long ago. They both make sense, both choices, and we as humans like to make sense. When it rains on a funeral, we say the universe is crying, and when the sun shines, we say the dearly departed is smiling from beyond. Rain on a wedding (like yours, Becca) they say is good luck, and yet on that sunny beautiful day, no one says, "Oh no, I was hoping for a little rain for good luck."

Today when I woke and snuggled in close to your father, I realized he smells different, the skin and dust of a much-older man, the pores no longer exuding whatever youth once gave off. It is not unlike the way a dog will know things. Remember when poor Margot was old and we got Rudolf to help see her through? I have never known if that was the right thing to do or not. I feared it hurt her feelings, because she stayed another two years, but there at the end, Rudolf often smelled her breath, and I think he was smelling death, that he knew it was coming. If we all opened our senses to it, we would see much more than we do in passing.

Sometimes I wake early and just watch your father sleeping; I lean close and breathe in, this new smell I have come to treasure as I once did that smell of youth and virility. He talks too much about death these days. I don't mind discussing the practical aspects; I think that's important. But he is discussing the hows, musing about when, his invitation for us to simply leave together there in the room like the big elephant. I'm always surprised when people ask those awful questions: Would you rather die suddenly of a heart attack, or after a long battle with cancer? And who plays such parlor games but the young, who believe they will always be young. People talk about premature deaths, but do they ever talk of mature ones?

Connie! That is the name of the woman from Filene's, and isn't it funny how pieces blow in that way and how I realize that sometimes when Gloria calls to tell me what is happening there at home, I picture Connie just as she looked walking past the Wilbur Theatre in 1950-something. Connie with her auburn bob and perpetual grin, selling hosiery while I sold cosmetics and perfume. Coty gift set? Prince Matchabelli?

Oh, it is so mysterious when the pieces blow in, like a window cracking to give the tiniest bit of air and light. Cold winter air and I am in the carpool line, windshield wipers batting the fat snowflakes, heat on my face and feet, making me drowsy, or I am there on the platform, waiting for the train.

Harvey

❦

SOMETIMES, HARVEY CRAWLS along and through the bushes so he can see where the ghosts come from. Maybe from the old manhole, like what the Ninja Turtles use. He told his mom how he found signs, like his dad taught him to do. He's seen broken sticks and tracks, a screwdriver. There are a lot of rabbit turds in there and Peggy eats those like a snack. Jason said rabbit turds is like Peggy's Raisinets but under the bushes is also where Peggy goes to the bathroom and that is what Harvey's mom wanted to talk about most. "You didn't wipe your feet!" she said, and pointed to the rug.

"I saw where they stay," he told her, but she was scrubbing with paper towels and saying his name the way she does sometimes—"Harvey, Harvey, Harvey"—so he didn't tell her he found a big flat piece of gold and some more matches. She asked didn't he smell what he stepped in? But, no, he didn't, because he was watching the manhole. You have to watch or they might come out and grab you. His mom was mad or he would have said what made her laugh one time, how she said dog doo-doo was white when she was a kid. She and Jason laughed and laughed and that's what Harvey likes to think about if scary things come in his head instead, like the Munchkins flipping your car and calling you things like *shit-butt* and *snothead*, or Lizzie with her axe, or those rich boys that killed their mama and daddy while they were watching television.

Super Monkey said, "Hey, you guys, c'mon, they're your mom and dad and you got a big TV and cars and stuff," and they said, "Well, sometimes a mom or dad needs to go away and there's nothing you can do about it."

"But they shouldn't go away," Super Monkey said. "A mom and a dad shouldn't go away ever and you need to just watch that big TV and you think about it."

And then they said, okay, they would think about it.

"Honey," his mama said, "I've got to go to work and you have got to go to camp. You can't do this every morning, okay? I had no idea where you were. And wipe your feet next time, okay?"

And he said, "Okay," and she said, "Maybe stay closer to the house," and he said, "Okay," but he didn't tell her he ran and put a note on top of the manhole. *Whos HEAR?* he wrote in red crayon and now he can't wait to get home from camp to go and see if they wrote back.

At camp, the teacher asked what kids like and when Harvey said turtles, they spent lots of time on turtles. The teacher told things that Jason already told Harvey, about how they lived with dinosaurs and how they could be huge, like two thousand pounds, like a car, and

how they can get really old if nothing kills them. But what he didn't
know is how a cool nest makes a boy turtle instead of a girl, and
a girl named Bailey said that wasn't fair until somebody else said
when the world heats up then there will only be girl turtles and then
she laughed and said, "Well, okay then. See? See?"

The best part was how a turtle can sometimes swim twenty miles
an hour and that's faster than this one kid says he can go in his
granddaddy's wheelchair that runs like a car. He said he can go ten
miles an hour and do doughnuts when his granddaddy is in the
bathroom and can't stop him. He says his granddaddy goes to the
bathroom all the time too. He said his granddaddy goes to the bathroom when his grandma talks too much, which is all the time. Even
the teacher laughed about that and it made Harvey wish he had a
granddaddy with a wheelchair, or just a granddaddy. He is the only
kid he knows without any grandpeople at all, not even an old one in
bed sleeping, like a bunch of them that live near here. He has peeped
in their windows before. Not too many kids have half people or if
they do they don't tell, and he knows they don't have ghosts in their
house so he tells he's got half of a brother *and* he's got a ghost that's
probably a dead old person trying to get back to that place they all
stay or to the cemetery. He asks if anybody has ever heard about
those boys that killed their mama and daddy while they were watching TV, and one new girl named Molly started crying. She's from
somewhere far enough that she talks funny and she has a hamster
named Cheeks. He asked why she was crying like a baby—was she
scared somebody would kill her while she was watching TV?—and
she ran to tell the teacher, and the boy who drives the wheelchair
fell back laughing.

"Guess what?" the teacher says and pulls Harvey by the arm.
He said Harvey had another chance yesterday. Harvey wants to say
what Jason taught him: *Guess what? Chicken snot—*

"What?" Harvey asks, and closes his eyes so he won't have to see how mad Mr. Stone is looking.

"Open your eyes, son," he says, and when Harvey does, he doesn't look so mean after all. He looks more sad, like when his mom was scrubbing the doo-doo rug or when she's looking out the window. He has one hair coming out his nose but Harvey doesn't laugh at that either. "I'm going to need to speak to your mom, again," he says. "You're a nice kid, a really good kid, and I want us all to get along." He says, "Do you understand?" and Harvey nods yes. Harvey asks does he want to hear a joke.

Frank

FRANK LOOKS BOTH ways, that endless flat stretch of rails as far as he can see—cotton, tobacco, soybeans all around him, and beyond, the straight line of spindly pines. How odd to be in this place on such a clear summer day, the sun so bright he has to squint; he sees dots if he stares too long, trying once again to imagine that dark, cold night, the sounds, the devastation. He steps carefully from one tie to the next, eyes on the spaces in between, where something shiny might catch his eye. He knows the train schedule and has since his childhood. Even all those years he and Lil lived in Massachusetts, working and raising their children, he knew the schedule through here, could imagine the whistle and the vibrations along these very tracks—the place of his adolescence, and now falling behind him in closed chapters, very few pages remaining.

Lil was the one who first suggested the migration southward and who, with their daughter's help, studied various communities. She had chosen this place to be near their daughter, a place with mild weather and four seasons; she had in mind that there are world-class medical facilities right down the road, places you don't want to have to frequent and where he has already spent way too much time. When they arrived, the politics suited them but now have taken a downward turn. There's a lot he has missed about their home, and lately he would prefer just about anything to pork and golf and ACC basketball. Bacon, barbecue, ham. Pork, pork, and more pork. Brackets for March Madness. Golf, golf, and more golf. I'D RATHER BE GOLFING, the bumper stickers say, and why would a person who doesn't play live on a course anyway, except that's where their daughter said they should be. She's a lawyer who had come to school in this state and never left.

"You know Richard Nixon went there," he told her when she was accepted and headed south.

"And you spent much of your childhood there," she had said. She said he had deprived them of a whole chunk of their history by never visiting, and now it was time.

HIS MOTHER HAD wanted to be where his father had died, his body never really found, just bits of bone and teeth and ash, and her health had been compromised; she had broken bones. And there was the baby to think about it; she couldn't afford to lose the baby—it was all that was left of him. Lil said she could understand this; she said it the first time he ever told her, and yet it is only now he feels *he* understands. How many times had he heard the story, how his mother's life had been spared by Frank's baby brother filling her womb and pressing on her bladder? She was six months pregnant but still discreet in her dress. She had said a person would have needed to stare rudely to see what was going on, and she had worn a full coat, which was the style anyway. It was out of character for his mother to leave home, but she did, and she was excited about the trip and bringing his father home, excited about the new baby.

The sun is hot as he picks his way down the tracks, careful of his footing. His eyes are tuned to the ground, but all he sees is litter—broken glass, scraps of fast-food wrappers. The collar of his shirt is wet, and he stops and pulls out a handkerchief to wipe his face. *O my heart of my mother! O my heart of my mother! O my heart of my different forms.* When he had students select and annotate from the *Book of the Dead*, spell 30b was by far the most popular selection. It was one of the easiest to memorize—he knew this was likely why—but he never discouraged it, perhaps because taking the time to imagine the judgment of one's own heart is not such a bad thing to do. Undergraduates often compiled a list of drunken brawls and sex with strangers and cheating on tests, which made for interesting reading, even if not worthy of a grade above a C.

"Could we weigh my paper one more time?" a stoned-looking smart aleck once asked, and Frank said sure, and pulled a feather from the drawer of his desk. He had done this many times, to the delight of all the others. He also had a small scale Lil had given him one Christmas years before, and he gently placed the feather on one side and waited.

O heart of my mother! O heart of my mother!

December 15, 1943. His grandmother had baked bread that morning, and the whole house smelled like warm, sweet yeast when he came home from Oakland School. It was a Wednesday, and as she did every Wednesday, his grandmother asked him to go with her so he could carry the bags. She was excited about his parents getting home. She was planning food for their arrival. Who knows what he was thinking about. It was the year they had to memorize so many different things, so maybe that—some verse of Longfellow or *Over the river and through the woods*—or he was thinking about Boy Scouts or what he wanted for Christmas; he is fairly sure that's the year he asked for a globe and a new baseball glove. But whatever it was vanished the next day.

They were all still in shock when they planned Frank's move in the late spring. "You'll be back soon enough," his grandmother said. "Your mother needs you."

In the beginning, it sounded like Frank and his mother and the baby would be home by late summer; he would miss baseball, but he would be back for school. But summer became fall, and fall became winter, and by then, Preston had voiced his intentions, and a whole new part of his mother's life began; that was the part Lil said she could understand, and for years they simply agreed to disagree, Frank a little hurt that she could so easily see his mother's point of view.

"But what about Grandmother?" he had asked when his mother delivered the news in a series of calm, quiet syllables while Horace wailed from his crib in the next room. "What about our house?" The house would sell, he was told, and his grandmother would move to live with Frank's Aunt Jenny in Worcester. His mother's family had dwindled to almost nothing: only a brother still in Maryland, where she had grown up. "What does it matter? We will be together—safe and together. As it should be," she kept saying, and he soon grew tired of the argument.

A STORY IS easier to fall into than your own life, which is why Frank was always taken with mythology, the explanations of all those unexplainable things: this is how the sun rises, and this is why the moon changes in size. The explanations of death, and what happens after, vary in different cultures, and so much of his life has been preoccupied with just that, the myths of death and all the ancient beliefs of the afterlife. "There was nothing for us to bury," his mother had said. It's hard not to think how different it would all be these days with DNA tests and research. Even now there might be traces of his father—his own DNA—in the dirt below his feet.

Early in his career, he had a wonderful library of books about canopic jars, and paintings and photographs of them; the whole process was so fascinating and guaranteed to hold a class's interest. Then of course, that silly fad of imitation canopic jars sprang up, and that's all anyone gave him for years, everything from the sentimental syrupy ones—wishes, dreams, desires—to the irreverent—ex-wives, grudges, felonies. Beware if you are a man with a hobby and anyone discovers it—you will get more urns than there are shelves; or if you like to fish, you will get fish that flap and sing and all kinds of silly rulers and signs about lying. Or baseball: you will get baseballs that talk. Whatever, all silly, and, what's more, it will taint your desire for this thing you love, which someone else is trying to claim *with* you. Part of having an interest is that it is *yours*—or should be—in a way that allows you to feel removed, instead of invaded, like the kudzu and wisteria overtaking the trees around him. He stops again to judge his distance from the car. So hard to find the right spot.

Years ago, when he sometimes practiced class lectures on Lil, he told her about the special ceremony that took place to open the mouth of a mummy so he could speak in the next life, and she immediately began naming all of the people she hoped they kept sealed up. She said, "Mum's the word!" Something she repeated a lot, especially after they moved. Now, he finds it all funny and has for a lot of years, but that night as he practiced, a young professor craving respect and recognition and tenure, he was irritated that she didn't listen better, that she didn't at least say something serious—*How did they do that?* or *Oh, how interesting!* or how smart his words were—before it became a conversation that was about her being funny. It was a time in his life when he really needed to be heard. He needed to be seen, to feel alive. He had just turned the age his father was when he died, and he woke each day with a tightening in his chest, a reminder that this could be his day. Of course, Lil also made him aware of *that*, since she herself had already experienced it.

"What haven't you experienced, Lil?" he asked her. "Anything? Is there anything at all?"

"I haven't been to the moon," she said. "I haven't gotten the Nobel Peace Prize," and then when she realized he wasn't laughing, she put her arms around him, the same way she did with the kids, when offering comfort. "Really, Frank," she said. "You'll be great. You always are."

IT WILL BE *great. It's just up ahead. It's around the corner.* Frank hates anticipation, hates waiting. Too often, the waiting is nothing but a lie, an undelivered promise. *You'll feel better soon.* No, no, I won't. *We'll be home on the sixteenth.* No, no, you won't. *You'll come home when your mother is better and able.* No, no, I won't. *You come first, Frank.* But, no, he didn't—not as a child and not when his own children arrived, and what sane and loving father wouldn't want his children to come first, and yet, every now and then, he wondered, When was it his turn? Would he ever get a god-damned turn? His mother didn't put him first, and neither did Lil during that span of years when she was determined to make up for her mother's life. "I didn't marry your goddamned mother," he had said. "I married you, and you aren't there anymore!"

And even this move. Why couldn't he just live to the end without having to visit what has haunted him all these years? It was so easy to ignore it when so far away, but now he can't *not* think about it, *not* revisit.

When the kids were young, they listened eagerly to all he had to tell them: how the heart was weighed against the feather of truth, how the hearts were then fed to the monster. And he showed them the many jars on his shelf, the silliness of their messages—enemies, fantasies, dreams—turned to the wall. Instead, he introduced them as Imsety, Hapy, Duamutef, and Qebehsenuef. Liver, lungs, stomach, and intestines. The kids loved hearing how all those good brains were tossed away, as if nothing more than a snot factory. Jeff liked the baboon, and Becca the raven, and Frank told Lil later he was predicting their future based on their choices—Jeff chose lungs, and Becca chose intestines, which he later turned into a family joke. *One full of a lot of hot air, and one full of shit.*

"I NEEDED TO stay there," Frank's mother had said. "He asked me not to leave. That was the last thing he said: don't leave."

"He was *dead*."

"No, he was *dying*."

She said, "I went to the restroom, and it saved my life."

What an odd fact to mark such a shift, and yet it had. And Frank has thought of it so many times when he excused himself to a lavatory in a public space or escaped a cocktail party or a heated discussion to collect his thoughts. Taking refuge there behind a locked door, eye to eye with himself in the mirror as he mouthed the familiar *I am here.*

His mother had described the moment so many times that Frank felt he had lived it as well. It was as if she had to keep telling it in order to believe it, as if some time she might tell it and find something new. And so he listened. To his knowledge, he was the only recipient of her going back through and over it all; she did it only when it was just the two of them all alone. When she died, Frank asked Horace and Preston if she had ever talked about it to them, and they said no, assuming that she hadn't talked to him either.

"He was sleeping," his mother had said. "He was wearing civilian clothes: a yellow cotton shirt with green flecks that he had bought as a souvenir, even though it was December. He thought it was funny and said he knew it would make his mother laugh when they got home." His hair was combed back. "Thick and black, just like yours, honey," Frank's mother always said. He was wearing Aqua Velva, like always. He had a newspaper on his lap, his hand—with his tapered, tan fingers—on top of the obituary of the man who had created Corn Flakes. She said it was an odd thing to remember, but she had, perhaps because she was thinking that after, if she still couldn't sleep, she would ease the paper from his hands and try to read a bit, in the dim light, about Mr. Kellogg, a detail that would be present in her mind forevermore, every trip to a market a reminder. She was thinking about reading the paper as she made her way through the car; she was thinking about how good it would be to get home, her body being jostled from side to side as she made her way into the small lavatory. She was wearing a skirt she could no longer button but had pinned to her slip; she was trying to straighten her stockings; she was reaching, the pooch of Horace filling her abdomen in a way that made it hard to bend over, when everything happened.

She closed her eyes as she told it all—"I'll be right back"—as if to conjure his father's face, an expression Frank never saw in the presence of his stepfather lingering there. It was a pause, an acknowledgment of all that rushed out of her life in that moment.

And why did this please Frank? He should have wanted her happiness, her comfort. Why did some part of him relish the pain and loss he saw on her face and heard in her voice?

"I'll be right back," she had said, "and then I hope I can sleep."

She whispered this in his father's ear; it was past midnight, and they were on their way home. They would have the whole train ride in the morning to talk and rest before returning to everyday life.

FRANK TRIPS AND falls forward, one knee landing on a cross-tie with a crack of pain that takes his breath, his palms outstretched into the gravel. "Please don't be foolish," Lil had said the day she came with him. "It's dangerous, and it's so hot." He catches his breath, hearing her say, *I told you not to do that.* His pants are torn, his hands scraped, but he can bend his knee. He can stand, and he waits for the pain to subside, for his vision to clear. He can see a small house in the distance, the roof caving at one end, where there is a big satellite dish; he hears a dog barking and the distant roar of a muffler in need of repair.

He takes another deep breath, knee sore but okay, but he has to pee, so he looks around to a spot where the pines are thick, offering shade as well as relief. *I went to the restroom, and it saved my life.* And is it any surprise that Horace grew up to be a nephrologist? Every time the two have gotten together over the years, the conversation always comes back around to kidneys and their mother's escape from death. "The kidneys should have been saved in one of those Egyptian jars!" Horace says. "The kidneys get more blood than the heart, brain, and liver. The kidneys, thanks of course to my presence, saved mother's life." And last year when Frank was in the hospital, complaining about all the tubes running in and out of his body, Horace had called from his place at Hilton Head and said, "Tapping a kidney's not so bad, big brother." *Tapping a kidney.* Horace said things like that, like he might still be at a fraternity party setting up a keg. "Tapping more than a kidney," he almost said, but chose not to go there. He was tired of the chatter. He simply thanked him for calling and wished him a great time golfing or sailing or whatever it was he was doing. Catheters, catheters, heart, bladder, enough. Enough with the slow drain.

Frank has always been grateful his mother was spared, even though as a boy he had sometimes—with enormous pangs of guilt—allowed himself to imagine his life if he'd been orphaned to his grandmother's care and stayed where he was—his house, his school, his life. *O heart of my mother!* And then he would find himself going to sit near his mother, to take it all back. He was so relieved she was there, even though it was hard in boyhood to see Horace, the little red-faced mewler with chronic cradle cap, as hero of the world. "Don't you go near those tracks," his mother had said, and he can almost conjure her voice as he makes his way from the edge of the woods back into the glare of the rails and the short distance to go.

Shelley

"HERE'S THE DEAL," the judge says when Shelley enters her office and is asked to close the door. There is a lawn mower passing right outside the window, and the judge holds one perfectly manicured finger skyward while waiting for it to pass. Shelley saw him as she was coming in, a man wearing aviator shades with a tattoo sleeve of snakes; this judge is big on hiring prisoners, giving chances for people to work and redeem themselves, which might be in Shelley's favor right now.

There is very little decoration to be seen, no personal photographs, nothing hanging on the drab beige walls; the venetian blinds behind where the judge is sitting are barely slanted, to let in a little bit of light. It's kind of like in *The Godfather*, and Shelley almost says that but then thinks better. The judge is already robed and ready to go. "It's short notice and slim pickings in the clerical pool these days."

"Okay."

"I have no idea what you were thinking the other day, but it was inappropriate. People may come in here gawking and acting like they've gone to the theater, but it is not the theater." She holds a hard stare and waits for Shelley to nod. The mower is far in the distance now, but it sounds like it might be circling back, and the clock on the otherwise bare mantel is ticking, ticking. "You know that, right? Not the theater."

Shelley nods.

"A woman was murdered. A child was orphaned. I take that seriously," the judge says.

"Yes."

"Yes, you know that I take it seriously, or, yes, you do as well? Yes, you know that this is no laughing matter? Not a soap opera or some silly form of amusement." The woman never blinks, and she leans forward with each syllable.

"Yes to all of that. Yes, I know."

"Do you have a personal connection to this case? Because if you do, that is something you should have disclosed in the beginning."

"No. No, I don't."

"This kind of case doesn't get nearly enough attention, in my opinion."

Shelley nods. She would love to tell her that that was the point of what she was trying to write. A murdered blond girl is more likely to get the attention, or a murdered rich person. But other people get murdered all the time, and nobody seems to care. People disappear or go missing, and nobody does anything; there are people in the world who have no one watching out for them, no one to hear when they ask for help.

"Are you listening?" The judge leans forward and slaps her hand on the desk.

"Yes, sir. I mean, ma'am. It was all an accident, really."

"An accident?" the judge asks. "There's no room here for *accidents*. You record what is said in my courtroom exactly as it is said, and nothing else. Nothing. Not what you think of the man on trial and not what toothpaste you're going to buy."

Colgate. Usually Colgate, Shelley was thinking, but she didn't dare say a word.

"You miss a beat and you're gone forever. Hear?"

"Yes. Thank you. Thank you so much." Shelley stands, and when she gets to the door, the judge calls out. "And someday . . ." She waits for Shelley to turn. "Someday, when I am retired and you see me out in the world in something other than my 'really expensive shoes' and without my hair 'about to burst into flames,' I might enjoy a conversation with you." She sits back, and her face softens just enough that Shelley feels like she might cry. "Just do your job, Ms. Lassiter. We all know life hasn't been easy for you either."

Shelley takes a deep breath, says thank you again, and steps into the hallway. Marva is waiting there with a worried look until Shelley gives her a thumbs-up and then heads into the bathroom to give herself a pep talk. She has to stay focused. She looks at her phone, and there is a message from Harvey's camp teacher and there is a message from Jason. The judge said the jury is ready, and everything is happening much faster than Shelley had thought it would, this second chance. She needs to listen to her messages but is afraid of getting distracted. But what if Jason got in an accident? What if the check she sent to him bounced—it shouldn't have bounced; she checked her balance several times and it shouldn't have bounced, but what if it did? Or what if Harvey has done something *really* bad or broke a bone, or what if Brent showed up and drove off with him? She listens, her heart slowing and her shoulders relaxing when she hears Jason's voice saying he's on his way home for the weekend. He has some things he wants to go over with her. A project. A family project.

Six more minutes. She takes a deep breath and stares at her reflection in the warped mirror. This courthouse bathroom looks like it never gets cleaned; every speck of that old tile would probably set off the black-light pee detector. Cooties in the air and on the old tall radiators, and metal doors all scratched up with initials and nasty graffiti: *Tony sucks. Patty fucks. For a good time call the asshole in office 247. Rick is a dick. Put a ring on it. Roses are red, violets are blue, I'm a schizophrenic and so am I.*

Now, she opens her phone and listens. "Hello, Ms. Lassiter. Harvey is safe—don't want to alarm you. But I do need to speak to you again about his behavior." Pause. "He's saying some things that upset some of the other children, and I'd like to help you figure this out." She stares up at the ceiling, where there are wet glops of toilet paper, and tries not to cry. Someone drew a penis in lipstick on the mirror, and someone else drew a cross on the wall, asking that we all be forgiven. Three minutes. "Please call me as soon as you can. Thanks."

Shelley wipes her eyes and heads out and into the courtroom, takes her seat, and waits, hands on the keyboard ready to go, like on the starting line of a race, like waiting for the spelling bee word to be called; on your mark, get set. The room is filled to capacity, the final act. The man's wife has returned to hear the verdict, but all those women who were called to testify are absent. The friend of the murdered woman, the one raising that orphaned son, is there in the front, and so are all the people from the retirement home who knew the young woman, who loved her, who called her "our girl."

Shelley shouldn't have said "accident" to the judge. What a stupid thing to say, and yet that word seems to fill her life these days and the judge acts like she knows things about her. Does she? Because lately, Shelley can't stop thinking about her brother and how he looked all those years ago, his shirt torn and face bloody, and how he whispered, "It was an accident," and how just last night, Harvey showed up scared and bare-legged and crawled into her bed in the middle of the night. "I had an accident," he whispered, and she told him it was okay, everything would be okay, and just try to get some sleep, but he kept talking; he was thinking of the Munchkins and how sad it was that they had to sit on that porch all day long and couldn't do anything when people were mean and said hateful things.

"They cussed," he whispered. "Jason said the Munchkins cussed all kinds of bad words."

"Of course they did," she finally said. It was three a.m., and she had not slept at all. "They were people born with problems, and hateful people teased them. They had every right to cuss and throw rocks." She rubbed her hand up and down Harvey's back, his bony spine startling her with his fragility, his little bird bones.

She has said everything she knows to say to soothe him; she has said that there are no ghosts, that everything is fine and he needs to try to do what the teacher at school suggested and focus on happier things. The pediatrician said he had "schoolitis" and sent her home with the name of a therapist and some harsh advice (she thought) about being a more direct and conscientious and demanding parent. She almost told Harvey what she once heard her grandmother say, "I don't fear the dead; I fear the living," but she didn't, because there are plenty of living people the child already fears. And so does she! She fears that asshole who any minute will be led into the courtroom.

Her grandmother was tired and washed-out, like an old gray rag—teeth missing but still dipping snuff and sucking on hard candies—and she'd whispered in Shelley's ear so Shelley's father wouldn't hear her—"I don't fear the dead; I fear the living"—and Shelley knew she was talking about him. He was a living man to fear, his own mother, who was mean herself, scared of him, his wife reduced to nothing, his son filled with hatred. But she can't tell Harvey any of that; she can't say how there are so many things and people to fear.

As a child, Shelley was a worrier, and then she worried about worrying—still does. And now she fears she has given this to Harvey, the way he is so cautious about what might jump out and grab him, the way he is so scared by ghost stories and obsessed with what happens when you die. He has his bird and fish and lizard cemetery, wooden blocks with names of the various creatures, and then he has a huge Lego structure that he says is a camp for runaway turtles and salamanders, who need to be loved. He once announced over dinner how much he loves skinks.

"You mean skanks?" Jason asked. This was at the old house, and Brent was still there.

"Skinks!" Harvey yelled. He didn't like that they were laughing at him, and he threw a buttered roll across the room. Peggy ate the roll in one bite and came over to the table in hopes of more.

This was when Brent still sometimes threatened the boys with a spanking, and she had said over her dead body. She knew all that bullshit about "This hurts me more than it hurts you" and other stupid things people who are three times your size say to make themselves feel better about their hateful ignorance. A man takes off his belt and beats the shit out of a kid who doesn't deserve it. Even a gentle swat from Brent sent her reeling. She had stood in her brother's room holding tight to a stuffed dog he had in there, one he won at the state fair when his school class went. He said a lot of boys gave what they won to a girl but that he really wanted to bring his home, and she got hopeful, thinking he was going to surprise her with it. But, no, he really *did* want it all to himself, but he would let her hold it sometimes, and she held it while their dad took him in the other room, telling him why he was not a good person, why there was a good chance he was always going to be a failure. And she counted the leather belt slaps on bare skin.

"Don't hit Harvey, and don't hit Jason. *Ever*," she said later when they were alone in their room.

"Discipline never hurt anybody," Brent said, and by then he had laughed with both boys. He had told Harvey a bedtime story and kissed him good night.

"But it *can* hurt," she said. "It hurts, and that shit stays with them, it chases and catches them, and you know what? It catches the parents who gave it, and they eventually come to a place where they have to face something really ugly and awful, because that's what they did to others; reap what you sow."

"Nice, Shelley," he said. And when he left, she thought how she would *not* miss *that* part of him, that part that was capable of hurting others.

Frank

He stops, waits for his breathing to settle. More and more these days, he thinks of his grandfather and all the diagnoses he made simply looking at teeth and nails, examining phlegm and piss and shit as if inspecting gemstones.

"Heart attack waiting to happen," his grandfather had said of old Mr. Kimes, the nice man who cleaned their fireplaces, who had little fatty sacs near his eyes, deep creases in his earlobes. "Good thing he's as thin as he is or he might've died years before. Wouldn't have seen his boy come home from the war. Wouldn't have seen his grandbaby." He could hear the rattle of a cough and call pneumonia before he even thumped a person's back and listened closely.

He talked of things many consider old wives' tales: the hiccups of death, the moment of brightening, the feet that will not get warm and keep moving, one over the other, like sticks rubbed together. "Well, I guess some old wife must have said it," he liked to say, often smiling big at Frank's grandmother when he did so. "Yes, some old wife probably said it right before her husband dropped dead, and so it became true."

And then everyone was surprised when he himself dropped dead, right there in the living room, without any warning at all; he came in saying what a very busy but good day it had been. He had successfully diagnosed a case of pneumonia and one of pleurisy, had removed a pinto bean from a toddler's nostril, and had changed the dressing of a man who'd lost his right hand to a saw in the lumber mill. He had complimented Frank's grandmother's cooking, said it smelled wonderful, and he was going to sit a minute by the open window and listen to the music someone was playing in the house next door. Then he took off his coat, sat down, and died.

She wasn't cooking, his grandmother said; the raw chicken was still there in the sink, alongside a colander of peeled potatoes, and there was no music coming in from the outside. This was her story and one she told for the rest of her life. "I witnessed him smelling and hearing another place," she said. "It makes me feel hopeful."

THE SUN IS so bright and hot he squints into the distance and to the place he needs to be. Not much farther. His shirt is completely damp, and he wipes his forehead with his handkerchief. He has walked this stretch of rail more times than he can count. To those seated on a passing train, this must look like the middle of nowhere. All those pennies on the track flattened—bitter copper—angering his mother, her face flushed when he had stood with the flattened piece in his hand. He can't stop thinking of all that, and wondering if they are still where he hid them. People talk about their bucket lists; well, there you go. His markers along the tracks have changed, but he knows he has reached the spot, and he stops and takes a deep breath. Birdsong fills the trees, and the distant cars come and go like ocean waves.

Preston is the one who had told Frank that it was believed most of the people in those cars died instantly. It was in the early years of their relationship, and Frank had questioned most of what his stepfather said. It seemed any acceptance was a direct affront to the memory of his father. The stories of those lost were too painful to hear, and yet what choice was there: so many young servicemen heading home, German immigrants from Long Island, probably so happy to have escaped their homeland before all the ugliness took it; a couple and their seven-week-old baby, and they were also from Lowell. His grandmother had read that part aloud from the paper, and he always meant to ask his mother if she had connected with that young family along the way, perhaps in the train station or while on board, if they had found this connection of babies and home. His mother would have asked where they lived, and then she would have said, "I live on Andover," and the street name would have been enough.

In the early years of their marriage, Frank and Lil had looked at a house on Trull Lane, right off of Andover. Lil loved it—the young neighborhood and families, the nice backyard, and it was so convenient to his teaching—but at the last minute, he realized that he hated the proximity to the life that got away. The house had been painted gray, and there were heavy-looking curtains up in his window, where there had once just been that simple shade with the bone ring. It was a relief not to have to pass by it each day.

• • •

"IT WAS A real lesson in goodness," Preston had told him when they stood in this very place all those years ago. "Everyone in the community turned out: doctors, nurses, veterinarians, guys like me." He told how he had brought tobacco baskets and ties, which were used to make gurneys, and how even children had brought food and water, the older ones running back and forth with information to be telegraphed to families far away. Coffee and food were delivered, and all public servants worked for hours and hours. The small brick hospital in a nearby town was filled to capacity, and so other spaces were used. People opened up their homes. The dead filled every morgue in the area, people slowly identified by their clothing and scars. Many were decapitated. When Preston told that part, he closed his eyes as if to will it all away. And then he stopped talking, turned the conversation to the tracks themselves and how they were constructed, and how he had grown up right there in that same place, always knowing those tracks and the sound of the train passing.

It was that day that Frank dared to ask about his dad, his hands filled with loose snaps and buttons he had picked up as they walked to the site. He had seen a speck of silver and, after digging, found a Captain Midnight badge—it belonged to a child or maybe one of the servicemen; maybe it had been sent to someone as the lucky charm that would bring them home. Maybe it had been among the many gifts that were scattered in the trees in the aftermath. Maybe it was his. His mother had told him they would bring him something, and when he found it, it occurred to him that it might have been *his*, but when he asked his mother, she just shook her head no; she didn't think so.

She said it was hard for her to remember, maybe because she was pregnant, but she did recall the yellow shirt his dad bought and how they had eaten conch. She told him she had a beautiful huge conch shell she was bringing to Frank—that was it, a conch shell—but it was lost there with his father. Still, the day Frank saw that flash of silver and pulled the badge from the dirt, he was struck by the coincidence that the night of the wreck he had listened to *Captain Midnight* on the radio, there in the living room his parents had furnished together, in the big brown chair where his father had sat, the back of which smelled of the oil he used in his hair. Frank had stood looking out at the cold December night and imagined his parents on the train. He was in the fifth grade at Oakland School, and his father had agreed to help with the science fair in February.

"I heard him," Frank's mother had told him at the end of her life, talking more and more when it was just the two of them. "I heard him calling me." She held tight to Frank's wrist. "He said, 'Don't leave, don't leave.'"

Frank's goal, his secret plan, had always been to go home. Home, northward—to ice and darkness, to wet sloppy springs and mild summers. He wanted to go *home*: his father's birthplace, his own birthplace, not the place of his father's death. He often sat there on his stepfather's back porch and looked out to the woods, where Preston had what he called a root cellar, a place to keep things cool and safe. "That's where we'd go if a big storm came," Preston had said. At first, Frank found the thought terrifying, climbing down into what really was like a vault, a tomb with a heavy iron lid, like a cistern or a manhole with a rickety ladder, but then the spot became more and more appealing, like a clubhouse, a secret spot. And it really was incredibly cool down there at the height of summer—six feet down, room enough to have his back against the cool brick and stretch his legs. Preston saw he was claiming it as his camp, and he let him; in fact, Frank came home from school one day, and there was a brand-new ladder attached, and a little wooden chair and table and a flashlight down below. "No wonder you got so interested in tombs," Lil had said, and laughed when he first described it to her.

It did feel like another world down there—removed from everything. When he had read about the Civil War and the Underground Railroad, he pictured tunnels growing out of a space like where he sat, the damp smell of earth and the darkness. And in later years, when people really were building fallout shelters, Preston claimed to be ready; by then, Frank was in school miles northward, the jar of flattened pennies and marbles still down there where he left them.

"We all want to leave something behind." Frank used to begin his introductory class that way. "We all want to be remembered." And then he asked that his students make a list of those belongings that defined them. A thousand years from now, what would it mean? A song, a sign, a secret message. *Kilroy was here.* Students were often too young to know the origin of Kilroy, even though they might have heard the saying, and he loved telling how some say the real Kilroy was from just south of Boston—Braintree—all roads leading back. *Kilroy was here.* A lot of people think that the little cartoon of Kilroy—peeping eyes—grew out of the omega symbol. The alpha and the omega, the beginning and the end.

There was a club at the high school he had attended, Alpha Omega: girls in their matching sweater sets and bobby socks and loafers, girls laughing and holding hands, clear-faced girls who thought this small town was the center of the universe. So much is coming back to him. Afternoons in a high school gym or walking the elm-shaded sidewalks to the movie theater, his youth and all that he failed to do in life calling his name.

So foolish what sticks in the brain—so inconsequential, so meaningless, and yet sometimes there is something in the glint of the sun on those rails and the thought of youth that makes him almost believe he can go back. It was like a part of him had also died on that cold night in December, and now it is just a simple continuation of that process, a signing over of all the other parts: *Here is my heart, and here is my brain.*

Frank was here. He had written that in charcoal there on the brick of Preston's root cellar. Perhaps today that fearful-looking young woman will finally let him in the house, and then he will say he just wants to wander there in the yard and adjoining woods, and he will look for his place, and if by fate it is there, he will climb down into it, like a dog making its bed.

Harvey

SOMETIMES WHEN HARVEY is asked to sit by himself a few minutes at school or at camp, he thinks about what Super Monkey might do. First, Super Monkey would be able to wear any mustache he wants to wear at school. It is not fair for a kid not to be allowed to wear a mustache whenever he wants to if he needs to. Second, Super Monkey can get all the money and jewels he needs anytime at all. He can buy his mama a car and a castle and any other stuff she wants and he guards where the rabbits are living in the tree and he guards where all the little fish and skinks is buried and he tells that bad man, "Don't kill the Dog House Girl," and "Don't kill or hurt Harvey's mama just because she has to write a report on you. That is her job and she does it good and you are not good, bad man. You eat poo-poo platters and murder people." And Super Monkey thinks the bad man should pick up trash for the rest of his life and he will be one nobody waves at.

Harvey's mama said, "Honey, don't wave at those men. Those are convicts." But to Harvey it was hard to tell, because none of 'em wear stripes like the Hamburglar. They look like regular people in blue jeans and shirts and hats, picking up trash. But his mama said, "Do you see those men standing at either end with guns? And if one of those men ran, then they would get shot, so it's better not to smile and wave at all."

Super Monkey could do it, but he can do anything. He could go right now and find Harvey's daddy and say, "Please come home. Please don't leave." Super Monkey would have saved those kids that got shot, too.

"You can join the group now, Harvey," Mr. Stone says, but Harvey tells him, "No, thank you." He's okay just sitting.

"Really, son," he says. "I want you to join the group."

"Can I wear this?" Harvey holds out the mustache he has kept safe in his pocket and finally the teacher tells him that yes, yes, *yes*, he can wear the mustache.

Shelley

$\backsim$

Now that man struts in, looking as relaxed as a person can be in an orange jumpsuit with his life on the line. He even whispers something to his lawyer and laughs. Months before the trial began, she and Harvey had seen the doctor in Lowes Foods and overheard him talking to the clerk about a party he was having. He was wearing a loud floral shirt, long pink shorts, and shiny black loafers. He was going to have a luau, and he talked about leis and pupu platters, which made Harvey bend over double in the checkout line, his face red with laughter. When he laughed that hard, you could see the thin white scar where his lip had been unformed. This was before Harvey went to kindergarten and still laughed openly; his hands clutched the sack of gummy candies he had begged to buy, instead of covering his mouth.

"Did I miss something?" The doctor looked at Harvey when he said this, and it made Harvey laugh even harder.

She thought at the time what a hateful stare he'd given to Harvey, and then he leaned in close to her, so close she could smell his aftershave or soap, something out of her league to know, and he said, "You know there are surgeons who can do a much better job with that." Harvey was still laughing, mouth wide, lip split, the thin white scar visible under his nose.

She has seen that same stare every day for weeks and weeks. In the piece she didn't mean to write, she described the doctor's eyes as being like dark slits in a fleshy melon. A jack-o'-lantern, a pumpkin head of hatred, fermented rot.

In the trial, he actually said he had never considered killing anyone. He added that he didn't care enough about any of them to kill them—meaning, he clarified, there was no passion there. He asked, Why would he sacrifice his life, not to mention brilliant career, in the kind of town that needs every ounce of brilliance and expertise it can get?

All she could think while taking notes was how humiliating it would be to have to go home and face the husband you cheated on, knowing that the asshole you cheated with didn't even care enough to kill you! The argument in her mind made her want to laugh, and she realized she had missed a beat or two, a few words, because she was remembering a woman on the stand saying how he'd said terrible things about his wife. He'd talked as if his wife was abusive to him, this woman said. But that woman is not in the courtroom today; none of them are. Today's show is just for the smart ones, the ones who did not go along with him, the ones who loved the young woman he killed, and the wife whose life he has temporarily ruined.

And how sad for his children to have to always know their father was capable of something so horrible, that they share DNA with such a horror show. A person might spend the rest of his or her life waiting for it to spring out of them without warning, in the form of a knife or a gun or a push from a precarious high spot.

One of the women who testified was someone Shelley had met several times, someone right there in their own neighborhood; she lived in that beautiful old house beside the cemetery and was the mother of a kid Jason knew, a sweet girl named Abby, who was Harvey's favorite babysitter and who Shelley hopes will have the good sense to move far, far away, where all this mess won't ruin her life. Sometimes the very best thing you can do is run, get away, shake the shit out of that snow globe you live in and never let it settle. Shelley herself had done that—of course she had—because she was like the canary in the mine, the thermometer in her childhood home. *Why don't you go in first, Shelley? What is the temperature, Shelley?* She was always so afraid she might fly in and never get back out. She might fly in and die that way, her soul nothing but a little sacrifice so the others could claim that her sad loss was the root of all the other problems and failures. But she did not want to sacrifice herself. The smart canary would learn to aim a little higher each time until finally one day, she just flaps and flies up above it all; she gets the fuck out of there.

It was hard to imagine how all the families affected by the orange-suit asshole wouldn't be ruined. And yet you would have to have no heart at all to see someone sit there and hear themselves and their sex lives critiqued and judged in front of a courtroom by a man who says he never gave a damn and not be moved, right? He even laughed outright at their stupidity to think he'd wanted anything more than to use them like disposable wipes. He used that word, *disposable*. Disposable company.

The woman who lives near Shelley had dressed like a grandma at church on her court day, a way that Shelley had never seen her look before. Usually, she was in short, tight dresses made for someone her daughter's age, and high heels like they all wear on the Real Housewives shows, the kind of woman who might loop her thumbs in the front pockets of that little dress like she's the cheese. *The cheese, the cheese. The cheese stands alone.* That woman had a daughter she should have been thinking about; children need to feel like someone is there. If Shelley's mother had ever been there to say nice things—the kinds of things Shelley says to Jason and Harvey— Shelley's life might have been different. She might have stood a little taller, taken more chances. Flown away sooner.

The man is getting restless, watching the clock, whispering again to his lawyer. It's like he's pissed off he's having to wait, like maybe he would have preferred to keep lounging in his cell instead. There is a low murmur of voices through the courtroom, and the tension is high. It feels a little like when Shelley went to see Madonna in concert that time.

Why didn't he just leave his wife and *then* date others? Then he could just break up, not murder them. Brent would call her *naïve*; he once told her that people *like* games. People *like* secrets. He paused then and asked, "Do you have secrets, Shelley?"

But instead of answering that, she did a whole routine she had thought up about a commercial on television—a drug for men, but what they show is a woman half his age lounging on the bed in something skimpy. We are led to believe the man has testosterone to spare but, uh-oh, he does sometimes need a little help from his friends at the pharmaceutical company, while the camera stays focused on the young woman as she slinks around the room in the same way the cheese does. Don't deny your passion—that's the focus, *passion*, as she stretches out on the bed like a cat and waits for the man in the bathroom, who must be waiting for things to happen. But then if you listen very carefully, you will hear the fast, low-volume murmuring of truth: "If you have shortness of breath or severe abdominal cramping or diarrhea, if you experience sudden blindness and loss of memory, if you have an erection that is painful and lasts over seven hours and you find it impossible to urinate, if you are vomiting and having life-threatening seizures, you may want to see your doctor." Read the fine print!

Once, when Brent found where Jason had written *SHIT* on the outside of the garage door, he made a joke over dinner, saying, "Well, the writing is on the wall." They all laughed, but when he asked a second time who did it and Jason still didn't respond, Brent got angry and made him get out there with Clorox and wash that door that had not been washed in a hundred years, but Jason had used a Sharpie, and when they left, it was still there—*SHIT*—faded but there. "Maybe your old man wouldn't give a shit about lying, but I do," Brent said, but Shelley told Jason how his father was one of the most truthful people she had ever known. "He was a hero," she said. "He was handsome and smart and kind and considerate, and he was a hero both in the marines and in life."

She didn't tell how she met Jason's father: at the end of a party with at least a hundred people, few of whom she even knew; by the end of the night, most were slumped around on the furniture or delivering nonsensical monologues, or so it seemed to her, and then there was this quiet boy on the couch, staring at an album cover— Fleetwood Mac—and without thinking, she went and sat beside him and said how it bothered her that they sang, "Thunder only happens when it's raining," because that isn't true. In fact, she once heard it thunder during a snowstorm, and many times she has heard it thunder without a single drop of rain. "A damn single drop," she said, and then repeated it when he laughed and offered her a hit off of his joint and then a sip of his drink. And she drank the whole thing out of sheer nervousness. It was raining, and she thought of being in a pup tent with her brother and how much fun they had once out in the yard and away from where their parents could hear their laughter. Their father had to get up early in the morning and would sometimes fly into a rage if he heard a floorboard creak or a commode flush or, God forbid, someone laughing. But there in the pup tent in the driving rain, they could relax and laugh and tell stories. Her brother was nice to her almost all of the time, like Jason with Harvey. These days, if she told how much she loved her brother, there would be some sicko trying to make something ugly of it, but that would be so wrong. He was like a parent to her; he was her best friend. He was all she had, her brother. His thick brown hair was wavy, and he pulled it back in a ponytail, which their dad hated.

Her brother told her to never touch the canvas of the tent when it was raining, because it would make it leak in that spot, something she still thinks about. She thought of all those times her brother got beaten; she knew lots of people who got whipped, and they used words like *spanked* or *switched*. Her parents always said that shit that tons of parents said about spare the rod and spoil the child, but her brother got it worse than anyone she had ever seen, their father doubling his belt over, letting the end with the buckle bite her brother's skin. When he came out of the room after the awful sounds, his face would be red but dry, not a tear shed, and she wanted to touch him but she didn't, because it seemed like touching that canvas tent during the rain. It seemed one touch might bring him crashing down, which it eventually did.

But that night with Jason's father, sitting there stoned, listening to Fleetwood Mac, her brother was already long gone, even though Shelley pretended he was still where she knew to find him, living with several other kids at the edge of town and driving pizza delivery. He was stoned a lot but was so much happier than he had ever been, and she was wishing for him the ease she'd felt in that tent, tucked in and far away from the rest of the world. Jason's father also had thick brown hair, and she asked was it weird he looked a little like her brother. He said he didn't know, and she gave a long explanation about how she didn't mean anything like that, like maybe all she meant is that her brother was someone she felt like she could trust and depend on.

"You can trust me," he said. "That's true." And he reached over, took her hand, and pulled her close, and they sat there like that until the needle was at the end of the album, a long, scratchy digging-in sound, until he got up and lifted it. Then he asked what her name was, and she told the truth.

There was a photo of a girl on Jason's father's dresser—a clean-faced girl wearing pearls. Jason's father's skin was dark, his origin hard to determine, with his black eyes and dark hair, and he smelled clean, like that soap Irish Spring or some kind of spearmint, which surprised her there in that place so saturated in alcohol and smoke and mildew. He bumped her with his elbow when removing his shirt and said, "Excuse me. I'm so sorry," and for that reason alone, she really did think that she could trust him. She felt the girl in the pearls was watching them, and wondered if she was somewhere wondering where he was, or if she was just some dream of a girl he was holding on to. Oddly, that was what she thought of when she missed her period, that the girl had watched and somehow knew Shelley was a failure in life, that she just longed to fit in somewhere, homesick for something she had never had.

"All rise." And then there she is, here comes the judge, stern and solid in a new pair of stylish heels Shelley has never noticed her wearing before, perhaps bought just for this occasion, but she is not about to make a note of that; instead, she rises and she watches the jurors file in, most looking straight ahead, as if to avoid having to see the hateful jack-o'-lantern sitting there. It's true that very few people look good in orange, which may be a reason to have chosen it in the penal system in the first place—that and, of course, it's easy to spot if someone makes a break. But this one isn't going anywhere, and neither is Shelley, and now she gets on the right channel, her fingers in anticipation of flying all over that keyboard, because that young woman he murdered could just as easily have been Shelley. So many times, that could have been Shelley. She's just that predictable.

Lil

New Year's Day 2016
Southern Pines
(Mild and sunny/we wish it would snow!)

FUN THINGS TO remember:

Jeff, you won in the punt, pass, and kick contest and got your picture in the paper (here it is). You were mad they didn't get an action shot. For weeks after, you did things like eat raw eggs and lift heavy bricks so you would be ready for the NFL, but first you had to go to sixth grade.

Becca in a Brownie troop. Do you remember the pledge? "To help other people every day, especially those at home." And now I am one of those people, but I have such a clear memory of you in your little brown dress holding up two fingers crossed by your thumb, that beanie off to one side, your book bag there on the kitchen counter, red Formica, the linden tree out the window.

Your father keeps pointing out what I don't remember, and I keep saying, "But here, look at all I do remember." He wonders where my memory has gone, and I keep saying it's not that it has *gone* but simply that I have run out of space. I have filled every nook and cranny with things I wish I could now box up and store elsewhere, to make room for the new. Like I remember making Popsicles out of Kool-Aid, filling the little plastic holders I got at a Tupperware party. And I can remember the Christmas one of you got a Vac-U-Form and one of you got Incredible Edibles, and the whole house smelled of sweet, burning plastic for days, and you both had scars on your arms from hitting those hot plates. I think those toys came with a warning and maybe got recalled, but you loved them while they worked. I remember Crazy Foam, and Fuzzy Wuzzy soaps, which grew fur and had a prize in the center, and those pretty jewel-toned bath oil beads that I think you two gave me every birthday or Christmas for several years, the fragrance Cachet and then Charlie.

I remember smells that way (a whole section of my brain seems to house them), and I love the memories, but I do need the space these days. I can't recall that your father has an appointment, but I can recall vividly the year we got a Christmas tree that was flocked in pale pink. I remember those temporary tattoos, skulls and crossbones and hearts and flowers, your tired, dirty bodies covered in them after long play days in the summer; I remember hosing you down on the back sidewalk and then filling a warm, soapy tub, Jeff surrounded by plastic boats, and you, Becca, with that bad-looking naked Tiny Tears doll that you took everywhere for years. I drew hopscotch boards for you, the big circular one like a snail, hopping round and round to the center, where we put a big H for "Home." And then you came home later and later, Becca, in your low-hanging bell-bottoms, which you spent a summer embroidering. I taught you French knots, remember? My mother taught me French knots and the running stitch, and then I taught you just as she'd taught me (hold tight to the needle and wrap, wrap, wrap), and you wore Indian moccasins and a beaded headband and a poncho like what is back in the stores now. You were no longer consulting your Magic 8 Ball by then; you weren't consulting me either.

I remember your father saying to Jeff, "Son, the only thing you should ever drink like water is water," and, Jeff, you were leaning against the refrigerator looking at us with one eye closed, I suspect to get us in focus. You were only 15 and reeking of marijuana and liquor. There are smells I'd rather not keep in my memories, but good luck with that.

Your father smelled like lemons that time I grew suspicious— lemons—and I knew it was something you had once had in the bathroom, Becca, and so I went down to Rexall and sniffed around. Love's Fresh Lemon—that was it. They also had Love's Baby Soft. You had both of those products when you went away to college. I unscrewed the cap and breathed it in, and I knew. I just knew without really knowing, if that makes sense. I wish now that I could delete it all from my mind, like that old electric typewriter we had for years, where you could put in a cartridge and retype all the words that you did *not* want, and they were magically lifted from the page.

I remember Rudolf and how there was a big smudge, like a shadow, where his body had pressed against our bedroom wall. Even after he died, I still thought I saw him from the corner of my eye. Even now, I think I see him sometimes, large graceful movements as he tiptoes down the hall, then rests in first position, naturally graceful.

More and more, I am always there in Boston when I write to you. And not even your Boston, but mine, the one of my childhood. I'm always there on the platform, waiting for the train; I put Christmas lights in the trees, and I hear laughter from people passing. I smell the river and the warm wool of my scarf, dampened by my breath. I think my mind takes me to that place where I still have things to work on. It is possible that there can be one thing in your life that you never stop working on. My wish is that you both are in lives that provide loving and trustworthy souls who can hear your story; I hope you are able to articulate with great passion all the things I did wrong in life and have great plans for how you will go forward and do it all better. Then I will know I did a good job. I love you more than the air I breathe. Always have. These days my air comes bottled, and they charge me for it.

June 2, 2015

We have been here a week, both of us exhausted from the move and the unpacking, still trying to adjust to the heat and the different light. We both needed a break, and so today we went to find the house where Frank had lived as a boy. He insisted I take that damn oxygen tank with us, but I won the battle, at least for today. I just wanted to roll down the window and breathe on my own, and I did fine. Down to only one cigarette a day, sometimes two. Frank said things looked so different to him, and he circled the block several times before stopping in front of the house; it clearly has not been loved, with paint peeling and some shingles missing; an old Honda

Civic (like we'd once had in our drive), bikes in a messy garage (we'd had that, too), and a circle worn into the dirt like a bike path. I waited in the car while he went to the door.

The young woman who answered said it wasn't a good day, so then we drove and parked along Highway 211 and stood at the edge of the railroad tracks. He said he wanted to walk down to the site, but he didn't do it that day. It was hot, and the sun so bright, broken bottles shattered and sparkling along the roadside. He told me how he used to put pennies on the rails, something I had heard him tell many times; one of the flattened pieces of copper was on his dresser, in the little jar where he put pins and paper clips. I can only imagine he was thinking of his father.

It's odd, isn't it, what we never outgrow. I think that those who forget being children have likely lost their souls; it's just that simple. Please don't forget. I hope these notes to you will help.

May 3, 1985
Newton
My father would have been 86 today, and I wish I could call him. TW3-3642. He almost always answered on the third ring and then called my name—"Lil!"—as if a complete surprise and delight to hear from me. There's so much I probably haven't told you about him.

He loved beef tongue, which I hated to see in the refrigerator, and he always wore a hat (many men did at the time). He once saw Houdini (I think he told you about that), loved crossword puzzles, and aspired to play chess after the '72 Olympics. He liked that there was a sport where you remained seated and more or less solitary, and he admired the way that each move reduced all the chances up ahead; he made little notations when he looked at the games in the newspaper, and I still have some of those notes that he kept squirreled away in a book called "How to Play Chess in Ten Easy Lessons." He had written "impossible" under the title with a big exclamation mark, but still he made his notes, and they are there in the book, just as he left them, things that make no sense to me: *Nc3 f5 e4 fxe4 Nxe4 Nf6 Nxf6+ gxf6 Qh5#.*

He once said he was sure he could be a better player if such concentration didn't make him want to drink and smoke so much. You wouldn't know all of that by those later years, the way he sat in his chair with so little to say, focused on whatever was on the television, a lot of silly shows like "The Gong Show," which he would never have watched back when he was teaching himself to play chess, and he certainly wouldn't have laughed. And yet there he was, laughing along with whatever silly thing Chuck Barris did. I checked on him daily for a long stretch of time (the rest of his life, I should say), the distance between us seeming longer and longer with each passing day, and especially in the winter. A broken hip that winter took him to the hospital and was the beginning of the end.

I never learned how to play chess, maybe because I associated it with those years right after my mother died, when it seemed that my father was looking for ways to fill his time, neighbors and friends at work encouraging him to have an interest or a hobby. Perhaps I also don't have the brain for it! I wasn't very good at bridge either. I was in a club briefly, but it became obvious that no one liked being paired with me; there was one woman, Naomi Brennan, who remembered every card thrown and talked the entire time, a Benson & Hedges cigarette always pinched there between her coral lips.

If I concentrated on the cards, I missed the conversation, and if I concentrated on the conversation, I made a million mistakes with the cards. Whenever we met at our house, you children were like mice, getting into my butter mints and mixed nuts and the little

Cokes. I even had skirts to put on the bottles (a gift from Naomi) and cloth napkins embroidered with the different card suits. My favorite part of being in that club was eating butter mints and smoking. I had smoked Salems for a long time, but then I switched to Virginia Slims, because I loved the commercials. I liked to think I had indeed "come a long way, baby."

Frank always asked if I really enjoyed that time with bridge group, and then he commented that it sounded like a henhouse brothel for the mentally impaired with talk of "tricks" and "rubbers" and "dummies." It seems such a joke would get old, but it didn't, or hasn't; it still makes me laugh, even though I gave up bridge to volunteer, and that made me feel better about myself. I think Frank *then* thought I was spending too much time in sad situations (the burn unit, where I read to children, the grief support groups, where I served coffee). And maybe I did get too close sometimes. Maybe I didn't have cheerful and uplifting things to tell when I came home. Maybe that's the difference between a game and reality.

My two cents: Go to the dentist twice a year. Floss. Get your physicals. Be honest. Be kind. Wear good, comfortable shoes. Let people know what they mean to you. Bring your children to see their grandparents. Always have extra Halloween candy. Drink lots of water. Make sure your children have pets and lots of free time. It's so important that they know how to be alone.

And thank goodness for you and your children that the days of laxatives are over! I saved several of my mother's magazines, just as they were by her bed, and over the years, I have enjoyed going back and reading what she was reading at the time, but I have been shocked by all the ads and columns about dosing your children with castor oil for anything that was wrong with them. It didn't happen to me, perhaps because my mother was not there, but it explains a lot of other people I know if that one psychology course I took in the extended-education program holds true!

What I love about looking at the magazines that were there by my mother's bed is to see what she had marked with a dog-eared page or a scrap of paper: the recipes and bits of news in Life magazine, like an article called "Men Lose Their Pants to Slack-Crazy Women." She also marked an ad about getting a canary and how it would lift your spirits and make you sing.

Sometimes, I take smoke deep into my lungs and I hold it there before I safely douse my cigarette in a pail of sand I keep by the back door, the same one that was by the door of my studio, the same one you children used at the beach and in your sandbox, Mother Goose barely visible on the rusted tin.

December 21, 1967
I am sitting on the floor in the studio at the end of the day, already dark at five as I survey my domain. I am so proud of the world I have built here, the little bodies in leotards and the great excitement when fitting them for their first toe shoes or picking out costumes for the spring recital. We all have fun with the recitals; the whole family pitches in with the props and the staging. I love to sit here in the dark, in the silence, the streetlight shining outside the window.

The kids want a puppy, and I think it is time. Margot is getting old, and aren't we all. I will turn 35 soon, older than my mother, and I'm both relieved and sad when I think of that. To be so happy! She would love knowing that I am, and who would have ever thought I could be? The tree at home is up and all decorated, and I have a tiny one here, as well. The shopping is almost done: G.I. Joe, Twister, Easy-Bake Oven, and that strange rubbery thing with his horse, Gumby. Frank and I are giving each other a Zenith stereo console. It will fill a whole wall, but Frank swears the sound is worth it.

My mother's cheese soufflé:

> ½ cup butter, ½ cup flour, 2 tsp salt, ½ tsp paprika, dash
> Tabasco, 2 cups milk, ½ lb American cheese (cut up), 8 eggs
> grade B (separated). Melt butter, add flour, and season. Stir
> until smooth. Add cheese and keep stirring. Beat whites stiff.
> Beat yolks and pour into cheese, fold over the whites, and
> put in casserole. 475F for 10 min, reduce to 400°F for
> 25 min or bake slow at 350F for hr.

She made a note that this should cost 63¢ and is supposed to
feed 6, but that they are talking about people who don't have a good
appetite, that our family of 3 licked the bowl clean. She wrote: *Fast
way is better! But don't leave the kitchen!*

Spring cleaning 1978
Here is a review my mother had torn from the paper, "The Deer That
Grew Up," about the movie "Bambi," which she had promised we
would go see. Of course we didn't get there, and then it was years
before I saw it. I took you two when it came through town in the late
'60s. "Bambi," "Dumbo," "Cinderella," "Snow White." So many lost
mothers! And as soon as Bambi's mother got shot, I started crying. Of
course, I never would have made you two leave, and so we sat with
our Milk Duds and popcorn, a grape Charms sucker for Jeff, you two
fixed on the screen and me studying that huge chandelier and hoping it
was securely supported. I studied that and the lovely red drapes at the
front of the theater, and imagined how nice that would be at the small
elementary school stage we borrowed each year for my recital. For a
long time after, we quoted Thumper: "If you can't say somethin' nice,
don't say nothin' at all"; certainly I have failed staying true to that one
too many times to count. But I have never eaten venison.

I also found the ad for the Darling Pet Monkey! $18.95, and
I am attaching it here. "Almost human," "likes lollipops," "FREE
cage" and "FREE leather collar & leash," it says, but, children, it
does not say what it will cost to clean all the rugs it will shit on or
the drapes will shred with those claws and teeth. Jeff named him
Zorro, but Demon was more like it. You were both terrified, and so
was I. Do you remember? Becca, you were crying hysterically, and
poor Margot was barking and whining and torn between wanting
to hide under the bed or kill it. I sent you both outdoors, for fear of
getting attacked while I finally trapped him in the small downstairs
bathroom. I called your father, but his office phone rang and rang
and rang, so I called the police, who came immediately but asked
me what were they supposed to do with it, and I said we didn't
care—just take it.

I did write to the Animal Farm in Miami Beach and try to get
my money back, but they never responded. The good news? We got
Rudolf, and though Margot wasn't thrilled, he grew into a graceful prince. If Nureyev had been changed into a dog, he would have
looked just like our Rudolf. I'm pretty sure that our Darling Pet
Monkey did *not* end up scaling the branches of the Franklin Park
Zoo, but that's what we told you two. In fact, we said there were
several Darling Pet Monkeys who'd welcomed him in.

February 2, 2012
Something I have never told you:

I called your young colleague on the phone several times to see
what I might hear in the background. Once, I held my nose and tried
to sound like Lily Tomlin on "Laugh-In."

"Hello?" I said. "Is Franklin there?"

Pause.

"I said, 'Is Franklin there?'"

"No one by that name lives here," she said, the words clipped and quick.

So the next time, I said, "Tell Franklin it's time." And I knew in the pause that she wanted to ask a question. She wanted to say "Time for what?" But I hung up.

And then I appeared at her door on a Thursday morning in early November. Her apartment reminded me of Becca's right out of college, only Becca has always had a way of pulling a home together, even with things like particleboard and cinder blocks, and this young woman did not; this one had no homey touches to speak of, and it reeked of patchouli, a little cone of incense burned to ash there on the table beside where she finally offered me a seat on a cot, covered in one of those cloths from India they used to sell at World Bazaar. Hers was covered in cat hair and some kind of crumbs.

She plopped down in a purple beanbag chair, and just the sight of it, just the imagined thought of you seated there, long legs out in front of you on that awful carpet people had to rake, made me pull my coat closer to my body. There is no telling what lived down in the deep pile of that rug, and yet I imagined you sprawled there, talking about this or that excavation and what had been unearthed, shards of china and peach pits in so-and-so's ancient shit house. The apartment was near a T stop, and I imagined you at her window, drawn to the clicks and clacks of passing trains.

I'm not sure what it was I thought I would find. Actually, I was disappointed for you. Such a foolish thought while there with this young woman glaring at me, hands crossed protectively over her chest.

"What is it you want?" she asked, a smirk on her young, lineless face.

"Oh, I think you know," I said. "So why don't you tell me what it is *you* want."

"I have no idea what you mean," she said, and pretended to care about those dried-up dead ferns she had hanging. She looked like she had just come in from a logging camp, flannel shirt opened over tight thermal underwear, jeans cuffed with those Wallabees the kids both wore. I hated those shoes, and I'm not sure why, but something about the shape and her wearing them made me hate them even more.

Her hair was all wild and tangled, like she'd stuck her finger in a socket. I felt drab and old, and had to rally myself to hang in there, to continue to think about what a ridiculous situation it was to begin with.

"Oh, yes, you do," I said. "Don't be coy with me. Don't hide there in your little lemony haze. I know your number."

"You know nothing," she said, and then I can't quite remember what else was said. I am pretty sure I told her that she was a little idiot and that you were a big idiot. I know I kept my hands in my pockets the whole time because they were shaking. I was more Marsha Mason/Jill Clayburgh, but I was trying to channel my best Glenda Jackson/Anne Bancroft, so somewhere in there I said, "Fuck you," at least twice, and then the last thing I said was that maybe after she fucked her way around the block several more times and gained some self-awareness, she might (I emphasized "might") be intelligent enough to have a conversation with me.

Then I turned and went to the door. I said, "I won't hold my breath," and she made some snide remark about my "behavior at the faculty party," and before I could say anything else, I felt the jar of the door slamming behind me.

The winter air was as brisk as a slap in the face, and I did something I have never done and probably never will again. I walked into a small bar there in Cambridge, all by myself before noon, and ordered Irish whiskey, my father's drink, and then I sat staring out at the cold gray day. I realized then that my hands were still shaking, and when I looked into the dark mirror over the bar, I saw that ugly face we all make when trying hard not to cry. So I took deep breaths and replayed the whole scene in my mind. Nothing about it made me flinch, and no part of me regretted saying what I had said. I still felt superior in that moment. I thought if that was what you wanted, then you had no business with me. People don't get stolen. People leave. They make choices, and choices have consequences. I said those exact words to you later that night, in fact.

For the longest time, I imagined telling you this—my version. I felt I had a card in my pocket to pull out and play. I even imagined reaching an age where we might shake our heads and laugh about it, marvel at how we survived such difficult, desperate times. But then once we were back in a good place, I wanted to stay there, just as I had done all those years with my father. Humiliating you or myself was the last thing I wanted, and so we kept moving forward, time eroding my hurt and anger.

You never said that you were sorry, but I knew you were. I knew by your attention, and your patience if I was having a bad day. I knew by the way you sometimes came and stood near me when I was cooking or doing the dishes, your hand on my back. I think you just never found the right words.

November 1999

When I was a girl, I wrote a letter to my mother. "Are you here?" I asked her. "Will you please let me know that you are?" And then I wedged it into a little hole in the kitchen cabinet we both knew about; we had decided one rainy afternoon that it was a wonderful hiding place, and she'd tucked a $10 bill in there and then held a finger to her lips. The money was long gone when I inserted my note.

• • •

Jeff, do you remember when you took a whole carton of my cigarettes and soaked it with the garden hose? I wanted to make you work and pay me back, but your father called it "an act of civil disobedience" and sided with your concern about my health and my recent case of bronchitis. You, who the very next year, when you were in high school, would start smoking yourself, probably to hide the fact that you were smoking marijuana all the time, and, no, cigarettes didn't work to mask the smell, and neither did the incense burning in your room, and neither did gargling Lavoris.

That was around the same time you were begging to go to church, much to my surprise and your father's delight, and you were playing electric guitar and drums in the sanctuary, and some were claiming to be high on Jesus, though I suspected that wasn't all. "Day by Day" and so on. It was when you both began questioning us, examining us, striving to find your own way and do it better.

As parents, we pack your bags and strap them to your little backs before you are even old enough to carry them, and then you have to spend the rest of your life unpacking and figuring it all out. Sometimes, I feel I can see it all spread out in front of me—dates and patterns, a clear path emerging, the design, the words that might define me, carved in stone.

November 28, 1982

I have never gotten over what I felt standing there at the Foundling Hospital, that wheel, wood scarred, the darkness up under the eaves, how hard to turn and leave a life behind. Once again, it is November 28—but 40 years later. I am stunned by the passage of these years and how there remains a part of me that is just the same.

A woman in my childhood neighborhood, Mrs. Rubinstein, told how on Yom Kippur she would throw bread on the water to cast away her sins and my mother said she wanted to do that but thought she might have to go into the city where there are a lot of ducks eager to eat them up! We all laughed. When I asked Mrs. Rubinstein if it really works, she assured me that if you were sincere, then indeed it did.

December 7, 2013

I miss how fast I used to be, my mind so sharp, like it was on fire, spitting out several ideas at once, and I could hold them all in the palm of my hand. Now I sometimes wake and it takes a minute to remember where I am. Just the other day, I woke to the sound of the snow shovel, and it was a calm peaceful sound, from the street in front of our house, and I imagined my father, and I knew just what he was wearing, that heavy black wool overcoat, shovel in his hand, my mother in the kitchen sipping a cup of coffee.

I really think my dad stayed alive because of me; a lot of people might have chosen a different course, but he hung in there, giving me all that he was able. I think it is why I write these letters. I want you to know things like that. Sometimes, I imagine myself on the platform waiting for the train. I stand there in the winter chill, and it is always dusk, with Christmas lights slung up into the bare branches of trees. I hear music and laughter and glasses clinking. And as I stand there, breathing into the warmth of the scarf around my neck, I think of you two.

If your father is still here when I am not, please remind him of our word. Tell him I said, "Just because the Houdinis didn't succeed doesn't mean that we can't." I feel my mother has come and gone so many times over the years. In my dreams, in the wind, in odd little meetings with strangers when just the right word is said.

I was 15 years old when I went to the Embassy Theatre with my friend Jean Burr, and we both sat there sobbing to watch poor Moira

Shearer dance to her death in "The Red Shoes." I remember looking up at the stars on the ceiling of that beautiful place and thinking how my mother had described the ceiling of the Cocoanut Grove, designed to make you feel you were under a warm summer sky, even on the coldest of nights. I held on to Jean's arm and thought how my mother would have loved that movie.

We stood there on Moody Street afterward, still wiping our eyes and blowing our noses, laughing at how we must look to those passing by and around us on the sidewalk. The streetlights were on, and we hugged before parting ways, and I remember I lied to my father when he asked about the movie. I said it was something silly based on an old fairy tale; I told him that he wouldn't like it at all but that there was a film coming soon that starred Johnny Mack Brown that I bet he'd want to see.

Then I'm on that wintry platform waiting for the train. I smell the river. I see the lights. And when the train approaches, the ground vibrates beneath my feet.

November 28, 1980
Every November 28 at 10:15, I stop and take a long inhale of my cigarette, and then I hold it as long as I am able. Some years, I have driven and parked there near Shawmut Street or sat in the lobby of the Radisson. Sometimes, I just walk outside to be alone. A lot can happen in 12 minutes.

November 28, 1991
Something I have never stopped thinking about: fate?

There was a handsome young man from Missouri whose photograph filled the newspapers in the aftermath of the fire. He became the face of survival and hope in the wake of so much grief. No human had ever been burned so badly and lived. Everyone, even the young man, asked how he had survived. He, himself, asked why. He wanted to die at times, and perhaps if he'd been able to walk, he might've just done that, flown from a window when no one was looking, like another young man had done when he could not live with his wife's death and the thought that he could have done more to find her that night. But the young man from Missouri lived, and after months and months of trials and failures, he rose from his bed and walked. And then he fell in love and got married and eventually returned to his beloved home in Missouri, only to be in a freak car accident 10 years later, pinned and waiting for help, when a gas leak engulfed him in flames. So, what does that even mean? Did some great soul out there simply delay fate so he could experience love and some happiness in his brief life? Did someone out there say, "Please, he's just a boy."

November 2015
Southern Pines

Sometimes, I wake thinking I am in my childhood bed. There is ice on the window, a hairline crack in the glass ceiling light. Home is that childhood bed on School Street, and home is Grove Street, where you grew up, and now home is here with your father, here in this humid world where I feel I live in a terrarium, a can of oxygen trailing me like an obedient dog.

I don't look like that girl on School Street, but I am still her.

I miss Grove Street. I miss the radiators, and the large mirror plastered into the wall. I miss the marks we left on the pantry door, measuring your heights over the years, the smudge on the wall I could never clean, where Rudolf curled each night. I miss going to Mount Feake, where my parents are buried, there on the river, there within sight of the building where my father worked his whole adult life. They are there side by side, as if nothing ever happened, and who would even know their story if I didn't tell it? Perhaps sometime you will go and visit them.

Becca, did I ever tell you that my mother always wanted an engagement ring and she wanted a Philco record player? She told me I should grow up to have both, and a lot of other things, too. I'm not sure why the ring meant so much to her (perhaps an expression of romance). She would have been disappointed that your father did not give me one either, that we went the more practical route and put a down payment on a car. But we have always had a stereo of some kind, and more important than that, we have had time.

I will always remember the day I looked over at your father, realizing how lucky that we had even found each other, and luckier still that we had survived some hard times. I suppose some of us have to see the edge before we understand how good it all is, and then if lucky, you still have time on the other side.

November 28, 1966
Newton
It's November 28, and I am out here on the back porch to remember the time. Frank is inside watching "The Big Valley," with the promise to get me up-to-date at the first commercial when I return. We let the kids watch "The Man from U.N.C.L.E.," since that's what all the kids are talking about at school these days. Becca says the girls in her class fight over who is best-looking: Napoleon Solo or Illya Kuryakin. I said I prefer the Russian (I think he's quite handsome, in fact), and she all but threw a tantrum, saying it was terrible for me to say that with her daddy sitting right there. I think this is what they call "a stage," but Frank laughed and said, Who knew there would be so many stages? He said "goddamn stages." He's going up for tenure, so it was good to hear him laugh, even if at her expense, because it has been a while.

I can see the blue light of the television in the Walkers' house, their cat sitting in a windowsill, begging to get in, and I don't blame her, because it's cold. I have my big coat over my nightgown. Boots, scarf, hat. It's tempting to go back inside, but I prefer the silence. It's cold but clear, with a slip of a moon. It is 10:15.

February 17, 2016
Southern Pines
Your father has said that when bad health comes his way, he plans to launch himself off the longest pier, take arsenic, tie a noose, or hold a gun to his own head. Not me, I tell him. Not me. I want to see Misty Copeland dance. I want to be a great-grandmother. I want to go back and walk Charles Street on a dark, snowy night just one more time, to peer in the windows of the card shop with the big fat cat licking her paws and then make my way across the Public Garden. I want to stand on the corner of Piedmont Street and listen: first, there is jazz, cool soul-defining jazz, and the clink of glasses and the murmured laughs, and then there is a hiss, a sizzle, a roar, a deafening roar, and somewhere in it all I will hear my mother; I will hear her as clear as a bell.

March 8, 2017
I woke today feeling afraid; I am afraid of losing your father. I am afraid of the distance he is keeping, and I feel it every time he walks out the door. I try to read or watch the television or the brightly colored Easter egg men passing by on the golf course, or I listen to music, but what I am really listening for is the door. He has promised that he would never do anything without letting me know, but as much as I want to trust him, there's something that keeps me off balance. After all, I have promised him not to go out and smoke when here alone, but I often do.

March 30, 2017
Dear Frank,
I am writing this note, and I want you to stick it in your
wallet. I want you to keep it and read it often. Do NOT
leave this house without telling me. Do NOT leave this
Earth without telling me. If you do, I will be so mad at you,
madder than I have ever been. I love you more than ever
—Lil

Shelley

SHELLEY HAS NEVER seen the courtroom so full, like something out of a movie. There is even a television crew from Raleigh, and she can see out the window that there are people waiting on the lawn. Her fingers are perched, like a concert pianist's, on the keyboard, so much better than that contraption she wore in Atlanta.

The jurors settle into their seats, twelve people looking very tired, like in that movie she loves so much with Henry Fonda. Jason had to read the play in high school, and the two of them rented the movie and watched it twice afterward. From the pictures early in the trial, Shelley has not been able to forget the image of the girl there naked in her chair with the needle in her arm. Her thin, pale body made

Shelley ache with cold, and she kept thinking how she wanted to take the afghan there behind the girl on the chair and wrap it around her. The friend, Joanna, had testified that was the young woman's favorite place to sit, that it faced the sunset and that the chair had once belonged to her mother, the only belonging she had from her mother, and Shelley realized that day that she really has nothing that belonged to her mother; at the time, she wanted nothing to remind her and took only a couple of things that had once been her brother's—the stuffed dog, the Saint Christopher medallion he wore one summer, not because he believed but because everyone was wearing them and a girl he liked had given it to him for Christmas. He said the girl had said it would protect him; he'd laughed and said, "Good luck with that," and yet he wore it faithfully that whole summer.

Who could leave someone that way? Cold and naked in a chair? Did she ask him to stay? Or did she tell him to leave her alone. "Leave me alone." That's what Princess Diana said when people tried to get her from the back of that car in the tunnel. Shelley had read that in a magazine. She said, "Oh my God." And she said, "Leave me alone."

Harvey doesn't mean to get in trouble, she will tell the teacher. *He's a sweet, good boy who is afraid. That's all.* Then she will tell how he built a Lego structure that was a camp for runaway turtles and salamanders and skinks who need someone to love them. She will say, *He's a good boy. He just really misses his brother.*

"HE TOOK AN innocent life," the prosecutor had said, "just because she was in his way."

The room is silent now, finally silent, and tense with the waiting.

"Guilty," the jurors all say. *Guilty. Guilty. Guilty.* And the courtroom rings with a thunderous applause that brings tears to Shelley's eyes. The friend, Joanna, runs over and hugs all the old people who have been there every day of the trial. Their girl vindicated—C. J., her name was C. J.—if not returned to life. And the nasty jack-o'-lantern smirks and looks at the judge like he'd like to kill her. And this is where on another day, if Shelley was working on her story version of it all, she would have the judge leap over that railing and beat the shit out of him, but she doesn't dare type that. She types, *Guilty.* She describes the thunderous applause that now has gone for over three minutes and scans the crowd for any sign of anyone she might recognize.

She reaches into her pocket for a Tic Tac, just in case she has to talk up close to anyone, and pulls out what Harvey must have slipped there this morning, an old empty matchbook from a place she's never heard of—the Lorraine Hotel—with a little note written on paper from his wide-ruled writing tablet: *You and my Dad shud go hear.* The matchbook looks about a hundred years old and says: 100 MODERN ROOMS, AIR-CONDITIONED FOR YOUR COMFORT. Where on earth does he find these things? And doesn't she wish they *could* be there in air-conditioned comfort, in a cool, dark room with crisp, clean sheets and a long worry-free afternoon up ahead. Another chance.

Frank

WHEN FRANK AND Lil rode over to see Preston's old house that first time, he was hit with a kind of sad longing that surprised him; perhaps it was simply the reminder of how many years had come and gone, and how for a long time it had been easy to fool himself, to continue to picture his mother alive and walking around that yard, tending to her flowers. She liked to cut blooms from the large magnolia tree that is no longer there, and float them in a silver bowl, the fragrance filling the small dining room. When Frank was a boy, it shaded a whole corner of the yard, the perfect climbing tree and an easy place to hide. The pods of the magnolia looked a lot like hand grenades, and Frank and the other boys in the neighborhood stockpiled them for when they played war.

There *were* good times, there *were* things he loved, and yet he had never revealed that to anyone, not even to Lil until that first day they came to look. That was when he told her how much he had loved that tree, and the river with its cold brown water, and the little pavilion that had a skating rink and swings. He loved the movie theater downtown and the way the whole town smelled like cured tobacco in the late summer. He liked that his mother seemed peaceful and settled with it all. Quite simply, he had grown to love the town, warts and all, but he'd never learned to have a foot in each place, an ability Lil had always possessed, half in the present and half in the past.

On the way, they had passed long stretches of flat, dusty fields, and he was aware of both the simple beauty and the poverty, neither of which he had noticed as a young man. There were small trailers and lopsided houses, some looking abandoned and left to deteriorate, and yet there was a car, a satellite dish—barren dirt yards and old recliners on front porches, discarded broken furniture in heaps alongside the road. And then in the midst of it all, there was life, work shirts and sheets on a line, a cheerful Easter wreath on a battered screen door; a barefooted child smiling and waving a dirty hand, an old woman watching him from the stoop, where she sat with a cigarette and a bag of chips. That's what he and Lil saw that first ride over.

"Don't look so sad," she had said, as if reading his mind. "There might be a warm, soapy bath at the end of that child's day, someone who loves him there to say good night." She said she thought that child might be standing there feeling sorry for *them*, old people out riding around because they were too old to play ball or swing from trees. "He might say, 'Did you see those old wrinkled people with nowhere to go? They didn't have any chips either.'"

THE YOUNG WOMAN had opened the door, chain lock still in place, and asked if she could help him, and that young boy, with a shock of dark hair that stood out in all kinds of cowlicks, squeezed against her and looked out as well. He was wearing a bushy fake mustache that hung low over his mouth and a bright-green towel tied around his neck like a cape. Frank has seen him in the yard other times when he passed, walking a figure eight with a big pine branch thrust forward like a sword—round and round, lemniscate, infinity. Frank had caught a glimpse of the inside of their house that day; the southern-facing window of the dining room where his mother had hung lace curtains now had venetian blinds that were closed tight.

"I lived here," he had told her. "My stepfather is the one who ordered this house from Sears; my mother planted the rosebushes." It was clear that she didn't want to ask him in. "I would love to come inside, show my wife." He had turned and pointed to Lil, who had lifted her hand and waved. "We wouldn't stay long."

The woman had paused then, one hand on the boy's head, as if she were considering it all, but then said she was sorry. "Another day would be better. My husband isn't home, and he knows more about the house," she said, and before Frank could say anything else, she closed the door.

FRANK'S MEMORIES OF Preston's house are as vivid in his mind as the house on Andover Street, as if all of his focus during those years was on whatever minutiae surrounded him. He recalled arriving and finding his mother in bed, her ankle broken, her shoulder broken, her stomach swollen with Horace, and this stranger catering to her every need. Frank had stood looking out on the backyard that very first day, fists stuffed deep in his pockets, and then he had turned to see a picture hanging on the wall of the dining room of someone laid out in a coffin. At first he couldn't believe what he was seeing and stepped closer to examine it. He had never seen a dead person except in the movies.

"That's my mother," Preston told him, as if there were nothing at all strange about the photo being there. "When she died, we realized we had no likeness of her. So we had that taken. She was a wonderful woman."

Frank didn't know what to say, so he just stood there studying the image: a padded casket lid open, an old woman in a black dress with her hands folded on her chest, where she had a Bible and some flowers. He waited until he heard Preston leave the room, and then he made his way outside into the sunlight and the baked brick stoop—the heat he grew to find comforting that summer, like being swaddled in down, the same way he was drawn to the distant shimmering mirages when he looked up and down the rails, urging him forward step by step.

The image of Preston's dead mother stayed with him for a long time, even though it was clear Preston had gotten the message, either from Frank's reaction or perhaps Frank's mother made a request, because the photo was not there the next day, replaced instead by a calendar from the local hardware store, which Frank's mother then later replaced with the coupling of those paintings *The Blue Boy* and *Pinkie*, like so many homes at that time. Lil called them "the Depressing Duo"—and during the only visit they all made when the children were young, Frank overheard her tell Becca and Jeff that at night Blue Boy left his frame and jumped into Pinkie's. She didn't tell them that Pinkie's portrait was to commemorate a twelve-year-old girl dead too soon, and he was relieved they never found out. In Lil's version, Pinkie was a party girl, talking and laughing so much that Blue Boy asked her to be quiet. Frank was also relieved the kids didn't discover the root cellar in the backyard, something he wasn't ready to share, not even with Lil.

That visit, he had pried open the lid and peeked into cobwebs and darkness; he had shined his flashlight to see his jar still there, the rickety chair.

Preston had dug and lined it like a vault—for keeping things cool or escaping a tornado or, God forbid, some kind of air raid—with a tiny ladder leading down to where no more than four people would even fit. "It's like a grave," Frank's mother had said, shaking her head and then turning away. Soon after, Preston more or less conceded that maybe it wasn't a great idea after all, and other than storing some canned tomatoes and peaches, he let Frank take it over as his camp.

AT THE END of her life, Frank's mother began talking when it was just the two of them, always with a kind of urgency, so that no one else heard her. "I'm so sorry, Frank," she said, Preston in the kitchen fixing a pot of coffee. It took some long minutes, and Frank's coaxing, before she finally completed her thought. "I'm sorry I took you from our home." She said that she had been so happy there it was too painful to imagine going back. She just couldn't picture that house without his father in it.

"Can you see?" she asked.

Preston came in about that time, and she closed her eyes again, easing into the faint shallow breath of earlier.

"She asks that a lot," Preston told him, his large fumbling hands more helpless than ever. "She says, 'Can you see?' But I'm not really sure what she means, and so I just say that I do."

And now, Frank does see. He understands how memories of what was good can be so painful you might choose not to look. He understands the desire to disappear, like an animal in hiding. When no one comes to the front door of the house, he walks to the far edge of the lot, through the brambles, blackberry thorns clinging to his clothes and scratching the backs of his hands. The tall, spindly pines tower over him, and there are all the sounds he loved as a boy: the squirrels and the birds. The small strip of trees buffers the highway noise, but when he was a boy there was no highway, just miles and miles of woods.

He had always kept the hatch open for light and air, and he could lie there and see the sky. It was a place to be alone—no baby screaming, nobody asking him to help with something. He kept his matchbook collection there, old marbles, flattened pennies, and in later years, right before he left to go to school, a can or two of Falstaff and a church key to open them. Frank's mother had called it a grave, but it was more like a tomb, or what he imagined someone waking to the afterlife might find. When he told Lil all of this on one of their early meetings, she said it sounded like his whole career could be traced right back to that time—a hole in the earth in a small town in eastern North Carolina, "a blip along the tracks." That's what *he* had called it, and he liked how closely she had paid attention, parroting the words right back to him. He liked that she didn't laugh.

The place is so overgrown it takes Frank a while to get his bearings; the sycamore tree at the back of the lot that had once stood over the cellar is no longer there. From here, he can see the screened porch has been closed in with cheap plywood, on which someone has written *Keep out*. A big dog is sprawled nearby in the sun.

What does Tomb Time mean? Lil had written that in a note. *Is that a course title?*

No, but it could have been a course title, the kind that would have drawn students, like when he used the subtitle "Skeletons in the Closet" for his undergraduate anthropology course on biological investigations. He still continues to think of topics and titles that would fill an undergraduate lecture hall: the recent excavation of an outhouse near Paul Revere's home; the Neanderthal cave paintings; that recent find of a horse from the Pleistocene Epoch right in someone's backyard. He has spent his adult lifetime studying such findings and is still shocked to learn that the bones of something that once lived and breathed have survived thousands and thousands of years. He kept a timeline in his office, stretching around the room, with that tiny half-inch mark that shows the miniscule life of a man.

What does Tomb Time mean?

He didn't answer that question; how could he even begin? It's hard to even answer it for himself these many years later. *Tomb Time*, a secret message, a silly buzzword for something that remained unspoken and removed from his real life. It was an escape, a call to flight, like what he had felt as a boy when he dreamed of jumping onto the northbound train, what he had felt during that time when Lil demanded so much of him, even though she was little more than a bitter ghost herself. And then something happened, something unplanned and surprising, and of course he responded to some attention; what dog wouldn't? Someone who listened to all he had to say. Someone who believed in his ideas and his thoughts. Someone who asked questions and wanted more and more of what he was able and willing to give, not someone to quip "Mum's the word" or come home from volunteering talking of death and decay, and smelling of all the hideous lotions and sprays people used to mask it. Of course he had had the fantasy of running, leaving all the heartache and sadness behind him and starting all over with a brand-new life and someone who would listen and care, someone who would make him feel important and loved, and, no, it also wouldn't have hurt if it were someone interested in sex and willing to explore or experiment.

He had been tired of a life so deeply rooted in grief. It was exhilarating to first allow himself to imagine it all, and then to actually act on the impulses. It was exciting; he felt alive, a gravitational pull that heightened all of his senses. But then even his imagination was crippled, every fantasy eventually broadening the lens to where he could see Lil standing there on the other side of the tracks— steadfast and loyal, opinionated Lil. And if he allowed himself to imagine the end of life, his body shriveled away, she was always the one there to witness it.

His mother had said things she needed to say at the end of her life, and so did Preston, whether Frank wanted to hear them or not, and both times he wondered, *Why now? Why tell me this now?*

Preston had said, "I fell in love with your mother when I saw her, and I felt bad, so help me God, because nothing in my life had ever happened to me like that." Preston was in his bed at home, and Frank sat beside him looking out the window to where he is standing right this minute. The sycamore was off to the left, and there was a picture of Frank's mother on the dresser looking as she did when they had first arrived here, a woman in her early thirties, the photo taken in Boston, in fact, on a day when she would have returned to their home on Andover Street and at the end of the day climbed into bed beside Frank's father.

"There she was, grieving and pregnant with another man's child, bloody with a shattered ankle and shoulder," Preston had said, "and

I thought she was the most beautiful woman I'd ever seen." He said he had always felt so ashamed of that, and then he told how he had always wished she would say that he had made her life so much better, but she never did. She said she was *grateful*. She said she was *comfortable*, but it was clear to him that none of it even came close to matching what she had once had. "I always hoped for more," Preston said. "Even though maybe I didn't deserve it."

"Why are you telling me this?" Frank had asked. He had come alone to see him, Lil back home with the kids and all their activities: Girl Scouts and football and carpools. When he'd called her early that morning, she had told him they had a big freeze, leaving the rhododendron drooped and coated in ice, but there in North Carolina, it was like spring, and he had left Preston for a minute to go and peer down into the vault, the hatch hinges rusty, cobwebs filling the space. He could see the mason jar of flattened pennies in the far corner, the old rusty church key, just as he had left it. He had planned to go down there later that afternoon after Horace arrived and when he had changed out of his good clothes, but everything had happened so quickly that he spent the afternoon making funeral arrangements instead.

"I convinced her to stay," Preston had said. The bag by his bed was filled with dark urine, and his hands looked nothing like Frank could recall; they were thin and pale, so different from those coarse tan ones searching for quarters behind ears and stealing noses.

Frank had put his hand on top of Preston's. "My dad asked that she not leave him."

But then Preston told him something else, something Frank has kept to himself all these years, simply because he didn't want to think about it or analyze or imagine.

There is a sound in the brush, and Frank pauses, listens, probably a squirrel or a bird. He knows the root cellar has to be close if it's still there at all. He takes a stick and pokes into the brush, the brambles catching his sleeve, but then he sees a small cleared area, and there it is, the lid covered over with loose pine straw and sticks, and a heavy rock, as if marking the spot, with a scrap of paper beneath. He steps closer and sees a makeshift tarp shelter under the low branches of myrtle, maybe the camp of that kid who lives here, or perhaps someone homeless who has wandered up from the tracks. The train is due in a little over an hour, plenty of time to try once more to see inside the house and then to return. From here, the brambles and hedge so high, he can see only the roofline, and the stone chimney Preston built himself.

"Can you imagine building a chimney like this, Frank?" his mother had asked one night over dinner—though then they would have said "supper." "Preston spent hours working, all those stones cut just right and then fitting them there." At the time, Frank avoided making eye contact with his mother or Preston, who was seated right across from him, his thinning hair slicked back from his shower, and Frank stared into his butter beans—he remembers so clearly the beans on that pale-yellow plate—and said that, yes, of course he could, but now he stares at the structure, thinking about Preston cutting and hauling stones—stone by stone—at the end of what had already been a ten-hour workday, and he feels that awful wave of regret, wishes he'd been kinder, had asked his advice and opinion about things, this man who stepped in as husband and father, his whole life relinquished to being the runner-up.

If Frank could talk to his mother now, he would want to say what Lil had said years ago: that she was young and afraid and grieving, and what else could she do? His mother had heard her dying husband say, "Don't leave me," and so she didn't, but Preston told Frank that what *he* had heard was "Please shoot me," someone trapped and begging to die. Frank wanted to ask why he was telling that. *Why now?* But he chose to just listen because what did it matter? "I didn't tell the truth," Preston had said. *Truth, Maat*—a word that originally referred to a measuring device, a stick or a reed. Measure it. Weigh it. *Heart of my mother.*

Shelley

❧

SHELLEY SCANS THE crowd as she makes her way to the car. Once again, she will be late picking Harvey up, so she takes a deep breath and calls the teacher to let him know and to hear what it is Harvey has done *now*. She gets his machine and, against her better judgment, leaves a message. She hates for her voice to be trapped there in someone's machine, waiting to be let out, but if she hung up, that would be worse, because he would know it was her. "I'm on my way," she says. "I'm so sorry I'm late."

She barely starts the car, and he calls right back, more interested it seems in the trial verdict than anything; everyone in town is. The word *guilty* feels good on her tongue, and she relishes

being the one who has something important to tell instead of just
being told.

"So about our boy, Harvey."

"Yes," she says, marveling for a second at the surge in her chest
with the use of that plural pronoun—*our*, our boy. She always loved
when she heard Brent say that: "Our son," "our boy." And then she
would add the *s* to the end of it: *Our sons, our boys*.

"I'm almost there," she says, and then, without meaning to,
drives slower and slower, tired and slow like when Harvey pretends
to be a turtle, scooching along and laughing as he inches his way
across the floor.

When she pulls up and parks, Harvey is over on the swings with
another child, pumping his legs and soaring as high as possible, a
bushy handlebar mustache lopsided on his face and obscuring his
grin each time he flies upward. Ned Stone is waiting for her there
on the curb. "Another kid has a late pickup, too," he says, "so let's
just sit right here." He motions to a bench in front of the school,
and they sit.

"Look," he begins. "Harvey is a really sweet kid, and I hope you
won't take this wrong."

"That's always a bad sign," she says.

"What I mean is that I feel I might be speaking out of turn, and
yet I think Harvey's acting out might have a lot to do with what's
going on at home."

He waits for her to look up and into his face, which is hard to
do, his green eyes unblinking like a cat's.

"Look, I don't want to intrude, but is his father coming back?
Do you know?"

"What?" She watches Harvey swinging higher and higher.

"Harvey said that you told him his dad is coming home soon. He
also said that he hears you crying at night because there's a ghost

in your house, and that he wets the bed." He pauses and waits until she looks at him again. "He says that he's saving his money for the Smile Train, and for you to go to a motel on a honeymoon. That he's scared of the ghosts and all the killers in the world, that Peggy can't hear and he wants to get her what old people stick in their ears to make them hear better. And, last but not least, that he has a turd collection." He shakes his head and laughs. "Oh, and he also has quite a wealth of knowledge about murders, and knows a lot of dirty jokes."

"Oh, yes, I've heard some of those. Lizzie Borden and a horse walk into a bar."

"Well, the one today was a little more risqué than 'Hey, why the long face?'"

"Oh?"

"One about a blow-up doll and the virgin? Except he said 'the Virgo.'"

"Oh no!" She shakes her head and puts out her hand to stop him, in case he was even thinking of saying the punch line; his face is flushed and he is not making eye contact with her. "Please don't go there." She could just imagine Harvey with a mustache, there in the center of a group of kids.

"So you've heard it?"

"No, but I can only imagine. I am so sorry," she says. "I am so embarrassed." She covers her face with her hands, her shoulders still shaking, first laughing and then crying.

"I'll probably get a call from a parent or two," he says. "There have been a lot of calls. One kid is scared to watch television because he's afraid that the Menendez brothers will kill him, and another told her mother she is scared of little people flipping their car over if they have to stop at a red light. Things like that."

"I am so sorry," she says into her hands. "I am so very sorry."

"I really think I can help," he says. "You know, spend some extra time with Harvey after school, maybe give him a job as my helper?"

"I did this to him. I did this. I gave him all these terrible fears and problems."

"You can't blame yourself," he says. "We all do the best we can."

It seems he's about to say something else, but a car pulls up and the other kid jumps from his swing and comes running over, Harvey right behind him, his mustache slipped to one side, and Ned excuses himself to go speak to the other parent, the kind of woman Shelley admires and also feels intimidated by—a "business casual" look, they call it, hands on her hips with great confidence, a sticker on her window that says she belongs somewhere. She sweeps her son into her arms and gives him a big kiss, while two other kids in the back seat watch a movie on a pull-down screen. She has a vanity plate that says MOM'S CAR, with a heart, and probably she parks it beside one that says DAD'S CAR.

Shelley is trying to imagine what that would even feel like when Harvey plops down beside her, his thin legs scratched and covered in bugbites.

"Am I in trouble?"

"Should you be?"

"No," he says, and presses his nose into her arm. When the woman drives away and Ned Stone walks back over, Shelley reaches in her pocket for the matchbook and note and holds it out for them both to see.

"Thanks for my note, Harvey," she says, and he tells her he has lots more of those. "A whole collection," he says, and looks at his teacher. "*Another* collection."

"I've never heard of the Lorraine Hotel," she says, and Ned tells her that's because it was torn down years ago.

"You'd have to go back in time to stay at the Lorraine Hotel," he tells Harvey, who grabs his hands and begins pulling him.

"Let's go. Let's go right now."

"Maybe tomorrow," he says, a steady calm hand on Harvey's shoulder. "But right now, your mom is waiting for you." He gives Harvey a gentle push toward her and then says goodbye.

"Thank you," Shelley tells him, and watches Harvey run ahead and climb in the back seat, relieved to know that she does not have to go back in time.

Harvey

❧

As soon as he gets home, Harvey gets his cape and his Fu Manchu and goes out in the yard with Peggy to see if the ghost left a note or more good stuff. He doesn't even get a snack. He's searching the ground for tracks and turds when he sees the ghost, all bent over, kicking and digging at the manhole. Jason said Harvey should never, *ever* go down that hole, even if it does look like the Ninja Turtle's, because it isn't safe. "They leave you stuff to keep you away," Jason had told him. "As long as you don't do something stupid, they won't hurt you."

"Hey there," the ghost says, and holds a piece of paper up. "Is this yours?"

Are you hear? Harvey wrote that, and somebody wrote, *NO!*

The ghost's pants is torn-up where his knee is bloody. Harvey nods. "Are you the ghost?"

It shakes its head no and laughs.

"A murderer?" Harvey asks. More shaking. "A shape-shifter or a zombie?" Harvey takes a step back.

"I'm just an old man, son. I used to live here when I was a boy. In fact, I've been here before but it wasn't a good time to see the house. Remember? You came to the door with your mother but you had a different mustache." He holds out his hand. "My name is Frank."

"Was it a handlebar or a walrus?" Harvey asks. Jason gave him a poster with all the names, like *horseshoe* and *chevron* and *Fu Manchu* but Harvey doesn't *have* a walrus, so it's a test.

"Definitely a handlebar," the man says. "And same towel. You have a green-and-white sofa in the front room—that's all I could see that day. When I was a boy, we had a brown one in the exact same place there in front of the fireplace." He puts his dirty hand out again. "How's that? Did I pass the test?"

Harvey reaches and shakes the hand. He shakes really hard, like he heard his dad tell Jason to do if he wanted to get something like a job or a good grade or maybe a girlfriend. "Did you write 'no' right there on my message?"

"No." The man looks at his watch, a big one like the kind that goes swimming and ticks real loud. "Must be somebody else."

"Are you sure you aren't a alien or serial killer?"

"Completely sure. You know a lot of dark things, son," he says, and looks at that big watch again. "Tell me about your mustache. You seem mighty young for facial hair."

"It's not real." Harvey takes off his mustache and starts to put it in his pocket with the penny and matches but the man is staring at him so he changes his mind and puts it back on. "But it *will* be when I'm a teenager. "

"I have a scar, too," the man says. "Several of them, in fact. I fell from a tree when I was about your age, had to get stiches in my chin. And I've got a great big one like a railroad track when they went in to fix my heart." He lifts his shirt just enough for Harvey to see part of the scar, big and purple, like on Frankenstein's head. He points to the middle of Harvey's Fu Manchu. "Do you know what this is called?" he asks. "This little dip right above your lip?"

"No." Harvey knows his mom wouldn't like him talking to a stranger, even if he did live here thousands of years ago.

"It's called a filtrum," the man says, and he sounds just like when the teacher says, "This is important, so be quiet and hear it," and everybody says, "Oh no," with their hands on their faces, like in the Christmas movie, because it will be boring. "In fact," he says, "there's a whole story about it."

"Is it boring?"

"I don't think so," he says, and then tells a kind of long story that's a little boring about how people know everything before they get borned and then an angel comes along and mashes her finger on your lip to make you forget it all.

"That sucks," Harvey says, and holds his mustache in place. "She mashed me way too hard."

"You must have known more than most," the man says. "And now you get to spend a whole lifetime remembering."

"I do know a lot of junk but she still hurt me," he says. "Somebody ought to mash her up hard too."

"I'm sure she didn't mean to hurt you."

"Well, I think she's a stupid shitty doo-doo bitch," Harvey says, and waits to see if the man is going to keep acting like a teacher and get after him, but he doesn't. He just laughs.

"What's that other note you got?" Harvey asks.

"Oh, just something I keep in my wallet—a little reminder my wife wrote me." He puts it in his pocket and goes back over to lift that lid Jason told Harvey never, ever to touch.

"Be careful," Harvey says, but doesn't go any closer. "What do you see? Skeletons? Half-eat animals and blood?"

"No." He shakes his head, one hand on that torn-up knee. "All I see is a backpack and some textbooks, a few beer cans, some old newspapers."

"Beer?" Harvey says. "Ghosts drink beer?"

"This one does. Eats granola bars and has a calculus book too. I see part of an old empty jar. That's all."

Harvey wants to see but is scared of falling in. He wants to be with Peggy, who's snoring in the sun, but he doesn't want to hear his mom say don't tell jokes, like the one about that doll fartin' and flyin' out the window. Peggy can't hear nothing, but Super Monkey can hear that old man breathing and something ticking like a clock, but the train will come soon and even Super Monkey has trouble hearing anything when that happens. The train is the best part of the day.

Shelley

❧

SHELLEY CAN'T SAY how long she has been sitting in the kitchen crying; it's such a relief just to get home and collapse. She is relieved to have her job back and that justice was served, relieved that Harvey's teacher is so kind and attentive, but also horrified by all the ways she is failing as a mother. She goes to get a paper towel to wipe her nose, and that's when she notices that green Toyota parked down at the corner by the woods. *Not today. He cannot come inside this house today.*

A door down the hall creaks on its hinges and then slams shut, and she nearly jumps out of her skin. The wind? She glances out on the porch, where Peggy is curled up in a pool of sunlight. Has

Harvey been spying on her? She tiptoes down the hall; the door to Jason's room is closed, and she stands, her ear pressed close, and she hears something in there. A radio? Someone talking? She puts her hand on the knob and, with a deep breath, pushes it open to see Jason sitting on his bed, headphones off to the side, a stack of papers and newspaper clippings spread out in front of him.

"Jason! Oh my God!" she says, both relieved to see him and sorry for him to see her looking this way. "You scared me!"

"You scared me," he says, and stares like he's looking right through her.

"Harvey will be so excited." She turns to call him. "Let me—"

"No. I don't want Harvey to hear this. I'll see him later."

"Hear what? What's going on?" She steps closer now.

"Why don't *you* tell me, Mom?" His voice is angry, shaking like he's about to cry, too. "Why don't *you* explain everything to me?"

"I'm not sure what you mean."

"Well, for starters, Harvey calls me every day, has since school started, saying he's scared because you cry every night."

"Not every night," she says. "I lost my job, but I got it back. I didn't tell you because I didn't want to worry you." She steps closer, shocked to see the headlines and dates of the newspaper articles around him: *June 1994—partly cloudy and humid—highs in the 90s.* "Harvey gets scared at night, but he's okay." DOMESTIC ASSAULT: 1 CRITICALLY INJURED AND 1 MISSING. "I'm so sorry I didn't tell you."

"I had to pick a topic to research," he says. "The professor said pick something you know practically nothing about, and so I chose my family." Jason pulls up a handful of the copied articles. "So tell me the truth. When I asked if you were getting a divorce from Brent, you said you weren't sure, and now I know that you were *never married.* Not to Brent, and not to my dad."

"But it was like we were."

"But *not*. And you told people he was your husband. You told *me* he was."

"I wanted us to be a family."

"But you lied." Jason stands and waves the papers in front of her. "You've never been married. You have two sons, and neither have fathers listed on their birth certificates." He thrusts copies of his and Harvey's birth certificates into her hand. "Do you even know who my dad is?"

"Jason."

"All those stories you told. The war hero. Big marine. Do you know how many people in this country are named David Moore? And I was just looking at the dead ones. So tell me."

"I don't know." She leans against the wall, eyes closed. "I'm sorry."

"What about that stuffed dog you said he gave me? Where did you get that, the thrift shop?"

"It was my brother's."

"Oh yeah. Your brother. Your wonderful, brilliant brother, who beat the shit out of your dad. There's a story." He's in her face now. *Don't blink, don't blink.*

"No wonder you read all that true-crime crap when I was a kid."

"I work at the courthouse."

"Or maybe you're interested in why people try to kill each other." His voice is so loud that now she has to turn away, wanting to cover her ears with her hands, but she knows she can't do that, and she's worried about where Harvey is, and that old man. Where is he?

"It was an accident." She takes a deep breath and opens her eyes. Peggy is still out there in a puddle of light, and she is relieved to see Harvey walking up from the woods, a stick held out in front of him like a sword.

"That's not what's in the papers," he says. "The paper says your crazy brother went nuts, and you hid under a bed while it all went down."

"No," she says. "My brother was scared—they hurt *him*. And he won that dog at the fair. He was a winner."

"Right. And what about my dad, huh? What's the DNA story there?"

"He was kind. And handsome."

"And what was his real name, Mom? Alive? Dead?"

"I'm sorry."

"No, *I'm* sorry because my whole life is a lie!" Jason shoves all the papers to the floor and starts pacing, fists clenched. "Do you even know where your parents are?"

"Dead," she says. "In my life, they are dead."

"He is, but for all I know, she's still alive somewhere. I didn't find an obituary."

"It doesn't matter."

"But it matters to *me*," he says. "My life is one big lie."

"That isn't true."

"Yes, it is. Your life is a lie, and that makes mine one, too. Are you even really my mother?"

"Yes, and I love you. I've always loved you. That is the truth, my truth." She reaches her hand out, but he shakes his head and keeps moving.

"I wanted to be a good mother," she says.

"And so you lied about everything?"

"I thought I was protecting you."

"Pretty sure you were protecting yourself."

"Yes. I see that."

Jason sits down on the edge of his bed, head in his hands. Shelley wants to go and sit beside him, but she's afraid he'll push her away. He tells her how he's been getting a ride back and forth from school

to come and check on them, see what he could find out; he's the
one who ate the bread and drank the milk. He has heard her cry
at night, watched Harvey wake and make his way to her room. He
took showers when she and Harvey left the house, sometimes even
slept a few hours in his own bed. Otherwise, he was in a tent out
there in the woods.

"I don't get it," he finally says.

"I was afraid." She steps closer, and he doesn't move, doesn't
raise his voice, just lets out a big breath and slumps onto his pillow, eyes closed. "I've been afraid my whole life. I know you might
never understand and you might never be able to forgive me, but I
just couldn't look back. I was so afraid it would all poison me, too.
I wanted to be a good mother. That's what I wanted more than anything. I was afraid anyone who knew the truth wouldn't want me,
or you or your brother."

After a long pause, he reaches off the bed to the floor and riffles
through the pages until he holds up the one that has her photo from
sixth grade; she's in navy-blue knee socks and her favorite plaid
skirt. It was wool, and she wore it even though it was springtime and
way too hot. "Honey, you're gonna burn up," one of the teachers
in charge had said, and offered to help her find something else, but
it was her favorite, and she felt best about herself when she wore
it—a kilt, like kids sometimes wear at schools where they all dress
alike so nobody feels different, and it had a big safety pin holding
the flaps together, and she liked the security of that pin, the sturdy
click of something that held things together. The teacher asked were
her parents coming, but she pretended not to hear and focused on
tying her shoes instead. Her features are blurred in the picture, but
she is smiling and holding up the ribbon they gave her when she was
the last one standing.

"C-o-n-v-a-l-e-s-c-e."

The boy before her had said "s-s," instead of "s-c," or maybe she wouldn't have gotten it right; maybe she would have made that same mistake. But the state competition got her the next month. All those hard words, and then she missed *parliament*—left out the *a*— and it was strange, because both of her parents smoked that brand of cigarettes, and so her whole life that word had been right there, all around her, in every room, on every table.

"There's a whole list here of what you spelled," he says, and leans in close to the blurred paper. "'Abysmal,' 'sepulcher,' 'hemorrhage,' 'hallelujah.'"

"Sounds horrible doesn't it?"

"Except for 'hallelujah.'" He pauses, never breaking eye contact. "What about 'verisimilitude'? Ever spell that one?"

Jason is staring, his fists still clenched. She will tell him everything. She will. She will take her time and hope that someday he will forgive her, that someday he might even understand how desperate she had been.

"V-e-r-i-s-i-m-i-l-i-t-u-d-e," she says, and perches on the edge of the chair across from him. "It's weird how well I remember that day so clearly but I remember almost nothing about the other one you read about." She reaches and picks up one of the pages and moves her finger along the date: *1994*. "I've tried. They questioned me for days, and I tried."

She is about to say more, the fragments she did recall—broken glass, the sirens, the blood, how she remembers staring at that tag—SEALY POSTUREPEDIC, DO NOT REMOVE, 658939347—and she remembers her brother calling for her, looking for her when the rest of the house was suddenly quiet, saying over and over, "It was an *accident*," and the way she saw his feet there by her bed, black Converse high-tops, his name inked in blue on one rubber toe, a star on the other, and there was blood where he had stepped and made his way into her room. She could hear him breathing hard. She could hear him whisper her name, telling her he was sorry, that it was an accident, that he would never hurt her. She is about to say all of that, to begin telling the story, how that was the last time she ever saw her brother, how as soon as she found a way to leave, she did, and how nobody looked for her and she never looked back.

The back door slams, and Harvey comes running into the house and down the hall, calling for her the way he sometimes does at night when he's afraid—"Mom, Mom, Mom!"—but then when he sees Jason, he claps and screams and jumps on the bed, with slow old Peggy right behind him. "You're home!"

"Hey, little dude." Jason holds up his hand for a high five and then, without looking at Shelley, grabs and collects all the papers and stuffs them into his dresser drawer, all the while promising Harvey that they will go get pizza and maybe even add some more stars to the ceiling. Peggy, with slow, consistent paws, has made a nest of the bedspread, and both boys sit there hugging her tired old body. Shelley wants to spell *probity*, *veracity*, *fidelity*; she wants to come out from under the bed and make everything okay. She wants to promise them good things, to say something important that they will always remember, but there is no word for all that she is feeling, so she just stands in the doorway and waits.

Frank

❧

FRANK BRAVES THE rickety ladder and then is standing below and looking up into the trees and sky. Perhaps this is the view he needed most, one that feels untouched by time. There are no initials written in charcoal on the wall—no more matches or pennies—just some broken pieces of that old mason jar and the familiar earthy smell, the clammy walls, the view up and out into daylight and air. Right before he ran off, that strange kid asked if Frank wanted to see inside their house, and he heard himself say, "Next time." He said that he needed to go soon, because he had left a note he shouldn't have left; the kid said his mom had left a bad note and almost got fired, and then he asked if Frank thought he'd live to be real old—"Way older than you even," the kid had said, "since so much stuff got mashed out."

"Yes," Frank had told him, "I think you'll be way older than me."

"I want to be as old as that turtle in China," he had said, and Frank was about to tell him he knew all about that turtle, as well as the turtle from sixty million years ago—one of the pelomedusoides—found by someone in this very state. But another time. *Next time.*

"You're just getting started," Frank said. "You have so much to remember."

And off the kid went, through the hedges and back into daylight, past the dogwood tree Frank's mother had planted so long ago, past the view Frank looked out at as he sat by his mother when she was dying, her body embryonic as she curled inward, not unlike the slides he had routinely shown his classes, those earliest-discovered bodies on their left sides, in the fetal position, with their hands covering their faces, as if not to see what comes next.

He picks up one of the pieces of the jar, draws a circle in the dirt as he did many times when shooting marbles, then slips it into his pocket. People often need closure; they need to see certain people or say words they have meant to say and, for whatever reason, didn't. His mother had apologized for taking him from his home, and Preston had to tell Frank what he had heard that night over seventy years before. Last words. People needing closure.

But not Lil. She just went to sleep and didn't wake. There were no hiccups, no hearing voices or seeing people off in a corner, no smelling or hearing another place, as Frank's grandfather had done. "Good night, Frank," she had said, as she did every night, with a pat on his chest, a kiss on the cheek, and then she turned on her left side and went to sleep.

Perhaps she had said all she needed to say—in her notes and scraps and reminders—and maybe if he sticks around and pays attention, he will hear their private word; maybe she will still have something more to say. Becca keeps asking about their word and probably will again tonight when she brings his dinner, as she has done for the past two months while they go through things, and now he is filled with panic that he left that note.

Lil would be furious with him, both that he left such a burdensome goodbye in Becca's hands and, more so, that he wrote their word for someone else to know. *I don't care if she is our daughter*, she would say. *That's* our *word*, our *business*.

The only thing worse than Lil mad was Lil afraid, and she had been afraid in this last year—a fear of loss, a fear of forgetting. He wants to tell her that he and Jeff have talked on the phone several times without a single argument, and he wants to assure her that he'll check the weather in Boston every day, just as she always did. He wants her to know that recent articles offer proof that the Neanderthals *were* communicating with others after all, and that he's sorry they didn't get back to Florence, he's so *sorry*, and he will *never* tell anyone their word and he will *not* hasten things. "Not today," he says. "Not today."

He looks at his watch and breathes a deep sigh; there's enough time to get home before Becca arrives, enough time to stand here a little longer, the wall cool against his back as he breathes in the familiar damp smell and waits for that faraway whistle, waits as the train comes closer and closer—vibrations coursing through the earth as it passes—and then fades into the distance of the late afternoon and disappears on that northbound track.

Acknowledgments

∽

I AM INDEBTED to archival reports from the *Boston Globe*, the *Fayetteville Observer*, and the *Robesonian* for facts pertaining to the Cocoanut Grove Fire in 1942 and the train wreck in Rennert, North Carolina, in 1943, as well as the 1959 publication *Fire in Boston's Cocoanut Grove* by Paul Benzaquin. Thanks to Chick Jacobs for directions to the train site, and immense gratitude to Bob Fisher, the former director of the Robeson County Library, who immediately searched the archives when he learned what I was working on. Thanks to the regulars in the Wesley Pines writing group for your shared stories and the inspiration you bring. For hometown memories, I want to thank Bill McLean, as well as the late Ann Culbreth, and the late Horace Stacey, who as a teenager ran telegrams in the aftermath of the crash. Invaluable thanks for feedback and conversation along the way to Wilton Barnhardt, Emma Beckham, Barb Bennett, Matraca Berg, Megan Mayhew Bergman, Belle Boggs, Marshall Chapman, Charlie Cuneo, Lisa Cupolo, Stephanie Donahue, Linda Dunn, Betsy Giduz, Marianne Gingher, Amy Hempel, Susan Irons, Elinor Lipman, Maureen Macneil, Louise Marburg, Allyssa McCabe, Jayne Anne Phillips, Steve Yarbrough, and Lee-Ann Yolin.

Thanks to my dear friend, Cathy Stanley, who has read my work in its roughest versions since we were fifteen. (Not enough thank-yous for that!) And to Lee Smith and Betsy Cox, who have generously given me their wise insights since 1977 and 1984, respectively.

Thanks to my sister, Jan Gane, for her continued love and support, and to our mom, who is an inspiration. The train wreck was a vivid memory from my dad's boyhood, and I have wished thousands of times that I could hear him talk about it—talk about anything—just one more time.

Thanks to Claudia and Rob—always—and to Alexander and Julian, Caroline and Julian, for the joys of family.

Great appreciation to my agent, Henry Dunow, and eternal thanks to my editor, Kathy Pories. What a pleasure and honor to get to work with you. Thanks to Elizabeth Johnson for her amazing copy editing and to Brunson Hoole and the entire Algonquin Staff.

And finally (but never least) thanks to my husband, Tom Rankin, whose love and support on our shared journey bring more joy and thanksgiving and adventure than I ever would have allowed myself to imagine. I am grateful.

HIEROGLYPHICS

Writing *Hieroglyphics*
An Essay by Jill McCorkle

Questions for Discussion

Writing *Hieroglyphics*

An Essay by Jill McCorkle

WHEN I WAS growing up, there was a train that passed daily not far from our house. I loved the sound of it and the whole neighborhood loved playing on the tracks. Even though we were told not to go there—admonished and threatened with the terrible things that could happen—we returned to put pennies on the tracks and watch them get flattened, waving to the conductor and the occasional man standing at the rail of the caboose. There was always someone saying how destroying a penny was against the law and we could get arrested, but that fear usually dissipated with the flat copper treasure in our pockets and the view of the many miles we could travel, crosstie by crosstie.

My dad told another train story, his childhood memory that then became laced with my own. He recalled the train crash that happened in our native county when he was an adolescent, a catastrophic event that made all the national papers, and left the survivors hospitalized and stranded far from home. He had gone, as many people had, to see the aftermath of it all, a memory that clearly haunted him. Though I knew it had happened fifteen miles away, I pictured it there just beyond our neighbor's backyard and the pine trees where I played. The details were impossible to forget: a freak snowfall, a stalled train crossing the track, a broken warning light, World War II soldiers heading home for Christmas. There were presents strewn, a bridal veil in the limbs of a tree, survivors filling every hospital bed in much of the state. I was an adolescent myself when I heard the story for the first time, sitting on our back steps with my dad and looking over the dark yard. He was grilling steaks, our dog was waiting for a bone, and so my memory is of his story but also my own story of that time with him. I imagined the crash and I imagined my dad as a boy witnessing the site, and I committed to memory the night I sat and listened to him, glowing coals, pipe smoke, the sadness in his voice as he described the loss. I was also haunted by the details and unfathomable grief, loved ones in other places waiting for news that would proclaim someone alive or dead: a clothing tag, a scar, a particular brand and size shoe—words and numbers and objects with the power to represent a life, convey a whole story. The dry-cleaning tag that looks like nothing but becomes an intimate object, as do the watch, the lucky coin, the button that person might have fastened in place before getting on the train.

During the many years I lived in the Boston area, I often heard references to the Cocoanut Grove fire with the same level of shock and reverence that all catastrophic events render. Lives end; time freezes. We look for clues and meaning and can't help but imagine the *what-if*s and *if-only*s. And then all those bits and pieces of life we often take for granted take on new weight and meaning. Just a couple of years ago I saw an obituary that made reference to the fire—someone who was supposed to be at the club that night in 1942 and then had a change in plans. The fire took place a year earlier than the train wreck, and quite a few of those who died in the crash were heading home to the Boston area. It was cold. It was dark. It was sudden. Loved ones were left waiting and searching through those personal items—a ring or necklace, monogram, card—that would lend information.

In the novel, two of my characters—Lil and Frank—are dealing with parents who died in these tragic events. His father was on the train going home; her mother went to the club without telling Lil and her father that was where she was going. These losses led them to each other in the beginning, and now they have a long marriage behind them. Still, there is so much they don't know about their parents, and likewise so much their own children don't know about them and their life together. And there is Shelley, a young mother trying to raise her sons and working as a stenographer in the courts, her shorthand and recordings of local crimes helping her blot out much of her own troubled past.

Everyone has a secret. Everyone has a memory that haunts or lingers. Everyone has the door they want to close but for whatever reason, time continues to blow it ajar. Frank has not wanted to look, and until now he has avoided going there. Lil flings hers wide open and goes in with a flashlight, determined to see and know all that she can. Shelley has locked hers multiple times, but the wind keeps rattling all that she cannot escape, while her son, Harvey, is just beginning to find his way, doing what all children do, imagining his future and along the way finding and collecting and hiding little things: matchbook covers and flattened pennies.

In the early days of writing this novel, I read that when sites of orphanages or schools are excavated, there are almost always little caches of toys tucked away and hidden, children wanting to claim and protect what belongs to them. There are also the many versions of *Kilroy was here*—graffiti, handprints, notes in bottles—the stroke of immortality and desire to be remembered. I was thinking of each of these characters in terms of the mark they leave on the world they inhabit, from the most visible and easily discerned knowledge to the tiniest keepsake or scrap of paper to what is consigned only to memory and perhaps never revealed. It is an endless excavation, each discovered item carrying its own story. My hope is that the readers of *Hieroglyphics* will be entertained by these characters and their lives, but I also hope it will lead them to think of various fragments and images from their own lives and to experience the oldest and purest form of time travel—memory.

Questions for Discussion

1. The catastrophic events referenced in *Hieroglyphics*—the train wreck and the Cocoanut Grove fire—really happened. Why do you think McCorkle used actual events? In what ways does that affect how you read the novel?

2. The character Lil says that we are all haunted by something. What do you think haunts each of the main characters and how do they each deal with it?

3. Harvey's sections, told from a child's point of view, are markedly different from Lil's, Frank's, and Shelley's sections. How does his point of view color our reading of the other sections?

4. There are many references throughout the novel to childhood games and toys and keepsakes. How do they function for each character?

5. Language—what is communicated as well as what remains unspoken—is a central theme in this novel, from Lil's notes and diary entries to Shelley's transcriptions to Frank's study of ancient cultures. How does this relate to the title of the novel?

6. At the end of the novel, Shelley is literally left standing in a threshold. How would you describe that threshold? What do you think lies ahead for her?

7. The present storyline focuses on a day in Frank's life. How would you chart his journey?

8. The characters all have interests woven into the storyline: Lil has her work as a dance instructor; Frank has his studies of ancient burial rituals; Harvey is obsessed with horror tales (real and imagined), his made-up superhero, and animal droppings; Shelley entertains a wholly imagined narrative (the book she would write) while also doing her job. How do these interests help us understand the characters' perspectives?

9. Frank, Shelley, and Harvey all have brothers who are key figures in their lives. Discuss what you know about each brother and how these relationships affect the central characters' lives.

10. Lil spends a lot of time thinking about her marriage to Frank, with particular emphasis on one period of time. How does she

resolve her feelings about his affair? How do you feel about her decision?

11. Grief is central in the lives of all four of the main characters. How has it affected the way they live?

12. In the aftermath of both the train wreck and the fire, people were identified by tags or scars or the contents of pockets. Discuss the relevance of these lists.

13. The four central characters' lives are all significantly influenced by their relationships with their parents. Which character's situation were you most drawn to? Even after we've lost parents, how do they live on for us and inform our lives?

14. Were you surprised by the ending? If so, why? If not, why did you expect it?

15. What kinds of things have you saved over the years, and why these specific things? Do you have any talismans? Would the meaning of these keepsakes be evident to anyone else, and if not, why not?

TOM RANKIN

JILL MCCORKLE'S FIRST two novels were released simultaneously when she was just out of college, and the *New York Times* called her "a born novelist." Since then, she has published four additional novels and four story collections, and her work has appeared in *Best American Short Stories* several times, as well as *The Norton Anthology of Short Fiction*. Five of her books have been *New York Times* Notable Books, and her most recent novel, *Life After Life*, was a *New York Times* bestseller. She has received the New England Booksellers Award, the John Dos Passos Prize for Excellence in Literature, and the North Carolina Award for Literature. She has written for the *New York Times Book Review*, the *Washington Post*, the *Boston Globe*, the *Atlantic*, *Garden & Gun*, and other publications. She was a Briggs-Copeland Lecturer in Fiction at Harvard, where she also chaired the department of creative writing. She is currently a faculty member of the Bennington College Writing Seminars and is affiliated with the MFA program at North Carolina State University.